**S   y
b   e
masked fac   nt
of the candlelight in his eyes.**

re was only the length of the pin between
. She did not resist when he took her
and deflected the sharp point away from
h   ody.

W   t was she doing? Alarmed, she dropped
th   rooch and put her free hand against his
ch   , but even as she opened her mouth to
sc   m he captured her mouth, kissing her
so   thlessly that her bones melted under the
on   ught. It was over in an instant. She was
sti gathering herself to resist him when he
r   sed her.

'Y   ' he said, his breathing a little ragged. 'I
w   ot wrong.'

'A   bout what?'

'Y   kiss like an angel.'

In   ne swift, fluid movement he turned away
fr   her, threw up the sash and slipped out
in   the darkness.

ity ran to the window, but there was no
s   of anyone and only the soft drumming of
hoofbeats fading into the night.

AUTHOR NOTE

I first 'met' Charity Weston when I was writing an earlier book, LADY BENEATH THE VEIL. Then she was a successful London actress, calling herself Agnes Bennet and not behaving at all well. However, seeing the true happiness Gideon and Dominique achieved was a turning point for her, and she decided it was time to make a new start.

I knew then that I wanted to write Charity's story—to show her facing up to her past and using her real name, despite the fact that it might bring her back into the sphere of her abusive father.

Actresses in the Regency period could be fabulously successful, but they lived on the fringes of polite society. Some married, and one or two married very well. Others acquired a rich protector and some, like Charity, earned enough to secure their independence and were loath to relinquish all their worldly goods to a husband.

At the beginning of this book Charity is still an actress, but she is aware that she wants something more from her life—in modern parlance we might say she is aware of her biological clock ticking away! Then she meets the mysterious highwayman, 'The Dark Rider', who is so fickle that sometimes all he takes from his female victims is one sizzling kiss. After that encounter Charity's life will never be the same again.

I do hope you enjoy Charity's story. She is a strong lady, determined to fight injustice, and when she meets her hero she proves herself to be a worthy partner for him!

Happy reading.

AT THE HIGHWAYMAN'S PLEASURE

Sarah Mallory

Printed and bound in Spain
by Blackprint CPI, Barcelona

Published in Great Britain 2014
by Mills & Boon, an imprint of Harlequin (UK) Limited,
Eton House, 18-24 Paradise Road, Richmond, Surrey, TW9 1SR

© 2014 Sarah Mallory

ISBN: 978 0 263 90944 9

Sarah Mallory was born in Bristol, and now lives in an old farmhouse on the edge of the Pennines with her husband and family. She left grammar school at sixteen to work in companies as varied as stockbrokers, marine engineers, insurance brokers, biscuit manufacturers and even a quarrying company. Her first book was published shortly after the birth of her daughter. She has published more than a dozen books under the pen-name of Melinda Hammond, winning the Reviewers' Choice Award from singletitles.com for *Dance for a Diamond* and the Historical Novel Society's Editors' Choice for *Gentlemen in Question*. As Sarah Mallory she is the winner of the Romantic Novelists' Association's RONA Rose® Award for 2012 and 2013 for *The Dangerous Lord Darrington* and *Beneath the Major's Scars*.

Previous novels by the same author:

THE WICKED BARON
MORE THAN A GOVERNESS
  (part of *On Mothering Sunday*)
WICKED CAPTAIN, WAYWARD WIFE
THE EARL'S RUNAWAY BRIDE
DISGRACE AND DESIRE
TO CATCH A HUSBAND…
SNOWBOUND WITH THE NOTORIOUS RAKE
  (part of *An Improper Regency Christmas*)
THE DANGEROUS LORD DARRINGTON
BENEATH THE MAJOR'S SCARS*
BEHIND THE RAKE'S WICKED WAGER*
BOUGHT FOR REVENGE
LADY BENEATH THE VEIL

*The Notorious Coale Brothers

AT THE HIGHWAYMAN'S PLEASURE
features characters you will have already met in
LADY BENEATH THE VEIL

And in Mills & Boon® *Undone!* eBooks:

THE TANTALISING MISS COALE*

And in M&B:

THE ILLEGITIMATE MONTAGUE
  (part of *Castonbury Park* Regency mini-series)

**Did you know that some of these novels
are also available as eBooks?
Visit www.millsandboon.co.uk**

To Willow, my beautiful dog.
Taking him for his daily walks over the moors
has helped me to write this story.

Prologue

June 1794

Charity closed her eyes and raised her face to the sun. It was blazing down from the cloudless blue sky while a skylark high above trilled joyously and a soft breeze stirred her hair, hanging loose and damp about her shoulders.

This is heaven, she thought, but when she opened her eyes she saw only the familiar fields around her, and in the distance, just beyond the river but before the rugged hills to the east, was the village of Saltby, no more than a little cluster of houses dominated by the stark square tower of the church.

How she wished she didn't have to go back there.

Charity tossed her head defiantly and felt the heavy weight of her hair rippling down her back. She would have to bundle it under her bonnet before they reached the village, but it was so good to have it loose, so deliciously *free*.

She heard a giggle.

'Lord, Charity, 'tis so thick it will never be dry before we reach Saltby.' Her friend Jenny lifted some of the blonde locks from her neck and let them fall again.

'But it was worth it.' She tucked her hand in her friend's arm. 'Come along now. Let's get home.'

They continued along a narrow valley, chattering as they went and swinging their bonnets carelessly from the ribbons. It was not until they rounded the next bend that they saw the activity in the valley ahead of them.

'Oh, heavens, I didn't know they would be here today,' muttered Jenny, coming to a halt.

On the flat land by the beck the sheep were being sheared. A stone-walled fold beside the stream was already packed with animals, while shepherds were driving more sheep into the water to wash the fat from their coats ready for shearing. A familiar black-clothed figure was standing on a boulder in the middle of the activity. His arms were raised to the heavens and he had a book clutched in one hand. Even at this distance Charity knew it was a Bible. He was reciting passages from the gospels, but the shearers paid him little heed, continuing with their work with a steady, dogged persistence that would see all the sheep sheared before dark.

'Oh, heavens, 'tis your father,' hissed Jenny.

'Yes,' said Charity bitterly. 'Phineas thinks himself another Wesley, preaching to the godless. Let's go back before he sees us. We'll take the long way over the hill.'

'Too late.'

The black-coated figure had jumped down from his makeshift pulpit and was striding towards them, shouting. There was no help for it. The girls stopped and waited for him to come up.

'And where might you be going?'

It was Jenny who spoke up.

'We are on our way home, Mr Weston. We have been to visit old Mother Crawshaw, to take her a basket of food. Now her son has gone for a soldier there is no one to provide for her and Mrs Weston thought—'

But Phineas wasn't listening. He was glaring, his face mottled with fury as he raised a shaking finger to point at them.

'You have been traipsing the countryside like that, with no kerchiefs to cover your shoulders and your hair down your backs like, like—'

'It was so hot we stopped on the way back to bathe at the secret pool,' said Charity, giving him a defiant look. 'We have done it many times before.'

'Aye, but you are not children now. You are fourteen years old and should know the Lord frowns upon women displaying themselves in such shameless fashion.'

'We did not intend anyone to see us,' she retorted. 'Our hair will be dry by the time we reach Saltby, and if it is not we will put it up beneath our caps before we get there.'

Even though he was still some yards away his fierce eyes burned into her and she could see the spittle on his lip as he ground out his words.

'And you would parade yourself here, before all these men, like the veriest trollop.'

'No, we intended to go the other way—' She broke off as he swiftly covered the ground between them and caught her wrist. 'Let me go!'

'God knows I have tried to teach you the ways of righteousness, but to no avail. "Even a child is known by his actions", and you are certainly known by yours.'

'But we have done nothing wrong.'

'I'll teach you to flaunt yourself in this way.' He made a grab for Jenny, but Charity clutched his sleeve and pulled him away.

'Run!' she shrieked to her friend. 'Run home now.' When Jenny hesitated, she cried, 'You can do nothing for me, save yourself!'

'Run away, then!' shouted Phineas as the girl fled. 'You cannot hide from the Lord's wrath, Jennifer Howe. I shall denounce you from the pulpit come Sunday!'

'Oh, no, you won't,' flashed Charity, struggling to free herself. 'You will see Mr Howe and he will give you three guineas for your parish fund and that will be the end of it.'

'You dare to censure me for doing the Lord's work?'

Her lip curled. 'I have seen too many times how a few pieces of silver will mollify your righteous temper!'

His eyes narrowed. 'Unnatural daughter!'

'*We* were doing the Lord's work,' she flung back at him. 'We were ministering to the poor, which is of more use than your preaching to them.'

Phineas waved his free arm towards the scene of activity by the river.

'You were using it for an excuse to come here and throw yourselves at these men. I know your wicked ways, girl.' He thrust his hand into her hair and Charity screamed as he tightened his hold. 'You know you distract men with this… this golden abundance, don't you? It is a vanity, girl, do you hear me, a vanity. "They that are of forward heart are an abomination to the Lord!"'

'Let me go!'

'Not until you see what becomes of those who mock the Lord and his servants.'

Ignoring her screams, he dragged her with him, back towards the sheep shearers. The men looked up warily as he approached, some muttered under their breath, but none dared protest. He hauled Charity to the boulder that he had been standing on moments earlier and forced her to sit.

'Jacob, come and hold her here.'

'Nay then, Parson, I don't—'

Phineas turned on the man with a snarl.

'Dare you gainsay a servant of the Lord?'

Jacob stepped up and took her arms.

'Sorry, lass.'

She hardly heard his muttered apology, for she was sobbing now, her scalp burning where Phineas had almost torn the hair out by the roots. She heard his hard voice boom out.

'Elias, bring me the dagging shears.'

'No!'

She screamed, cried, pleaded, but it was no use. She heard the rasp as the shears cut through her hair, handful by handful, and all the time Phineas was reciting from the Bible.

It was all over in minutes, less time than it would take a man to shear a sheep. There was a curious lightness to her head; she could feel the burning sun on her scalp. Jacob released her, but she did not move. She sat hunched on the rock, her eyes dry now, staring unseeing at the ground.

Phineas stood back.

'And the Lord said, "Withhold not correction from the child".'

His words fell into silence. The men were milling around, uncertain what to do. The skylark had gone, and even the sheep had ceased their bleating.

Slowly Charity got to her feet. She stared around her. The sky was still an unbroken blue vault and the hills looked the same, but everything was different, as if her world had tilted and she was looking at this scene as a detached, indifferent observer. She raised her eyes to look at her father. His face was still an angry red and he was breathing heavily, his arms by his sides and the cruel steel shears clasped in one hand.

'But I am not a child,' she said slowly. 'Not anymore. And that is the last time I will let you lay a finger on me.'

With that she turned and walked away, leaving her hair, those long, silken tresses, lying at his feet like a creamy golden fleece.

Chapter One

January 1807

It was trying to snow, the bitter winds blowing the flakes horizontally across the carriage windows. Charity Weston felt a flicker of relief that there were no passengers riding on the top of the Scarborough to York cross-country mail. Black, low-lying clouds were making the winter day even shorter and soon the familiar landscape would be lost in a gloom as deep as that which filled the carriage. It was very different from the bright limelight in which she spent most of her days—or rather her nights—on stage.

She wondered what her fellow passengers would think if they knew she was an actress. The farmer and his wife might not have smiled at her quite so kindly when she took her seat, but then, all they saw was a fashionably dressed lady accompanied by her maid. She had even gone back to using the soft, cultured voice of a lady, having thrown off the rather flat, nasal tones of the south that she had assumed, along with another name, whilst working in London. It would be no wonder, therefore, if they thought her a lady of some standing. However, if they lived in or near Allingford it was quite possible that they would realise their error in the next few months, for she had accepted an offer from her old friend to join his theatre company.

A new town, new roles and a new audience. Once the idea would have filled her with excitement, but for some reason Charity could not raise any enthusiasm.

Am I getting old? she wondered. *I am seven and twenty and all I want is a place of my own—not the lodging houses I own in London, but something more....*

The carriage was rattling through a village and she saw a little cottage set back from the road. Golden light shone from the downstairs window, and the door was open. A woman was standing in the threshold, arms thrown wide to welcome the two little children running up the path towards her. Charity watched her catch the babes in her arms and look up at the man following them. Even in the dying light it was pos-

sible to see happiness shining in her face, and
Charity felt something clutching at her heart.

That was what she wanted: a home and a
loving family.

She turned in her seat, pressing her head to
the glass to look at the cottage until it was out
of sight. The scene had been a happy one, but
it was no more than a single moment, and she
knew only too well how deceptive appearances
could be. Once they were all indoors, out of
sight, the children might shrink behind their
mother's skirts as the man towered over them,
Bible in one hand and riding crop in the other.
He would demand complete obedience and reward any defiance with a thrashing. Shivering,
Charity huddled back into her corner and closed
her eyes, struggling to repress the memories.
Perhaps it had been a mistake to come back to
Allingford, so close to her roots.

The sudden slowing of the coach and raised
voices from outside caused the farmer's wife to
shriek. Charity heard a mutter from Betty, her
maid, who was sitting beside her.

'Oh, lordy, what's amiss?'

'Most likely a cow on the road,' Charity replied calmly. She let down the window and
leaned out. 'No,' she said with equal calm. 'It
is not a beast. Well, not a four-legged one, at
any rate. It is a highwayman.'

Betty gasped and the farmer's wife began to gabble hysterically, her hands clasping the silver locket resting on her ample bosom, but Charity felt nothing more than a mild excitement as she regarded the horseman who was standing beside the road and brandishing a pistol towards the driver and guard. In the gloomy half-light he presented a menacing figure with his hat pulled low over his brow, throwing his face into deep shadow. Everything about the highwayman was black, from his tricorn to the hooves of the great horse that carried him. In a rough, cheerful voice he ordered the guard to throw down his shotgun and hand over the mailbag.

Charity felt a touch on her arm.

'I pray you, madam, come back into the shadows,' muttered the farmer in an urgent whisper. 'Mayhap once he has the mail he won't bother with us.'

She sat back at once but made no attempt to put up the window again, lest the noise and movement should attract the man's attention.

'I think it pretty poor of the guard,' she whispered. 'He's made not the least attempt at resistance.'

'There must be a gang of them,' breathed Betty.

'No, I don't think so.' Charity leaned closer to the window again. 'I can only see the one man.'

The rider dismounted and picked up the mail-bag, throwing it over his saddle. Charity turned to the farmer.

'Surely between you and the two men on the box, you could overpower him?'

The farmer immediately shrank back farther into his corner.

'Not if he's armed,' he declared, a note of alarm in his voice.

'He's coming over,' hissed Betty. 'Oh, lordy!'

She clutched at Charity's sleeve as the door was wrenched open and the stranger said jovially, 'Well, now, let's be seein' who we have in here. If ye'd care to step down, ladies and gentleman!'

The farmer's wife whimpered and shrank back against her husband as the lamplight glinted on the pistol being waved towards them. With a little tut of exasperation, Charity climbed out, sharply adjuring Betty not to dawdle. The farmer and his wife followed suit and soon they were all four of them standing on the open road, with the winter wind blowing around them. She glanced towards the box, where the driver and guard were sitting with their hands clasped above their heads.

'Will that be everyone?'

'Unless there is someone hiding under the seat,' retorted Charity, rubbing her cold hands together. 'If you intend to rob us then please get on with it so we may be on our way.'

The man's face was in shadow, but she could feel his eyes upon her. Now that she was closer to him she could see the deeper black of a mask covering his upper face. It did not need Betty's little gasp of dismay to tell her that drawing attention to herself was not the wisest thing to do.

'And who might you be, ma'am, to be making demands?'

'That is none of your business.'

'Ah, well, now, beggin' your pardon, ma'am, but I have to disagree with you.' He waved the pistol. His voice was still cheerful, but there was no mistaking the note of steel in his tone or the menacing gesture. She drew herself up.

'I am Mrs Weston.'

'The devil you are!' He stepped a little closer and she had the impression that she was being scrutinised very carefully. 'You'll be on your way to Beringham, then?'

'I have no business in Beringham.'

'No?'

'No, I am going to Allingford.' She hesitated. 'To the theatre. I am an actress.' She held out her reticule. 'Here, if you are going to rob us, take it!'

She saw the flash of white as he grinned.

'No, I don't think I will. 'Tis a charitable mood I'm in this evening.'

'Are ye not going to rob us, then?' The farmer goggled at him.

'I am not. I've decided I'll not take your purse, nor the ornament that's a-twinkling on your lady wife. Get ye back into the carriage… ah, except you, ma'am.'

Charity's heart lurched as he addressed her. Not for the world would she show her fear, and she said with creditable assurance, 'I have nothing for you.'

'Oh, but I think you have.'

Betty stepped up, crying, 'You'll not touch my mistress!'

Charity caught her arm. 'Hush, Betty.'

The pistol waved ominously.

'Send your maid back to the carriage with the others, Mrs Weston.'

'Do as he says, Betty.' Charity held her maid's eye and put her hand up, her fingers touching the discreet pearl head of the hatpin that held her bonnet in place. 'I'll deal with this.'

She saw the understanding in the older woman's eyes and with a grim little nod Betty walked away, leaving Charity alone with the highwayman.

'I've changed my mind,' he told her. 'I'll take that fancy brooch you have pinned to your coat.'

It was a small cameo and of no particular value. Charity supposed he would present it to his sweetheart and found the idea did not please her. He reached out his hand to pluck the brooch from her breast and she forced herself to keep still while his fingers fumbled with the catch, but after a moment, and with a huff of exasperation, she brushed his hands aside.

'Here, let me.' She unfastened the cameo and held it out to him. 'There, take it. Now may I go?'

'Not just yet, lady.'

He stepped closer and she was enveloped in his shadow. Charity was a tall woman, but he towered over her, the caped greatcoat making his shoulders impossibly broad. A tremor ran through her, but she told herself he was only a man, and in her profession she had dealt with many such situations.

She said calmly, 'Surely you will not attack me here, in front of everyone.'

He laughed, and again she saw that flash of white teeth.

'Attack? Faith, me darlin', that suggests you ain't willing.'

'Indeed? Well, I—'

Her words were cut off as he reached out and

dragged her to him. She found herself pinioned against his chest, one arm like an iron band around her shoulders. She looked up to protest and at that moment his head swooped down and he kissed her.

Through luck or expertise his mouth found hers immediately and her senses reeled from that first, electric touch. She could not move and he continued to kiss her, his tongue plundering her mouth and causing such a rush of sensation through her body that it was impossible to resist him. The stubble on his face grazed her skin but she hardly noticed, her mind spinning with such irrelevant thoughts as the fact that he did not smell of dirt and horses. Instead her head was filled with a succession of scents. First there had been the unmistakable smell of leather and the wool of his greatcoat, but when he pulled her closer she recognised the pleasant tang of soap and lemons, spices and clean linen. As his tongue explored her mouth her bones dissolved and hot arrows of pleasure drove deep into her body. The sensations were new and unnerving. She wanted to cling to him, to push herself against that hard, male body.

Time stopped. She was his prisoner, fighting her own desire to kiss him back rather than struggling against his embrace, and when he finally raised his head she was strangely disappointed. She remained in his arms, unable to move and staring up at him. Her eyes had grown more accustomed to the darkness and she could make out his features a little better beneath the shadow of his hat. The smiling mouth and lean cheeks, the strong lines of his jaw that ran down to the cleft of his chin, the hawkish nose and most of all those dark, dark eyes, gleaming at her through the slits of his mask.

'Mmm,' he murmured, soft as a sigh. 'Heavenly.'

Charity had forgotten her surroundings, the icy wind that was even now scattering tiny flakes of snow over them, the fact that he was a stranger. She had even forgotten that he was a highwayman, until he raised his head and barked out an order to the coachman and guard.

'Keep yer hands on yer heads, me fine friends.'

His rough warning brought her back to reality. She pushed him away—no, *he* did not move, it was she who stepped back, hiding the trembling of her hands by vigorously shaking out her skirts. A glance behind her showed the coach still standing on the road, the driver and guard still sitting motionless on the box and the white faces of the passengers visible at the coach windows. It could only have been a min-

ute that had passed, maybe two, yet Charity felt
as if something momentous had occurred. She
gave herself a mental shake. Good heavens, it
was only a kiss, and she had been kissed before,
but never had it had such an effect.

It was the excitement, she told herself sternly.
*Fear set your nerves on edge and made you feel
the experience all the more keenly.*

The highwayman was holding out his hand
to her.

'Having exacted my price from you, madam,
you are now free to go on your way.'

Silently she took his hand and let him help
her back into the carriage. He closed the door
and she saw the glint of amusement in his eyes
as he touched the barrel of the pistol to his hat
brim in a mock salute. He stepped back and
glanced up at the box.

'Now, me lads, I'll thank you to sit where
you are a while longer.'

He whistled and the black horse trotted up to
him. Charity noted the athletic way he leaped
up into the saddle and galloped away, leaving
everyone in a shocked, immobile silence.

As the hoofbeats faded, the spell was broken.
The farmer began to rage about the impudence
of such rascals while his wife fell back in her
seat, fanning herself vigorously and declaring
she could feel a seizure coming on. Betty mut-

tered up a prayer of thanks and the guard clambered down to retrieve his shotgun and to ask if the passengers were all right.

'All right? Of course we are not all right!' shouted the farmer. 'What're you about, to let one rascally knave with a popgun cause us all such terror? Look! Look at my wife. Right terrified, she is. 'Tis a disgrace, I tell 'ee. One man on the road and all you can do is drop your gun!'

'Aye, I dropped it right enough,' replied the guard, affronted. 'He were threatenin' to shoot me head off.'

'So you let 'im get away with daylight robbery!'

'As I recall, he didn't take anything o' yours,' the guard retorted.

'He stole the mail,' countered the farmer's wife.

'And he assaulted my mistress,' added Betty.

'Which is why I came to enquire if she was hurt.' The guard turned his attention to Charity. 'Well, ma'am? Have you suffered any injury?'

Charity was reliving the memory of being imprisoned in those strong arms and her lips still burned from the highwayman's kiss, but she would never admit that to a soul.

'N-no, I am a little shaken, but I am not hurt.'

'The rascal stole your brooch, Miss—'

'Hush, Betty. It was a mere trinket.' She turned to the guard. 'Please, it is not important. Let us get on.'

The guard seemed satisfied with that. He nodded.

'Then we'll be on our way. We're stopping at Beringham to change horses, so we will report the incident then.'

He closed the door and the carriage rocked as he climbed back onto the box beside the driver.

'Aye, and I'll be reporting this to the mail company,' muttered the farmer as they set off again. 'Never seen the like, a guard and driver made to look no-how by a lone horseman— why, between the three of us we could have taken him!'

'That's just what my mistress sug—'

Charity dug her maid in the ribs. She summoned up a bright smile.

'Well, I for one am glad we came off so lightly. I pray we will have no more excitement before we reach our destination.'

Her prayers were answered, and the short journey into Beringham was uneventful. The passengers were invited to go into the inn while the constable was summoned.

After the chilly carriage, the sight of the inn's blazing fire was very cheering, and when the landlord had supplied them all with a cup of hot coffee, even the farmer's mood improved. The local constable turned out to be a stolid individual called Rigg who painstakingly wrote everything down, explaining that the magistrate would want to have all the details reported to him. Once the guard and driver had given their version of events, he turned to the passengers. Charity glanced at the clock. They should have been at Allingford by now, but the delay could not be helped, so she stifled her impatience and gave her attention to the matter in hand.

'He got down off his horse and ordered you all out o' the coach, you say?' The constable looked at his notes. 'So you had a chance to get a good look at the fellow, eh?'

The farmer shook his head. 'Nay, 'twere too dark to see out by then.'

'That's true,' affirmed Betty. 'And he soon ordered us all back inside, except Mrs Weston.'

'Weston?' The constable looked up, all attention. 'Mrs Weston, you say? Are you—?'

'I am an actress.' She smiled to atone for interrupting him. 'Mrs Weston is my stage name.'

The farmer's wife sniffed, her earlier smiles replaced now with a more haughty stare.

'Ah, I see.' The constable looked even more interested in that. 'You'll be on your way to

Allingford, then.' He added, with something like a sigh, 'We have no theatre in Beringham.'

'Nor any other entertainment,' grumbled the farmer. 'Even the inns ain't what they was.'

'But she was closest to the villain,' put in the farmer's wife, ignoring her husband. 'In his arms, she was, and he was makin' free with her—'

'I beg your pardon, but it was no such thing,' declared Betty, bristling in defence of her mistress. 'He ravished her, quite against her will.'

Charity blushed and shook her head at the bemused constable.

'He stole a cheap brooch, that is all.'

'And he kissed her, too!' cried the farmer's wife in outraged accents.

'Very understandable, ma'am, if you don't mind my saying so,' returned the officer of the law, then coloured to the tips of his ears.

'It means she saw him better than the rest of us,' said the farmer. 'Right tall fellow, he was.'

'Ma'am?' The constable turned his eyes towards Charity, who shrugged.

'I would not have said he was that tall. About medium height, I think.'

'Bigger, surely,' argued the farmer's wife. 'He towered over you!'

Charity remembered it only too well, but she shook her head now.

'I was cowering a little.'

It was a lie. She had felt no fear in her encounter with the highwayman. There had been anger, yes, and excitement, but she had never felt afraid of him. The farmer's wife was continuing.

'A big man, all in black and astride a great black 'oss. And he had right broad shoulders.'

Charity remembered him coming close, the feeling that he was enveloping her in his shadow.

'His coat was very large,' she said. 'It had several capes on the shoulders, which gave the impression of width.'

'Did you see his face, or his hair—did he wear a wig, perhaps?'

'He never removed his hat. And he wore a mask, so I could not see his countenance.'

That much was true. She could not even say with any certainty what colour his eyes had been, only that they were very dark and had bored into her, as if he could see into her very soul.

'His horse, though—that should be easy to find.' The coachman tapped out his pipe upon the hearth and set about refilling it. 'It was a stallion, a great dark beast, pure black from mane to hoof.'

'And he weren't from around these parts,' added the guard. 'Irish, I do reckon.'

'Aye,' agreed the farmer. 'Definitely Irish, no mistaking that brogue.'

Charity said nothing. She had spent her life working with actors and mimics and suspected that lilting Irish accent had been as false as the inflection she had adopted in London to make everyone think she had grown up south of the Thames. The landlord, who had been hovering by all the while, nodded sagely.

'The Dark Rider. They say he comes from Dublin.'

'Oh, Lord bless us!' exclaimed the farmer's wife, falling back in her chair. No one paid her any heed.

'Nay, I thought it was Shannon,' said the coachman, 'But that's who I guessed it might be. I've never seen him afore, though.'

'The Dark Rider?' asked Betty nervously.

'Aye.' The landlord nodded. 'He's been working the roads around Beringham for a year or so now. Robbed Absalom Keldy and his wife afore Christmas, he did.'

'And I was told he took fifty guineas off Mr Hutton only last month,' put in the coachman.

The farmer snorted. 'Well, he can take what he likes off Hutton, with my blessing. Self-serving old scoundrel that he is!'

'Aye,' agreed the landlord, 'but the Dark Rider's capricious, see. You never know what he will take. It might be no more than a kiss from a pretty woman, other times it's a purse.'

'He always takes the mailbag,' added the constable, 'although they turn up again at the roadside after he's looked through 'em. Searching for money, I dare say, although who'd be foolish enough to send money in a letter, I don't know.'

The landlord winked at Charity. 'He's got the ladies around here all of a pother. They all wants to meet 'im. Many think he's a gentleman in disguise, kicking up a lark.'

'Gentleman or no, he'll be dancing on the gibbet when he's caught,' growled the constable. 'I think that's all I needs for now, so you can be on your way.' His unhurried gaze swept over the passengers. 'You'd best tell me your direction, in case we needs to speak to you again, or to ask you to identify the culprit.'

'Well, you'll find us at Broad Ings Farm.' The farmer's buxom wife stood up and shook out her skirts. 'And we've paid our fare to the next crossroads, so the quicker we get moving the better.'

'And you, Mrs Weston?'

Charity spread her hands.

'I have no idea where I shall be living in

Allingford, but you can always find me at the theatre.'

They were ushered back to the coach. The driver was anxious to make up time and they rattled quickly through the darkness to the crossroads, where the farmer and his wife alighted, leaving Charity and her maid with the carriage to themselves.

'Well, well, what a to-do, mistress! We should have been in Allingford three hours since.'

'I know, Betty. I hope Hywel has a dinner put aside for us. All this excitement has given me an appetite.'

Betty gave a disapproving sniff.

'Don't know how you can be thinking of food when you were ravished by that scoundrel! Still, it couldn't have been that bad, since you didn't have to make use of your hatpin, and I know full well that you've used it on more than one occasion when an admirer has been a bit too familiar.'

Charity did not reply, but settled back in her corner and closed her eyes. To be truthful, she had not even thought of her hatpin when the highwayman had pulled her close. She had not thought of anything. She had known ladies in the audience to swoon at the sight of a particularly handsome actor, but had always considered them very silly beings. Now she could understand them a little better, for the powerful attraction she had felt for the audacious rascal had made her light-headed, and she had come very close to swooning herself.

Heavens, what was she about?

You are *growing old, my girl,* she told herself sternly. *Old and lonely, if you must needs faint at the attentions of a stranger.*

The lights of Allingford interrupted her musings and Charity was grateful to put aside her disturbing thoughts. A servant was waiting to escort them the short distance from the inn to a modest house where they were admitted by a very superior manservant who announced that Mr Jenkin was waiting for Mrs Weston in the parlour. As the servant opened the door she saw a tall, distinguished-looking man with silver hair standing before the fire. Upon her entrance he came forward to greet her.

'I was beginning to think you had changed your mind about coming to work for me.'

Laughing, she gave him her hands and pulled him close to kiss his cheek.

'Not a bit of it, Hywel! And good evening, my dear. We were delayed on the road. A highwayman, no less!' She turned away to remove her cloak and bonnet so that Hywel would not see her face; he knew her so well he would see in an instant that there was more to the encounter than she was telling him. 'He is well known in this area, I believe—the Dark Rider. A very poor example of his kind, in my opinion.'

'I have heard of him.' He handed her a glass of wine as she came back towards the fire. 'What did he take from you?'

'He stole a trinket, a cheap brooch of mine.'

'And did he demand a kiss from all the ladies?'

She blushed.

'Yes.'

'Of which you were by far the prettiest.'

Her mouth twisted in a little moue of distaste.

'Blonde curls and blue eyes! You know I do not rate my milk-and-water colouring.'

'You are a fine actress, my dear, but your beauty—your *milk-and-water colouring*, as you call it—has contributed no small part to your success.' He invited her to sit beside the fire and lowered himself into a chair opposite. 'How did you like Scarborough?'

'Very much.' She sent him a twinkling look. 'I was compared very favourably with Mrs Siddons.'

'And now you will take Allingford by storm. I am very grateful that you have deigned to grace my little theatre with your presence.'

'Nonsense, you know I owe everything to

you. When you wrote to tell me you had lost your leading lady, how could I refuse to help you? After all, I owe you everything, for taking me in and looking after me all those years ago.'

'I had my reward—you are a natural actress and your success reflected well upon my travelling players, so well that investors were persuaded to join me in building the theatre here.'

'Yet still you encouraged me to try my luck in London.'

'Your talent deserves a wider audience.' He sat back, smiling. 'I looked out for you in the newspapers—Agnes Bennet, darling of Drury Lane! How long ago was it, five years?'

'About that, yes.'

'But you quit London just as you were making a name for yourself. Why was that, my dear?'

Charity cradled her wine glass in her hands.

'I fell in with a bad crowd. When I realised how bad I was disgusted, with myself as well as with them. I decided to leave that life, and Agnes Bennet, behind me.' She gave a wry smile. 'It was a miracle that I escaped with my virtue intact.'

'So you are Charity Weston again.'

'Yes, and I have spent the last few years touring the country, building a new career for myself.'

'And doing very well, if the reports are to be believed.' Hywel got up to fetch the decanter and refill their glasses. 'So why did you come to Allingford, my dear?'

'Why, because you asked me—your leading lady had contracted inflammation of the lungs and retired to Worthing with her husband.'

'When I wrote I hardly expected you to accept.'

She spread her hands. 'I wanted to come back to the north.' Her eyes twinkled. 'Being able to play in a theatre rather than an inn or a barn is very welcome, Hywel, and when you told me you were the owner *and* manager here I could not help myself!'

'Away with your flattery, baggage! Please do not mistake me, my dear, I am delighted to have you rejoin my theatre. Many of your old friends are still working for me. But it is very close to your old home. And to your father.'

She shrugged. 'Saltby is several miles away. I doubt Phineas ever comes to Allingford, and it is even more unlikely that he would visit the theatre.'

'But he is no longer at Saltby, my dear. He lives in Beringham now.'

She sat up. 'So close?' She chewed her lip, frowning, then said slowly, 'It matters not. I am no longer afraid of him. Besides, I am tired of my wandering life, Hywel. I am minded to settle down, and where better than Allingford, where I can continue to work in the theatre?'

'But using your real name—is that not rather a risk? Weston is bound to take it amiss when he discovers you are here.'

'I have hidden behind a stage name for too long. I have accepted the courtesy title of *Mrs* Weston, but I will go no further. I want to be myself now.' She sipped her wine. 'I have heard nothing of Phineas since I left.' His brows lifted and she continued, 'I stopped calling him "Father" years ago. He does not deserve the title. Is my stepmother still living?'

'No. She died several years ago, before he moved to Beringham. He is a man of property now. It appears your stepmother left him a tidy sum.'

Charity looked up, surprised. 'Really? I knew he had married her for her dowry, but I had thought it was all spent.'

'Apparently not, since he came to Beringham a man of some means. He has married again and his wife brings with her a small fortune. He is now a magistrate, too.'

'Is he indeed?' She grimaced. 'Poor Beringham.'

'Very true. Thankfully we have a county border between us. He rules with a rod of iron and will allow no theatres or entertainments in his area.' He grinned. 'All the better for me, of course, since those who want to see a play must come to Allingford.'

'It must irk him dreadfully to know people are free to enjoy themselves here. I wonder if he is aware that the theatre in Scarborough was built by a clergyman? He would certainly not approve of *that*! Phineas believes salvation can only come about through suffering.'

'As long as it is not his own.'

She laughed and said bitterly, 'Of course. He was always able to justify his own comfort.'

'He and his wife live in very grand style now,' Hywel told her. 'He has a fine house in Beringham. It is stuffed full of works of art, I am told, some of quite dubious quality, but expensive nevertheless. And he has set up his own stable, with a fancy carriage to take him and his lady about the country.'

Charity gazed into the fire, wondering if this third wife was any happier than the first two. She had never forgotten her mama's anxious careworn face, the way she would jump at shadows, always afraid of incurring her husband's wrath. When she died, Phineas had immediately taken another wife, a kindly woman who had soon been broken by his cruelty and become a meek, silent figure in the house. Charity shuddered.

'Thank goodness I am no longer part of that family.'

'Yet the connection is sure to be made,' said Hywel. 'Some in Beringham will remember that Phineas once had a daughter.'

'That was thirteen years ago, Hywel. *I* will never acknowledge the connection and I doubt Phineas would want it known. The past is dead to me.'

He looked unconvinced.

'Do you still suffer the nightmares?'

She shrugged. 'Rarely. Although, I did wonder, coming here—'

Hywel laid his hand on her arm.

'You are safe enough here, Charity. Weston has no jurisdiction in Allingford. And you can rely upon my protection.'

She reached out and briefly took his hand.

'I know that, Hywel. You have always been a good friend to me. But enough of this dull talk. Tell me how you go on here and what you have chosen for my first role!'

'The theatre is doing very well—my players are good and reliable. I thought, for your first appearance, you should play Mr Sheridan's sentimental heroine, Lydia Languish.'

'And will you be Captain Absolute?'

He shook his head, laughing. 'I am too long in the tooth now to play the lover. Will Stamp takes those roles now.'

'Young Will? I remember he had just joined you when I left.'

'And proved himself a good actor,' said Hywel. 'I shall play his father, Sir Anthony.'

'Do you have a script for me? It is a while since I played Lydia.'

'Of course. I shall furnish you with one to-morrow when I take you to the theatre to meet my cast.'

'And I must find myself somewhere to live.'

'You are quite welcome to stay here for as long as you wish.'

'Thank you, Hywel, but I thought to rent a little house for myself.'

'You will need a manservant. I know just the fellow—'

'No, no, at least, not yet. Betty can do all I need—Betty Harrup, my maid and dresser. She has been with me for several years and is upstairs even now unpacking for me. We have been used to fending for ourselves and I shall be quite content.' A mischievous chuckle escaped her. 'And I shall not be asking you to fund me, Hywel. I have invested well enough and have a comfortable income now.'

'In that case, I shall find for you all the most

suitable properties for a woman of substance. I shall puff off your fame quite shamelessly and Allingford's landlords will be falling over themselves to provide a house for you. We have three weeks before we open again, so you have plenty of time to make yourself at home here. But enough of that. I had dinner put back and I am sure you must be hungry.'

'Ravenous, my dear. Shall I go upstairs and see if Betty has unpacked for me, or will you allow me to dine with you in all my dirt?'

He laughed. 'Let us dine now, by all means! A little dust on your skirts will do no harm.'

They passed the rest of the evening comfortably enough, catching up on all that had happened since they last met, and despite the nagging worry of knowing her father lived in the neighbouring town, when Charity retired to bed there were no nightmares to disturb her slumbers. Instead she dreamed of a masked man on a black horse.

Charity soon found a home of her own in Allingford. In less than a week she had moved into a snug little house in North Street. It took only a couple days to make it comfortable, and on the third evening Charity was able to sit down in the little sitting room to study her script of *The Rivals,* ready for the rehearsals, which were to start in earnest the following day.

'I've brought in more coals for the fire, Miss Charity.'

'Thank you, Betty. You need not wait up for me, I shall see myself to bed.'

The maid dropped the bucket on the hearth and straightened, bending a fond but frowning gaze upon her mistress.

'Now, don't you be sitting up 'til all hours straining your eyes, ma'am.'

'I promise you I won't,' said Charity with a smile. 'Goodnight, my dear.'

Betty went out again and soon she heard her stumping up the wooden stairs. Charity turned back to her script, but she could not give it her full attention, for she was aware of the creaks and sighs as the unfamiliar house settled down for the night. Once she heard a soft thud and she took her candle into the back room to check that the door into the yard was secure. Her candle flickered and she looked around a little nervously.

Everything was strange and new, but she comforted herself with the thought that soon she would know every nook and creaking floorboard of the little house. She went back to the sitting room, but the fire had died down and she decided she would not waste more coal on it.

'I shall go to bed,' she told the shadowy corners. '*The Rivals* must wait until tomorrow.'

She went upstairs and as she passed the first door she heard the rhythmic snores coming from her maid. There were two more rooms in the attic, but Charity had insisted Betty should sleep in one of the two chambers here on the first floor. Smiling, she made her way to her own chamber. It was at the back of the house, and she had chosen it because she thought it would be much quieter than the room overlooking the street. As she entered, her candle flickered and she saw that the window was not fully closed. She crossed the room, leaving her candle on the dressing table as she passed. She pushed down on the heavy sash and was just slipping the catch into place when she heard a soft chuckle behind her and a deep voice said, 'Faith, me darlin', but I'd forgotten how beautiful you are!'

Charity swung round, a startled cry catching in her throat. Behind the door was the shadowy figure of a man in riding dress, a tricorn pulled low over his face.

'The Dark Rider!'

She saw the flash of white as he grinned.

'The very same, me lady.'

'Get out.' She backed against the window. 'Go now before I call my maid.'

'Sure, now, I'm thinking you'd have screamed before now if you was going to.'

Charity was wondering why she had not done so. She said, 'So are you a common housebreaker, too, or did you know this was my house?'

'Oh, I knew, Mrs Weston. Word travels fast when a celebrated actress takes up residence in a small town like this. Are ye not going to ask me what I'm doing here?'

A trickle of fear ran down her back as she supplied her own answer to that question. She kept her eyes resolutely away from the bed as she stepped closer to the dressing table. 'I want to know how you got in.'

He waved to the window. 'Over the lean-to roof.'

She rested her hand on the silk-and-velvet bonnet thrown over one of the mirror supports.

'Well, you may leave the same way.'

'I will, when I'm ready.'

'Now.' She pulled a hatpin from the bonnet. Its steel shaft was some eight inches long and glinted wickedly in the dim light. 'Do not think I will not use this to defend myself,' she added, when he did not move. 'It would not be the first time and I am quite adept, you know.'

'I don't doubt it,' he said, his voice rich with laughter as he strode over to the window. 'But you mistake me, Mrs Weston.' He put his hand in his pocket. 'I came to return this.' He held out her cameo brooch. 'Well, take it, me darlin', before I change my mind.'

Warily she reached out and plucked it from his open palm.

'I thought to see it adorning some pretty young serving wench,' she told him. 'Why did you bring it back?'

'Guilty conscience.' He moved a little closer. 'And the prospect of a reward.'

Suddenly she felt very breathless, gazing up into the masked face and seeing the glint of the candlelight in his eyes. There was only the length of the hatpin between them. She did not resist when he took her wrist and deflected the sharp blade away from his body.

What was she doing? Alarmed, she dropped the brooch and put her free hand against his chest, but even as she opened her mouth to scream he captured her mouth, kissing her so ruthlessly that her bones melted under the onslaught. It was over in an instant. She was still gathering herself to resist him when he released her.

'Yes,' he said, his breathing a little ragged. 'I was not wrong.'

'A-about what?'

Her eyes were fixed on his mouth, fascinated

by the sculpted lips and the laughter lines engraved on each side that deepened now as he gave her a slow smile.

'You kiss like an angel.'

In one swift, fluid movement he turned away from her, threw up the sash and slipped out into the darkness.

Charity ran to the window, but there was no sign of anyone, only the soft drumming of hoofbeats fading into the night.

Hywel clapped his hands. 'Very well, everyone, let us begin by reading through the first act. Mrs Weston—are you with us?'

Charity started. 'I beg your pardon, Mr Jenkin. I am ready to rehearse, of course.'

He looked closely at her. 'Did you not sleep well last night?'

'No, as a matter of fact.' She paused and said casually, 'You told me you could recommend a manservant for me. Someone to be trusted.'

'Aye. There is a fellow called Thomas who is presently doing odd jobs for me, but he would prefer regular work, I know.'

'How soon can he start?'

'Today, if you wish. Shall I send him to you when we have finished rehearsals?'

Charity nodded.

'If you please, Hywel.' She touched the little cameo pinned to her gown. 'I shall feel happier with another servant in the house.'

Chapter Two

It was opening night and the theatre was packed for the new production of *The Rivals*. The playbill pasted up at the entrance announced boldly that the role of Lydia Languish was to be played by the celebrated actress Mrs Charity Weston, fresh from her successful season in Scarborough. Ross Durden took his seat on one of the benches in the pit and soon found himself squashed by bodies as the pit filled up.

'Should be a good night,' remarked the man in the brown bagwig who was sitting beside him. 'I read that this new leading lady's being compared to Mrs Siddons.' He pulled a nut from his pocket and cracked it expertly between his fingers. 'We shall soon find out.'

'Have you ever seen Mrs Siddons?' asked Ross, mildly intrigued.

'Once.' The man cracked another nut and

munched meditatively. 'In York, in the role of Lady Macbeth. Excellent, she was. Never seen the like. Just hope this lass is as good as they say.'

'But this is a comedy,' Ross pointed out, recalling that the great Sarah Siddons was renowned for her tragedies.

His neighbour shrugged. 'A play's a play and if the lady's no good then we shall soon let her know!'

Ross said no more. He had come into Allingford on business today, and had bought himself a ticket because he had wanted a diversion before returning home. *The Rivals* was one of his favourite plays and the fact that Charity Weston was making her debut in Allingford had not influenced him at all.

At least that was what he told himself, yet somehow this evening the familiar prologue and first scene did not captivate him, although the rest of the audience seemed to be enjoying it. He realised he was waiting for Mrs Weston's appearance in Scene Two.

Then she was there. Powdered and bewigged, but there could be no mistaking that wonderful figure nor the brilliance of her blue eyes, visible even from his seat halfway back in the pit. Her voice, too, held him spellbound. It had a mellow, smoky quality, redolent of sexual allure. It

should not have been right for her character—
Lydia Languish was meant to be a sweet young
heiress—but there was an innocence about
Charity's playing that rang true.

Ross glanced about him, relieved to see the
audience was captivated by her performance.
Smiling, he turned back to the stage and settled
down to enjoy the play.

The first performance in a new theatre was
always exciting, but nerve-racking too, and
Charity breathed a sigh of relief when it was
over, knowing it had gone well. The audience
was on its feet, clapping and cheering. She
dropped into a low curtsy, smiling. The applause never failed to surprise her. When she
reached the wings, Hywel caught her hand and
led her back to the stage.

'They will not settle down if you do not
grant them one last bow,' he murmured, smiling broadly.

She sank into another deep curtsy. Someone
had thrown a posy of primroses onto the stage.
She picked it up and touched it to her lips before
holding it out to the audience, acknowledging
their applause. The crowd went wild, and they
were still stamping and clapping and cheering
when she accompanied Hywel into the wings.

'Well, that is the first night over. I only hope they continue to enjoy my performances.'

'Oh, they will,' replied Hywel confidently. 'Now, I must go and get ready for the farce and you must prepare yourself to be besieged by admirers when the show is over!'

Charity exchanged praise and compliments with the rest of the players, then went back to the dressing room to find Betty waiting for her. Her handmaid's austere countenance had softened slightly, a sign that she was pleased with her mistress's reception.

'Help me out of this headdress, if you please, Betty. Heavens, it is such a weight!'

'If you'd been born twenty years earlier, Miss Charity, you'd have had your own hair piled up like this for weeks on end.'

'I cannot believe this monstrous, pomaded style was once the fashion.' Charity gave an exaggerated sigh of relief as Betty carefully pulled away the wig, which was curled, powdered and decorated with a confection of feathers and silk flowers. 'Put it aside, Betty, and help me out of my gown, if you please. Mr Jenkin thinks there may be a crowd in the green room once the farce is ended.'

'Not a doubt of it, madam, the way they was cheering you. Now, I brought the rose silk and your embroidered muslin. Which will you wear to meet your admirers?'

'The muslin, I think, Betty. And they are not my admirers. Mr Jenkin tells me that it is the custom here at Allingford for all the cast to gather for a reception in the green room.'

'Aye,' muttered Betty, 'but there's no doubt who will be most in demand!'

Charity was exhausted and longed to go home to bed, but she knew Hywel would expect her to join the other members of the cast and 'do the pretty', as he phrased it, talking to those wealthy patrons who were invited backstage to meet the players. She was grateful for the supper that was laid on and managed to eat a little cold chicken and one of the delicious pastries before Hywel carried her off to introduce her to the great and the good of Allingford. He began with Lady Malton, who looked down her highbred nose at Charity and afforded her the merest nod.

'In a small town like this we cannot rely upon one rich patron like Lady Malton to support the theatre,' Hywel explained as he led her away from the viscountess. 'We depend upon the goodwill of a large number of gentlemen—and ladies—of more moderate means. People like the Beverleys. They are a delightful couple and the backbone of Allingford life. Sir Mark is the local magistrate and his lady is very good-natured and likes to fill her house with actors and artists.'

Having presented Charity to Sir Mark and Lady Beverley and spent a few minutes in conversation, he led her away to meet a bluff, rosy-cheeked gentleman in a powdered wig, whom he introduced as Mr John Hutton.

'Mr Hutton has travelled from Beringham to be here,' said Hywel.

Conscious of her duty, she gave the man her most charming smile.

'I am sure we are very grateful to you for coming so far.'

'And I am glad to see you here,' replied Mr Hutton, taking her hand and pressing a whiskery kiss upon her fingers. 'Especially glad to know that *you* did not take any hurt getting here.' He laughed at her look of confusion and squeezed her hand. 'Why, ma'am, it's all over Beringham that the Scarborough coach was held up.'

'Ah, yes.' So that was where she had heard his name before. Her excellent memory recalled the coachman mentioning that a Mr Hutton had been robbed by the same highwayman.

'There is no doubt that this "Dark Rider" is having an effect on business,' Hutton continued. 'Many are afraid to make the journey between

Beringham and Allingford.' The whiskery jowls quivered with indignation. 'The sooner the fellow is caught and strung up, the better it will be for all of us.'

Such serious talk was not what was needed, so Charity summoned up her brightest smile.

'I am very glad *you* were not discouraged from coming tonight, sir. I hope you enjoyed the performance and will come again.'

'Aye, I did enjoy it, ma'am, very much, and very pleased I am that Mr Jenkin here has seen fit to open his theatre in Allingford.' He made a little bow towards the actor/manager. 'By Gad, sir, we need something to distract us from this dashed war.'

'And there is nothing like a good play to do that, Mr Hutton,' agreed Hywel. 'Let me tell you what else we have planned....'

With a word and a smile Charity left the gentlemen to their conversation. She worked her way through the crowd, smiling and charming them all in the hope that they would return to the theatre for another evening. There were a couple baronets and one knight, but the rest were landowners or wealthy tradesmen from the town, many with their wives who were prepared to be jealous of a beautiful actress, but a few minutes in Charity's company persuaded these matrons that there was no danger of the *celebrated Mrs Weston* stealing their husbands away from them.

As an actress in London, she had grown accustomed to fighting off the admirers who wanted to make her their mistress. It had not been easy, but with skill and quick thinking Charity had managed to maintain her virtue, generally without offending her admirers, and in the past few years while she had been touring under her own name, she had perfected her role. To the married men and their wives she was charmingly modest and at pains to make them understand that she was interested only in her profession and would take compliments upon her performance, but not her person. She succeeded very well and all the ladies agreed that she was a very prettily behaved young woman, although not, of course, the sort one could invite into one's home.

However, the single young men who clustered about her were treated to a very different performance. She gave each one her attention for a short time, laughed off their effusive compliments and returned their friendly banter, refusing to be drawn into anything more than the mildest flirtation. Yet each one went away to spend the night in pleasurable dreams of the unattainable golden goddess.

The crowd in the green room showed no sign

of dispersing. Charity smothered a yawn and was wondering how soon she could slip away when she was aware of someone at her shoulder. Summoning up her smile, she turned to find herself staring at the snowy folds of a white neckcloth. She stepped back a little to take in the whole man. He was soberly dressed in buckled shoes and white stockings with the cream knee breeches that were the norm for evening wear, but his plain dark coat carried no fobs or seals and he wore no quizzing glass. Yet he carried himself with an air of assurance and she guessed he was one of the wealthier inhabitants of Allingford.

His athletic figure and deeply tanned skin made her think he had spent a great deal of time abroad. His face was not exactly handsome, but it was arresting, with its strong jaw, hawkish nose and those dark eyes fringed with long black lashes that any woman would envy. When he bowed to her she noticed that his black hair was cut fashionably short and curled naturally about his head and down over his collar.

'May I congratulate you on an excellent performance, Mrs Weston?' The words were slow and measured, very much in keeping with his sober appearance, but there was something in his voice that was very attractive and strangely familiar. A memory fluttered, but was gone before she could grasp it.

'Thank you. I am glad you enjoyed it.... Have we met before?'

'How could that be, when you have only just arrived in Allingford?' There was an elusive twinkle lurking in his dark eyes that was at odds with his grave tone. 'Besides, if we had been introduced before, I would surely not have forgotten it.'

She wanted him to speak again, just so she could enjoy that deep, velvet-smooth voice.

'You live in the town, sir?'

'Close by. At Wheelston.'

'Ah, I see. Is that very far from here?'

'A few miles.'

His answers were annoyingly short. She looked up into his face and felt again that disturbing flutter of recognition.

'I beg your pardon, sir, but are you sure we haven't—?'

He took out his watch and broke in upon her.

'You must excuse me, Mrs Weston, it is getting late and I must cut and run. I wanted only to compliment you upon your performance. Goodnight to you.'

With a bow he was gone, leaving her dissatisfied with the brevity of their conversation. Sir Mark and Lady Beverley claimed her attention, but although she responded civilly to their praise and conversation, her eyes followed the tall stranger as he made his way across the room.

'Tell me, Sir Mark,' she interrupted the magistrate's flow of small talk. 'Who is that gentleman?'

'Who?' Sir Mark glanced up.

'The one by the door.' Charity felt a slight ripple of disappointment. The man had sought her out, but had obviously not been enamoured, since he was leaving so soon.

'Oh, that's Durden, not the most popular man in Allingford.' Sir Mark turned back to her, his whiskers bristling. 'He wasn't rude to you, was he, ma'am?'

'No, not at all. I was merely...curious.'

'You are intrigued by his blackamoor appearance,' suggested Lady Beverley. 'That comes from his years in the navy, I believe. He was a sea captain, you know, but he came home two years ago, when his mother died.'

'He is certainly not popular,' Charity remarked, watching his progress towards the door. People avoided his eye, or even turned their backs as he passed. 'Why should that be?'

Sir Mark hesitated before replying, 'His taciturn manner, I shouldn't wonder.'

'Poor man,' murmured Lady Beverley. 'I am

surprised, though, that Mr Jenkin should invite him—he has no money to invest in the theatre.'

'Jenkin invited him for the same reason I make sure you send him a card to each of your parties,' replied Sir Mark. 'The property may be run down and its owner may not have a feather to fly with, but Wheelston is still one of the principal properties in the area. Unusual for Durden to turn up, though. He keeps to himself as a rule.'

'Is that any wonder, given what happened?' said Lady Beverley, shaking her head. 'But I am not surprised that he should come this evening when we have such a celebrated actress in our midst! Ah, Mr Jenkin—let me congratulate you on your new leading lady. I was just telling Mrs Weston that I have never laughed so heartily at one of Mr Sheridan's comedies…'

Charity wondered exactly what had happened to make Mr Ross Durden so unsociable, but the conversation had moved on and the moment was lost. Stoically, she put him from her mind and returned to charming the theatre's patrons.

By heaven, what a damned uncomfortable evening! Why did I put myself through it?

Ross strode back to the livery stable to collect his horse, still smarting from the slights and outright snubs he had received from the worthy people of Allingford. Apart from the actor/manager, who knew nothing about him, and Sir Mark and his good-natured wife, no one else had made any effort to speak to him. He knew his neighbours thought he deserved their censure, and that was partly his own fault, for he had never done anything to explain the situation, but damn it all, why should he do so?

He turned his mind to the much more pleasant thought of Mrs Charity Weston, and a reluctant grin tugged at his mouth. If he had talked to her much longer it was very likely she would have recognised him. Perhaps it was because she was an actress and used to playing parts herself that she noticed the similarities between the quiet, respectable gentleman farmer and the boisterous, lawless Dark Rider. Hell and confound it, he thought the way he disguised his voice and changed his whole manner would fool anyone, but apparently not. He had seen her fine brows draw together, noted the puzzled look in those large blue eyes—by God, but she was beautiful! Aye, that had almost been his undoing. Kissing her when he held up the Scarborough coach should have been enough for him. Why in heaven's name had he gone to her house? Madness. He put up his hand to rub the white blaze that ran down the great horse's face.

'Well, Robin, no harm done this time, my old friend, but we will need to be more careful. We'd best give Mrs Weston a wide berth in future, I think.'

Ross rode back to the farm, the familiar cluster of stone buildings rearing up blackly against the night sky as he approached. A solitary lamp glowed in the yard and he found Jed dozing in a chair in the stables. Leaving the groom to take care of Robin, he went into the house.

Silence greeted him when he entered through the kitchen door, but a cold wet nose pressed against his hand.

'Back in your box, Samson, good boy.' He scratched at the dog's head before the animal padded off into the shadows.

Mrs Cummings, his housekeeper, had gone to bed without leaving a light burning, but the sullen glow in the range showed him that she had banked up the fire against the winter chill. Lighting a lamp, he also noted with a burst of gratitude that she had left a jug of ale on the table and on a plate, under an upturned bowl, was a slice of meat pie.

The woman was a treasure. He must increase her wages—when he could afford it. He poured himself a mug of ale and threw himself down in the chair beside the fire. As he devoured the pie he thought about his situation. That it had come to this—a captain in his Majesty's navy, decorated for bravery under fire, now struggling to pay his way. He picked up the poker and stirred the coals with rough, angry movements while a quiet, insidious voice murmured in his ear.

What about those coaches you hold up? You could take more than enough to live comfortably.

He shook his head to rid it of the tempting thought. He was no thief; he wanted justice and would take only what had been stolen from him. Why, even the mailbags he searched through were always left at the roadside, where they would be found intact the next day.

Then you're a fool, said that insistent voice. *If you're caught, you'll hang for highway robbery—no one will care about your justice.*

'I will,' he said aloud to the empty room. 'I'll care.'

He drained his mug to wash down the last of the pie, then took up his bedroom candle to light his way up the stairs. The echo of his boots on the bare boards whispered around him.

Fool, fool.

Charity liked living in Allingford. Her fellow players were friendly, as were the townsfolk. Of the more noble families, only Sir Mark and Lady Beverley afforded her more than a distant nod if they saw her in the street, but she was accustomed to that. Actresses were not quite *respectable*. Her first appearance at the theatre was followed by equally successful performances in the tragedy *Jane Shore* and another comedy, *The Busy Body*. Charity knew both plays very well and they did not overtax her at all, so when she was not rehearsing and the weather was clement she enjoyed hiring a gig and driving herself around the lanes. She had grown up not fifteen miles from here, in Saltby, and although she determined not to visit the village, nor to go anywhere within her father's jurisdiction as magistrate, the countryside around Allingford was familiar and welcoming. Her maid did not approve of these solitary outings and tried to dissuade her, but Charity only laughed at her.

'What harm can come to me if I stay close to Allingford?'

'There's highwaymen, for a start,' retorted Betty. 'They still haven't caught the rogue who held us up on the Scarborough Road.'

'The Dark Rider.' *The rogue who kissed me in this very house.*

Charity had neither seen nor heard anything of him since. She had scoured the newspapers for reports of the mysterious highwayman and had spoken to her fellow players about him, but there was no information. However, she had no intention of explaining any of that to her maid.

'Surely a highwayman will be patrolling the coaching road and I mean to explore the by-ways. I shall not see him again.'

Charity was not sure she really believed that and even less sure that she wanted it to be true. Betty tried again.

'You might meet your father.'

That thought was much more alarming. Charity wondered if she had been wise to confide so much about her past to Betty, but the maid had proven herself a good friend over the years. However, Charity would not be dissuaded.

'I doubt it. And as long as I stay this side of the county line he cannot hurt me.'

Betty frowned, her usually dour countenance becoming positively forbidding.

'He must know by now that you are in Allingford. Someone will have told him that Charity Weston is appearing at the theatre.'

'Mayhap he will think it a mere coincidence that an actress has the same name as his daughter.'

'And mayhap he is planning some mischief.'

'Nonsense, Betty. It is more than a dozen years since I left Saltby. Phineas has probably forgotten all about me.'

'Not he, mistress. From all you have told me of the man, he will not rest while you are in Allingford. Your success will be like a thorn in his flesh.'

'Well, that is a pain he will have to bear,' said Charity stoutly, 'because I am not going away.'

Nevertheless, she made sure that when she travelled north or east she kept within the bounds of Allingford, although she felt confident enough to venture farther afield on the other side of the town, and one sunny March day she set out to explore the land to the west. The air was bracing and a covering of snow on the distant hills told her that winter had not yet gone for good, but the blue sky lifted the spirits and Charity was glad to be out of the town. At a crossroads she stopped, debating whether to explore further or to go back to Allingford. After all, it was the first night of a new play tonight and she would need to prepare.

While she was making up her mind, a pedlar came round the corner, leading his donkey laden with leather packs. The gig's pony snorted and shifted nervously. Charity quieted the animal and pulled a little to the side to allow the pedlar to pass.

He tipped his hat, his bright, beady eyes alight with curiosity.

'Good day, missus. Hast thou lost tha' way?'

'No,' she replied cheerfully. 'I am exploring and cannot decide which route to take.'

'Ah, well, then. I tek it tha's just come from Allingford.' He stopped and pushed up his hat to scratch his head. 'If tha' teks that road to yer right, you'll reach Kirby Misperton. The way to the left leads to Great Habton. And that track there—' he pointed to a wide lane bounded on either side by ditches '—it looks best o' the lot, but leads to nobbut Wheelston Hall.'

'Thank you, that is most enlightening.'

With a toothless grin the pedlar touched his hat again and went on his way. Charity looked at the three lanes before her. She had an hour yet before she needed to turn back. Kirby Misperton, Great Habton—the names were intriguing, but Wheelston.... She frowned slightly, wondering where she had heard the name before.

Then she remembered the quiet stranger who had attended the opening night reception only to leave after the briefest of words with her. Ross Durden. He had said he lived at Wheelston. Of the three lanes before her, the track to the hall was by far the widest and had been well made, but showed signs of neglect with the ditches overgrown and hedges straggling untidily on either side. A prosperous property, perhaps fallen on hard times? She remembered Lady Beverley's words. There was clearly some sort of mystery about Mr Durden. She set off again.

You cannot drive slap up to someone's house just because you are curious!

Charity ignored the shocked voice of her conscience and turned the pony. She had set out to explore, so why should she not go this way? The crossroads had no signposts, so it was not unreasonable for her to take the most interesting route.

After what felt like a good half mile she was beginning to wish she had listened to her conscience. An accumulation of cloud had covered the sun, making the air very chill, and a sneaking wind cut through her fur-lined pelisse. The unkempt hedges hid her view and had overgrown the road so much that it was too narrow for her to turn the gig.

'I shall turn round in the next gateway,' she said aloud, causing the pony's ears to prick. 'Yes, I know,' she addressed the animal. 'You want to go back to your warm stable. And I confess that I, too, am beginning to think longingly of my fireside and a hot drink.'

No convenient gateway presented itself and she was obliged to drive on around the bend, only to find herself at the entrance to a substantial property: Wheelston Hall.

It was a rambling, many-gabled house built of

grey stone, with a simple portico over the wide door. A curving drive swept around the front of the building, but it was heavily rutted and covered in weeds. Without waiting for Charity to guide him, the pony turned onto a narrower path leading around the side of the house. It was in much better condition and Charity made no effort to restrain the animal as it trotted towards the numerous outbuildings.

Charity found herself in a large cobbled yard; in the far corner someone was chopping wood, but he had his back to her and was unaware of her presence. She guessed from the man's size and the curling black hair that it was Ross Durden. Despite the icy wind, he wore only his shirt, buckskins and boots, the shirtsleeves rolled up high to display his muscled arms.

He picked up a large log and placed it on the chopping block, then raised the long-handled axe and brought it down on the log in one smooth, powerful arc. She was struck by the fluid grace of the movement, the slight shift of legs and hips, the flutter of his billowing white shirt as his arms circled, the flash of the blade as it cleaved through the air and the satisfying crack as the wood was split asunder and the pieces fell onto the cobbles. One of the logs had rolled behind him, and as he reached around to pick it up, he spotted the gig. He straightened slowly and turned. Tossing the wood into the basket, he began to walk towards her.

For a brief moment Charity wanted to flee, but she fought down her panic. Not only would that be very cowardly behaviour, she doubted she could turn the gig and whip the little pony to a canter in time to get away. The man looked so much larger, so much less civilised than he had done at the theatre. Untamed and rakish was her impression of the man, but that was curiously at odds with his appearance in the green room.

Another memory nagged at her brain, but it was elusive; she could not quite catch it. She forced herself to sit still and watch as this large gentleman with his wild hair and dark, dangerous eyes approached the gig.

'Mrs Weston.'

The words, uttered deep and slow, sent a quiver running down her spine. There was neither welcome nor enquiry in his tone. It was a mere statement of fact that she was here.

'Mr Durden. I, um…I was exploring and took this lane quite by chance.' She gave him a bright smile, but nothing in that harsh, dark face changed.

Foolish girl. You should have stayed away.

She gathered up the reins. 'I am very sorry. I did not mean to intrude—'

He put out his hand and gripped the pony's head collar.

'It is no intrusion, but you are a long way from Allingford.'

Again the quiver ran down her spine. He was pointing out to her how vulnerable she was.

'You are cold,' he said. 'Perhaps you would like to come in and warm yourself by the fire?'

No! It was not to be thought of. May as well enter a tiger's cage.

He turned and called to someone in the stable, his voice echoing around the yard, then he stepped up beside the gig and held out his hand.

'Jed will take care of the pony until you are ready to leave. He will lead it into one of the empty barns, where it may wait for you out of the cold.'

Her conscience clamoured with warnings, but they went unheeded. With his eyes upon her and his hand held out so imperiously, she felt obliged to let him help her down and escort her into the house. The old wooden door opened onto a short corridor and from there into a large kitchen, at one end of which a fire slumbered in the range. A large shaggy dog jumped up and came to greet them, wagging its tail and sniffing at Charity's skirts.

'Easy, Samson, don't frighten our guest.'

Charity leaned down to scratch the animal behind its ears.

'I am not frightened. Is he a gun dog?'

'Gun dog, sheepdog, companion. Whatever is needed.'

He snapped his fingers and sent the dog back to its box in the corner.

'How useful,' murmured Charity, stripping off her gloves. After the chilly air outside, the kitchen was blessedly warm. He waved towards an armchair beside the fire.

'Sit there while I make you tea.' He stirred up the coals and swung the trivet holding a large kettle over the fire. 'I presume you would prefer tea to ale? I'm afraid there is nothing else here suitable for a lady.'

His voice was perfectly serious, but she noticed the disturbing glint in his dark eyes when he looked at her. Again she had a flash of memory, but he was expecting an answer and she must concentrate on that—and the fact that she was alone with him.

'Yes, tea, if you please. I confess I am a little cold now.'

'I, on the other hand, am quite warm from my exertions. I hope you won't object if I take a mug of ale?'

Without waiting for her reply, he turned away

and picked up the blackjack sitting on the table. Charity heard the kettle singing merrily and was a little reassured by the familiar sound. She knew she should keep her eyes averted, but could not resist glancing up under her lashes as her host filled a mug with ale and drank deeply. She watched, fascinated, as he swallowed, watching the muscles of his throat working, noting the strong lines of his neck, the hard, straight jaw and lean cheek. There was power in every line of his body and it seemed to call to her, an attraction so strong she found it difficult to keep still.

As he lowered the mug and wiped his hand across his mouth he met her eyes, holding her gaze with his own near-black eyes. Charity's heart began to pound and her hands gripped the arms of the chair. The space between them seemed charged, like the heavy air that preceded a thunderstorm. Surely he must hear the thud of her heart, or even see it, since it battered mercilessly against her ribs.

She should say something, but her breath caught in her throat. She was in thrall to that dark predatory gaze, unable to look away. Unwilling to look away. She had to acknowledge that the perilous attraction was all on her side, the man before had not moved or spoken, so how could she blame him for the danger she felt now?

Was it the rattle of the kettle lid and sudden hiss of steam that broke the spell? Or was it the fact that she was no longer subject to that dark stare? He turned to the fire and proceeded to make the tea. With a conscious effort Charity made herself release her grip on the chair arms. She watched as he lifted a rosewood tea caddy from the shelf and spooned leaves into a silver teapot before pouring in the boiling water. She was desperate to break the silence, but when she spoke she almost winced at the inanity of her words.

'Tea making is more commonly a woman's role, Mr Durden.'

'Since my housekeeper is not here it falls to me,' he said shortly. 'I could ask you to do it, but I am not in the habit of making my guests work.'

Charity thought his manner suggested he was not in the habit of entertaining visitors at all, but she did not say so. Instead she watched him fetch out of the cupboard a beautiful tea-cup and saucer.

'I do not have much call to use these,' he re-marked, as if reading her thoughts. 'There is sugar, if you want it?'

'Just a little milk, if you please.'

His strong hands were remarkably gentle with the fine porcelain.

As if he was caressing a beautiful woman.

A hot blush raced through Charity at the thought and she sat back in her chair, away from the direct heat of the fire. She took the cup from him with a murmur of thanks, but did not look up, conscious of an unfamiliar ache pooling deep inside her.

He refilled his tankard and drew up a stool for himself. It was a little lower than her chair, she noted, and thought she would be grateful that he was not towering over her, but when he sat down his face was level with her own, which was somehow even more disturbing. Desperate to avoid his gaze, she looked about the kitchen. The room was large and high ceilinged, big enough to accommodate a cook and at least half a dozen servants. She recalled Lady Beverley's comment that Mr Durden had no money at all. However, even with a lack of staff, the long table was spotless and on the dresser the copper pans gleamed.

'I beg your pardon, madam, for bringing you into the kitchen, but it is the only room in the house with a fire.'

'Oh, no, no, I am very comfortable, I assure you.' She smiled, forgetting her unease in her eagerness not to be thought critical of his hospitality. 'I was merely thinking how much work there must be, maintaining a house like this.'

'It would take an army of servants to do so,' he replied frankly. 'Most of it is closed up until I have the funds to restore it. I have an excellent housekeeper in Mrs Cummings, but she can only do so much. She insists on keeping one parlour tidy for me, and my study, but I spend very little time indoors so there is no point in having a fire anywhere but here during the day.'

'Very sensible.'

Charity sipped her tea. It was good. However poor he might be, her host did not buy inferior bohea. Sitting by the fire, with a hot drink to revive her, she began to relax a little.

'I enjoyed your performance in *The Rivals*.'

'Thank you. It was very well received.' She gently replaced her cup in its saucer and would have got up to put it on the table, but he forestalled her, reaching out to take the saucer, his fingers brushing hers as he did so.

It was as much as she could do not to snatch her hand away. She was so aware of him that her skin burned at his touch and little arrows of excitement skimmed through her blood. It was like the heady excitement of a first night, only worse, because she had no idea how to deal with this. Nervously she began to chatter.

'We open in a new play tonight, *The*

Provok'd Husband. Do you know it? I am very much looking forward to it, because I play Lady Townly. Hywel—Mr Jenkin—is to play my long-suffering husband. We have played it together before, but not for many a year. Perhaps you will come and see it.'

'No, I won't.'

His response was so blunt she blinked at him, but it also made her laugh.

'Fie upon you, Mr Durden, I did not expect quite such a strong rebuttal.'

'I beg your pardon. What I meant was that I rarely go into Allingford, save when there is business to attend to.'

'Of course, and pray do not think that I shall be offended if you do not come. I am not so conceited as to think people cannot go on quite well without attending my performances.' Smiling, she rose to her feet. 'I have taken quite enough of your time and must be getting back. Thank you, Mr Durden, for your hospitality.'

He grimaced. 'Such as it was.'

Sympathy clenched at her heart. She did not think him embarrassed by his straitened circumstances, but he was most clearly aware of how it might look to others. Impulsively she put her hand on his arm.

'A warm fire and a warming dish of bohea— I would ask for nothing finer, sir.'

He was staring at her fingers as they rested upon his bare forearm and Charity wondered if he, too, felt the shock of attraction. She could almost see it, a dangerous current rippling around them. Carefully, she removed her hand and began to pull on her gloves. The dog had left his box and was looking up at them, ears pricked expectantly. Glad of the distraction, Charity smiled down at him.

'Goodbye, Samson.'

Embarrassed by the nervousness that had her addressing a mere animal, she hurried to the door, biting down on her lip as Mr Durden reached past her to open it. He was so close that if she leaned towards him, just a little, their bodies would meet. Stifling the thought and the heady excitement that came with it, she swept past him along the corridor and opened the outer door herself.

Charity was almost surprised to step out into the cobbled yard. Some part of her—the part that remembered her upbringing, she thought bitterly—had almost expected to find the door opened directly into the fiery jaws of hell. She welcomed the chill air; it gave her something to think of other than the presence of the man beside her. She buttoned her pelisse and smoothed her gloves over her hands while he called for Jed to bring out the gig. Anything to fill the awkward silence. Her eyes fell upon the basket and the large pile of unsplit logs by the chopping block.

'I interrupted your work, sir, I—'

'It is no matter, the break was very welcome.' The words were polite, his tone less so. He handed her into the waiting gig and shook out the rug before placing it over her knees. She held her breath, not moving lest he think she objected to his ministrations when in fact it was quite the opposite. A strange, unfamiliar awareness tingled through her body as he tucked the rug about her. She did not want him to stop.

'It looks like rain.' He glanced up at the sky before fixing her with his dark, sober gaze. 'Go directly to Allingford, Mrs Weston. No more exploring today!'

She tried to smile, but her mouth would not quite obey her, not while he was subjecting her to such an intense stare. With a slight nod and a deft flick of the reins she set off out of the yard. The track was straight and the pony needed little guidance. She could easily look back, to see if he was watching her.... No! She sank her teeth into her lip again and concentrated on the road ahead. It was a chance encounter, nothing more. To turn and look back would give Mr Durden completely the wrong idea.

But her spine tingled all the way to the gate

of Wheelston Hall and she longed to know if he had watched her drive away.

Ross stared at the distant entrance long after the little gig had disappeared. He heard Jed come up beside him and give a cough.

'Who were that lass, Cap'n? I've not seen her hereabouts.'

Ross kept his eyes on the gates.

'That,' he said, a smile tugging at his mouth, 'was the celebrated actress Mrs Charity Weston.'

'Actress, is she?' Jed hawked and spat on the ground. 'And were she really explorin', think 'ee?'

Ross turned and walked back towards the woodpile.

'She said it was so.'

'And you invited 'er indoors.' Ross looked up to find Jed regarding him with a rheumy eye. 'Never known you to do that afore, Cap'n. Never known you to show any kindness to a woman, not since—'

'Enough, Jed.' He beat his arms across his chest, suddenly aware of the cold. 'If you've nothing to do, you can carry that basket of logs indoors and bring me an empty one.'

'Oh, I've plenty to do, master, don't you fret.'

The old man shuffled away, muttering under

his breath. Ross returned to the woodpile and began to split more logs, soon getting into the rhythm of placing a log on the chopping block and swinging the axe. He tried not to think of the woman who had interrupted his work, but she kept creeping into his mind. He found himself recalling the dainty way she held her teacup, the soft, low resonance of her voice, the bolt of attraction that had shot through him when she met his eyes. He had felt himself drowning in those blue, blue eyes…. Ross tore his thoughts away from her only to find himself thinking that the gleaming white-gold centres of the freshly split ash boughs were the exact colour of her hair.

'Oh, for pity's sake, get over her!'

'Did ye call, Cap'n?' Jed poked his head out of the stable again. 'Did ye want me to get Robin ready for ye tonight? There's a moon and a clear sky, which'll suit ye well…'

'No. That is—' Ross hesitated '—you may saddle Robin up for me this evening, Jed, but no blacking. I'm going to Allingford!'

Chapter Three

By the time Charity arrived back in Allingford, her disordered emotions had settled into
a state of pleasurable exhilaration—very much
as they had done after she and some of the other
players in Scarborough had made an excursion
out of the town and walked on the cliffs overlooking the sea. It had been dangerous, especially for the ladies, because the blustery wind
had snatched at their skirts, threatening to drag
them off the cliff and dash them into the angry
seas below, but the excitement was to see the
danger and know that it was just a step away.
That same thrill pulsed through her now. It
puzzled her and she wondered just what it was
about Ross Durden that set her so on edge. He
was not conventionally handsome—and she had
had experience enough of handsome men in the
theatre. He had said nothing that could be con-

strued as improper, yet his very proximity had
set the alarm bells ringing in her head.

She was still pondering this conundrum as
she left the gig at the stables, and was so lost
in thought that she did not notice the Beverleys' carriage standing outside the gun shop,
nor hear Lady Beverley calling to her until she
was almost at the carriage door. Charity begged
pardon, but Lady Beverley waved away her excuses.

'No matter, my dear, you are the very person
I need.' She alighted from her carriage. 'Do you
have ten minutes to spare? Sir Mark is inside
inspecting a pair of pistols he is minded to buy.
He will doubtless be an age yet and I have seen
the most ravishing bonnet in the milliners, but I
am not at all sure the colour would suit. Would
you be an angel and come along to Forde's with
me now and give me your opinion?'

'Why, yes, if you wish....'

'Excellent.' She turned to her footman. 'Wait
here with the carriage for Sir Mark and then tell
him to pick me up from the milliner's on High
Street.' She tucked her arm through Charity's,
saying with a smile, 'There, that is all settled.
Come along, my dear, it is but a step. You shall
give me your arm and tell me what it is that has
you in such a brown study.'

'If you must know,' Charity began as they set off, 'I was thinking about Mr Durden.'

Lady Beverley stopped to stare at her.

'Heavens, what on earth has brought this on?'

Charity felt the colour flooding her cheek and gently urged her companion to walk on.

'I was exploring today and came across the lane leading to Wheelston.' No need to say she had actually driven to the Hall. 'It looked so run down and forlorn....'

'Yes, well, the whole estate is in dire need of repair.'

'I remember seeing Mr Durden at the reception for my first appearance at the theatre. You said then something had happened to him....' Charity let the words hang.

Lady Beverley did not disappoint her. She leaned a little closer, saying confidentially, 'It was such a prosperous estate in old Mr Durden's time, but after he died the son continued in the navy and left his poor mama to run the place. She was very sickly, you see, and died in... Now, when was it? Two years ago, almost to the day. Young Mr Durden came home to find the place nearly derelict. But then, what did he expect, leaving an ailing woman to look after his inheritance? Quite shameful of him. A dutiful son would have sold out when his mother became so ill. Of course, that is easy for us all to say after the event, and Mr Durden was a very good sailor, I believe. Certainly, he reached the rank of captain and was commended for bravery on more than one occasion, that much I know is true, for it was reported in the newspapers.'

They continued in silence for a few moments and Charity tried to reconcile this picture of Ross Durden with the man she had seen an hour or so earlier.

'I cannot believe— That is,' she continued cautiously, 'he did not look like a man to neglect his duty.'

'No, well, I believe he was truly grieved when he came back and discovered just how bad things were at Wheelston. But then, if he had shown a little more interest in the place when his mother was alive…' Lady Beverley stopped. 'Ah, here we are, my dear, Forde's, and there is the bonnet I like so much in the window. The green ruched silk, do you see it? Let us step inside and I shall try it on.'

Charity spent the next half hour with Lady Beverley in the milliner's, and by the time the lady had made her purchase, Sir Mark was at the door with the carriage. Charity realised there would be no more confidences today. She took her leave of her friends and made her way back to North Street, ostensibly to rest and pre-

pare for her performance, although it took all
her willpower to force her mind to the play and
away from the enigmatic owner of Wheelston.

The ride into Allingford restored some sense
into Ross's overheated brain. What was he
thinking of, paying his hard-earned money for
a theatre ticket? He should have been on the
road tonight; who knew what luck he might
have had? At least there was a chance that fortune might have favoured him, whereas this
way he knew that his pocket would be several
shillings lighter by the time he went home.

It was madness, he knew that, but having
come all the way into Allingford it would be
even more foolish to turn round and ride all the
way back again without doing something. The
thought of risking his money in a gambling den
or drinking himself senseless at the George held
even less appeal for him.

'Damnation, I have come this far, I might as
well watch the play.' Savagely he kicked his feet
free of the stirrups and slid to the ground. The
stable lad at the livery took charge of Robin,
and Ross made his way to the theatre. He was
early, so he went into a nearby tavern, called
for a mug of ale and took a seat by the window,
where he had a good view of the theatre's entrance.

It appeared this comedy was very popular, for a large crowd was gathering. A number of carriages drew up on the street and disgorged the wealthier country gentlemen in smart wool coats and embroidered waistcoats and their fashionable ladies wearing a startling array of headwear, some with so many ostrich feathers that Ross felt a twinge of sympathy for anyone unlucky enough to be sitting behind them that evening. He continued to watch, deriving no little amusement from the scene, then, suddenly, all his senses were on the alert.

A smart travelling carriage had pulled up outside the theatre. Very few people in the area owned such an equipage and he knew of only one who affected a hammer cloth on the box seat. It was pretentious in anyone other than the nobility, but the gentleman Ross had in mind was all pretension. The footman opened the door and Ross's lip curled as he watched a young woman alight, the flambeaux on the street sparkling off the gold thread in the skirts that peeped from beneath her short, fur-lined cloak. Even at this distance he could see that she was strikingly pretty, with large dark eyes and dark curls that were piled high and adorned with gold ostrich feathers.

Ross felt a surge of loss and regret, but it was quickly succeeded by bitter anger. How

could he feel anything more than contempt for
the woman after what she had done to him? He
stared more closely at her, observed that despite
her rosy cheeks and creamy skin, there was a
frown between her brows and her mouth was
pursed into a look of discontent. She glanced
around her with disdain and held up a nosegay
as if to protect herself from the offensive smell
of the crowd.

Ross turned his attention to the man who
followed her out of the coach. He was some
years older than the woman, a tall, portly man
in a wine-coloured coat with stand-up collar,
beneath which his starched neckcloth was so
wide it seemed to be holding his head up by the
ears, while the ears themselves appeared to be
supporting his powdered wig.

A gold waistcoat strained across his bulging
stomach and white satin knee breeches were
stretched over his thighs, the breeches tied at
the knee with gold ribbons that dangled against
his embroidered stockings. Everything about
the man screamed opulence, but not elegance.
He walked with an air of self-importance that
would have been amusing in anyone else, but
Phineas Weston was a magistrate, and as such
he wielded terrifying power over the common
people.

Weston! Ross struck his palm against his

forehead. When Charity had told him she was an actress and had no business in Beringham, he had immediately assumed Weston was not her real name and had dismissed all thoughts of a connection. But to see the Beringham magistrate and his wife here in Allingford—surely that was more than a coincidence. Especially when it was well known that Phineas considered theatres dens of iniquity and would not license any such entertainment in Beringham. Ross downed his drink and went out to join the crowds making their way into the theatre. He could see the gold ostrich feathers dancing some way in front of him, but he kept well back—he had no wish for them to remark his presence just yet.

He bought his ticket and made his way to the pit, but did not sit down immediately. He waited for the ostentatious couple to appear in one of the boxes, then chose for himself a seat on the far side of the pit, where he could keep them in view. It was providential, he told himself, that he should see them here. It made the journey worthwhile. Certainly it eased his conscience in coming to Allingford. However, once the play began he forgot all about gold waistcoats and nodding ostrich feathers, for Charity Weston was on stage and he found it impossible to think of anything else. Her last performance had been as a young heiress; this time she was equally convincing as a rich man's wife with a penchant for gambling.

It was hard to believe the assured woman on the stage was the shy, nervous creature he had entertained at Wheelston that afternoon, but perhaps that had been an act, too. He was suspicious of her beauty. The luxuriant blonde hair and deep blue eyes belonged to a fantasy, far too good to be true. He had been caught before by a pretty face only to find a grasping nature and a heart of flint beneath. He glanced up at the box where Phineas and his wife were sitting. Mrs Weston—Hannah—was laughing and applauding the comedy, until her husband admonished her and she subsided into stern-faced silence.

It must have cost Phineas a great deal of soul-searching to come to the theatre, and he certainly could not be seen to approve of the entertainment. Ross had no such qualms, but he was on his guard. He would enjoy the performance but not—most definitely he would not—allow himself to be captivated by the actress.

The play ended to enthusiastic cheers and applause from the audience. It was clear that Mrs Charity Weston was hugely popular. A number of nosegays were hurled onto the stage and she gathered them up, lifted the flowers to her face as if to inhale their delicate perfume then smiled her thanks towards the audience. One had to admire her technique. Ross glanced up at the boxes again. Phineas and Hannah Weston were the only ones not applauding.

There was a short interval before the next part of the programme, which according to the handbill promised amusing songs and recitations. Ross noted that the Westons were leaving their box and he joined the throng heading for the foyer. Few people paid him any heed; those that did recognise him gave him no more than a disapproving stare before moving away. He took no notice, for he had spotted those golden ostrich feathers a little way ahead of him. The wearer was standing alone and Ross was at her side before she had even seen him.

'Good evening, Hannah.'

'Ross.' Alarm flashed across her face, but she quickly concealed it. 'I didn't expect to see you here.'

'Nor I you. I thought your husband considered entertainments like this an affront to the Lord.'

He noted the wary look in her eyes, but before she could reply he heard an angry voice behind him.

'Durden. I might have known we should find

you in such a place as this. Get away from my wife, damn you!'

A hush fell over those nearest them and people edged away. Ross turned slowly to find Phineas Weston at his shoulder. His lip curled.

'You should try for a little civility, Weston. You are not in Beringham now.'

The older man's eyes narrowed and his face turned a dark angry red, almost the same colour as his coat.

'The law is the law, whichever side of the county border you may be.'

'And is there a law now about speaking to an old friend?' drawled Ross. His tone was deliberately taunting and he saw the flush deepen on Hannah's already rosy cheeks.

He allowed himself a contemptuous smile as Weston struggled with his temper. A bell rang out, summoning everyone back to the auditorium. Phineas took his wife's arm.

'Come, my dear, this way. I have fixed it….'

Ross watched them go, then with a shrug he made his way back to his seat.

'Another successful first night, Miss Charity.'

Charity cleaned the paint and powder from her face while Betty eased the heavy wig from her head.

'It isn't over yet. We have still to play the

farce.' Charity met her maid's eyes in the mirror and smiled. 'But we have made a good start. Can you work your magic on the wig again for tomorrow night's performance? The *papillotte* curls looked very well, I think.'

There was a knock at the door and the stage doorman looked in, his old eyes twinkling.

'Mrs Weston, I have a lady and gentleman here who are very desirous to meet you and don't wish to wait until tonight's reception.'

Charity glanced at the little clock on her dressing table. Smudgeon must consider these patrons important—and very rich!—if he was prepared to allow them backstage between performances.

'Of course, Mr Smudgeon. I have a few minutes to spare before I need to change my gown for the farce.' She sent Betty away and rose to greet her visitors.

Her smile froze when the couple walked in. She gave no more than a cursory glance to the woman in her glittering, overdecorated gown and gilded feathers before fixing her eyes upon the man at her side.

For the first time in thirteen years she was face-to-face with her father.

It took Ross a few minutes to realise that the Westons had not returned to their box. He recalled the magistrate's words as he led his wife away. *I have fixed it....* Mayhap there was some advantage to be gained here. Quickly he slipped out again and made his way to the stage door. He bribed the boy standing guard to let him in and depleted his meagre purse even further to be directed to Mrs Weston's dressing room.

He made his way through the main room where the ladies of the chorus were changing their gowns. There were a few good-natured shrieks and one or two saucy comments, but he ignored them and continued on to the narrow passage and series of doors that had been described to him. The first, so he had been told, was for Mr Jenkin, the actor/manager. The second was reserved for the theatre's new leading lady.

An elderly man was standing in the doorway to Charity's room, and Ross recognised him from his previous visit to the green room as Smudgeon, the stage doorman. A shout went up and Ross stepped back into the shadows, rehearsing the reason he would give for being there if he was challenged. Smudgeon stepped out into the corridor and pulled the door closed behind him, then to Ross's relief he set off in the opposite direction. As the footsteps died away, Ross could hear the rumble of voices coming

from the dressing room and was almost certain
that one of them belonged to Phineas Weston.

Charity was aware of the familiar icy dread
stealing through her when the doorman withdrew. Her smile faded and she remained standing, determined to keep the meeting short.

'This is one place I did not expect to find
you,' she remarked, to break the silence.

'I would not have come had I not heard such
disturbing intelligence.'

Phineas glared at her, his fleshy jowls working angrily. She thought he had aged considerably since she had last seen him. His whiskers
were grey and he had put on weight, but he still
had an imposing presence, and now he pulled
himself up to his full height to declare, 'How
dare you come back here, dragging my name
through the mud?'

She remembered that deep, resonating voice
of outrage—she had heard him use it many
times to great effect from the pulpit—and
was obliged to ignore the chill it sent running
through her.

He cannot hurt me. He has no power here.

She raised her brows and forced herself to
remain calm.

'It is my name, too, and if the reports are to
be believed I am raising it *out* of the mire. Not

that I have told anyone of the connection be-tween us.'

His eyes snapped.

'When people told me that an actress—' he almost shivered with revulsion as he spoke the word '—that an actress calling herself Mrs Weston was playing in Allingford, I could not believe it was you. Then I heard talk that my daughter—my daughter!—was *exhibiting* her-self on the stage. I tried to put an end to such rumours, but it is too widely spoken of, so I judged it was time to come and see for myself.'

Charity spread her hands.

'And now you have seen,' she said coldly. 'Are you satisfied?'

His brow darkened. 'Still the same pride, still that same stubborn wilfulness that I tried so hard to dispel—'

'That you tried to beat out of me!'

'Aye, and I should have thrashed you harder,' he snarled. 'As it is I have to watch you prostitu-ting yourself—'

'I am *acting*. That is all it is.'

'It is a monstrous abomination and you are the purveyor of evil.'

She managed a laugh.

'Good heavens, one would think you were speaking of Bonaparte himself!'

Phineas drew back, glaring at her from under beetling brows.

'The Emperor has his faults, but he is God's instrument.'

'Bonaparte?' she said, surprised. 'He is a tyrant. An enemy of England.'

'England has more enemies within,' roared Phineas. 'Sinners and those who wish to see the country once again under the heel of the Pope! Bonaparte is the scourge of the papists. There are some who think he is an agent of the Messiah, whereas *you*, madam, are an agent of the devil!'

'Now, Phineas, don't you be getting yourself in a bother about this.'

The woman standing beside Phineas spoke for the first time. Charity assumed this was his wife, the third Mrs Weston, and when she took a moment to study her she was surprised how young she was, possibly even younger than herself, but a constant look of dissatisfaction had left permanent lines upon her once-pretty face. She smiled, although her brown eyes held a calculating look.

'My dear Charity—may I call you that? After all, I am your mama now.' Her affected laugh grated upon Charity's ears. 'We did not come to quarrel with you, dear, but you must see that to have you here, not fifteen miles from our home, is a little difficult for your papa. After all, he is a justice now.'

'I don't see that my being here has any bearing upon you at all,' replied Charity. 'Allingford does not come under your jurisdiction.'

'But to have you parading yourself on the stage, for all the world to gape at and ogle—'tis an outrage.'

'I am an actress, and a respectable one,' retorted Charity, putting up her chin.

'You are little better than a trollop from the streets,' Phineas declared. 'If you had any proper feeling, you would be using a different name rather than disgracing mine.'

'It is my name, too, and I am not ashamed to use it,' she said coldly. 'No one has asked me yet if we are related, but if they do I will deny it, if that is what you wish.'

'So you would add lying to your many sins.'

Charity raised her brows and said sweetly, 'If you denied the rumours, were you not just as guilty? Now, if you will excuse me, I have to prepare for my next performance.'

Phineas glared at her, his nostrils flaring.

'Unfeeling, *unnatural* child. To be flaunting yourself in this den of vice—'

'If you are so disgusted with my performance, I suggest you leave now,' Charity interrupted him.

'I shall, immediately, but don't think you have heard the last of this—'

'Now, now, my dear, let us not be too hasty.' His wife caught his arm. 'We should stay for the farce, don't you think? After all, we paid good money for our box and I wouldn't want to waste it.'

Charity watched as her father was torn between his righteous indignation and his dislike of wasting money. She had to give his latest wife some credit for being able to handle him so well. She watched as the new Mrs Weston said in a coaxing tone, 'Come, sir, let us go back to our box and leave dear Charity to think over her position.'

'There is nothing to think over,' retorted Charity. 'I do not intend to leave Allingford.'

Scowling, Phineas stalked to the door.

'Come, my love. I shall escort you back to your seat.' He ushered his wife out of the room, then turned once more to Charity.

'So you will not leave, eh?' His smile and the final softly spoken words chilled her more than all his earlier raging fury. 'Dear little Charity, the Lord has brought you back into my sphere. I should be thanking Him, for it is clearly His will that you are here and He means for me to deal with you once and for all. Daughter.'

* * *

From his place in the shadows Ross heard only the final word but it was enough. He gave a little grunt of satisfaction. So she *was* his child—but there was no time to ponder how that might help him just yet. Phineas and Hannah were walking his way and at any moment they would come upon him. There was no way to escape without being seen. Then, suddenly, the problem was solved. A distant voice called for the chorus to go on stage, and the gaily costumed flock of laughing, chattering dancing girls crowded past him. Phineas and his wife were obliged to flatten themselves against the wall to make way. Grinning, Ross slipped back through the now-empty space and was out of sight even before Phineas and Hannah had moved.

Long after her father had left the room Charity remained rooted to the spot, fear charging through her limbs and leaving her trembling. She barely heard the excited chatter of the chorus as they rushed by her door. She should have expected this. She had always known that in coming to Allingford she risked contact with her father. What she had not expected was the raging, unreasoning fear that she had experienced in his presence. It was as if she was a child again, in his power and unable to defend herself any more than she had been able to defend herself or her mother from his savage punishments, delivered while he recited passages from the Bible.

You are a woman now. You are of age. He has no power over you. He has no power over you.

She repeated the words over and over again, but still her limbs would not work and it was not until Betty came in that the spell was broken.

'Bless us and save us, madam, what are you doing standing there?' She took one look at Charity's face and said quickly, 'Oh, my lord, whatever is the matter?'

Charity forced her stiff, aching throat to work. 'My father was here.'

Betty threw up her hands. 'What, that gentleman and his wife who came to see you? Well, I never did. You may be sure, Miss Charity, if I'd known I would never have left you alone with him. But come now, dearie, the singing and recitations are finished and you have to be on stage in five minutes!'

'I do? Oh, yes, of course.' Charity struggled to bring her mind back to the present. 'Quickly, Betty, help me into my gown.'

Charity made her way up to the wings, all the time taking deep, steadying breaths. If she faltered, then the other actors would suffer, too. She forced herself to think of nothing but the performance. It worked. She was word perfect as always, paying no heed to the audience, concentrating upon the stage, upon the next line. Afterwards, she joined the others in the green room and was relieved to find that Phineas and his wife were not there. She circulated amongst the patrons, smiling and laughing as if she had not a care in the world. Only Hywel noticed anything amiss.

'You are very pale, my dear. Are you quite well?'

She took his arm, leading him aside to say quietly, 'My father was in the audience tonight. He came backstage during the recitations.'

'The devil he did! What in heaven's name was Smudgeon thinking of—!'

'You mustn't blame Elias, he did not know.' She tried to smile. 'Most likely he thought my father was a rich patron that we should butter up.'

'Well, I'll make dashed sure he doesn't let him in again,' muttered Hywel. He realised that she was upset and covered her hand with his own. 'Don't worry, my dear. He can't hurt you here. He has no authority in Allingford.'

'That is what I keep telling myself. And with

Betty and Thomas living in I know there is nothing to fear.'

He squeezed her fingers.

'My house has rooms and to spare—you could always move in with me.'

'Thank you, Hywel, but no. I came here because I wanted to settle down, to be done with running away. I have faced my father. He was all bluff and bluster, nothing more. As you say, he cannot hurt me now.' She straightened her shoulders and smiled up at him. 'He is merely the ogre of my nightmares, and I will not allow him to intimidate me. I shall go on as I have done so far and…and be *damned* to him!'

After the performance, Ross collected his horse and rode home slowly. He had been tempted to remain for the reception, but had decided against it. Charity Weston was too alluring, and he needed to be free of her presence if he was to decide what to do with the knowledge he had gained that evening—the knowledge that she was the daughter of the man he hated most in the world.

Chapter Four

Charity tried to push all thoughts of her father from her mind and was helped considerably by her busy life. There were theatre performances every evening and any number of breakfasts and suppers with friends from the theatre, to say nothing of the invitations to parties and soirées from Lady Beverley, who liked to fill her house with the writers, poets and artists living in the area. She thought occasionally of the Dark Rider and found herself wondering where he was and what he was doing. She had not seen him since he had appeared in her bedchamber and returned the brooch.

'And that is a very good thing,' she told herself, putting him resolutely out of her mind. 'Consorting with a highwayman would do your reputation no good at all!'

The current production continued to play to

packed houses and Hywel reported that even more people than usual were coming over from Beringham. When Charity learned of it she wondered aloud why, if that was the case, none of the newspapers had picked up that she had the same name as Beringham's repressive magistrate.

'I had expected some rumours and gossip by now,' she told Hywel. She threw a shrewd glance his way. 'As manager of the theatre I thought you might have made use of the connection.'

They were sitting in his office at the theatre, taking a glass of wine together before preparing for the evening's performance.

'That you are Phineas Weston's daughter?' He grinned and gave one of the expansive gestures that were his trademark. 'I might have done so if he had been a justice in Allingford, but our local newspaper is not interested in what happens in another town. However, in Beringham it is a different matter.' He reached around to pull a folded newssheet from the shelf behind him. 'This is a copy of the *Beringham Courant* from a few weeks ago. You will see that it hints at a connection between you and Phineas Weston.' He continued in a colourless voice, 'The editor of the *Courant* is now in the House of Correction for one month's hard labour.'

Charity stared at him, aghast.

'You think there is a connection, that Phineas punished him for this? Why, that is preposterous.'

Hywel shrugged. 'Preposterous or not, the day after that piece was published the editor was charged with stealing a bundle of wood and brought before the justice. The landowner, Sir James Fryton, just happens to be a close acquaintance of your esteemed father. After last night's performance I got talking with a group of men from Beringham, respectable tradesmen. They told me that the editor is an honest man and not a poor one, either. He has no need to steal wood.

'They believe Fryton and the witnesses to the act were all in Weston's pay. The *Courant* has been challenging Weston's iron grip on the town for some time and attacking his extreme religious views—the penalties of which always seem to favour Weston and his friends financially, I might add. It would appear Phineas was eager to bring down the editor. However, it is also a warning to prevent anyone else taking up the story.'

'But that is monstrous!'

'The man is mighty powerful within his own area.' Hywel chuckled. 'However, in this case his little scheme has not worked, because word has spread and Beringham is now rife with the rumour that the justice's daughter is an actress and is performing here in Allingford. That is why the theatre is so full, night after night—the people of Beringham are coming in droves to see you.'

Charity's eyes twinkled. 'Oh, dear, poor Papa will not like that at all!'

'No, and there is nothing he can do about it,' declared Hywel. 'His jurisdiction ends at the county border and Sir Mark Beverley, our own magistrate, is a great supporter of the theatre and will have no truck with Weston's religious bigotry. But it is all good news for us. The play still has a week to run and we are already showing a healthy profit.' He grinned. 'Perhaps we should send complimentary tickets to Phineas and his wife to thank him for helping us to fill the theatre.'

'I pray you won't. He is so grasping he would feel obliged to use them.' Charity gave an artistic shudder, but it was not completely false. 'I would not have that man within a mile of me again if I can help it!'

Charity tried to put Phineas Weston completely from her mind, but when Mr Smudgeon pressed a note into her hand a few nights later, as she was returning to her dressing room, she felt a chill of apprehension.

'It was given me by a young woman, ma'am,' the doorman quickly reassured her. 'She's waitin' at the stage door now to know if you will see her.'

Charity's initial fear changed to pleasure, and she said now, 'Yes, yes, of course. Give me time to change my gown and I will send Betty to the door.'

Some ten minutes later she sent her maid out and waited, her mind full of nervous excitement. She heard a soft knock upon her door and a plump young woman peeped in, her eyes wide with apprehension.

'Charity? Is it really you?'

'Jenny!' Charity pulled her into a fierce hug. 'Oh, my dear, it is so good to see you again after all these years! Let me look at you.' She held her friend away and studied her carefully. The thin fourteen-year-old she remembered was gone, replaced by a plump matron, dressed in a sensible gown of sober hue. However, Charity was reassured to see the same kindly twinkle in those green eyes.

'I didn't think you'd remember me,' Jenny confessed. 'After all, it's been so long, and you never wrote—'

Charity pulled her into the room, saying contritely, 'I know, Jenny, and I do beg your pardon for that.' She scooped up a pile of abandoned skirts from the velvet-covered daybed and tossed them aside. 'Come and sit here with me and tell me how you got on.'

'Nay, I've nothing to tell,' said Jenny shyly. 'You are the famous one and must have seen and done so much since you left Saltby. I did envy you, you know, walking away from everything like that. The shearers talked of it for weeks after.'

'I hope you did not suffer for it.'

'Nay, not a bit. Your father was furious, of course, but Papa gave him a generous donation to the church so he never bothered me more, save to ask if I had any news of you.'

'That is why I did not write to you,' said Charity. 'I guessed he would try to find me. I was very lucky when I left Saltby. I met Mr Jenkin, who took me on with his travelling players, and I found the life suited me very well. But what of you, Jenny? You are looking very well indeed.'

'Well, I'm married now, you know, with three lads of my own. I married Jedediah Rigg—do you remember him? His father was the clog and patten maker and Jedediah has taken over his business. We are doing very well, although you wouldn't recognise Beringham now, Charity. 'Tis not the happy place it was when we were children. The inns are closed, and there's no music or dancing allowed in the town.'

She looked uncomfortable and Charity said quickly, 'You need not be afraid to tell me that this is all down to my father.'

Jenny nodded. 'He closed all the places of entertainment and has withheld licences from all but a couple inns—those that can pay him a generous fee for his goodwill! We don't like it much, but what can you do? He has the richer townsfolk in his pocket, and as long as they support him...' She plucked at her gown. 'Jed says it is forcing everyone to find their amusements out of town, or outside the law, which is not a good thing. I worry so for my boys...' She shook off her melancholy and smiled at Charity. 'But enough of this, tell me instead all about you!'

They spent a comfortable hour together, chattering non-stop, until Jenny jumped up, glancing at the little bracket clock that Charity kept on her dressing table.

'Heavens, I must go. I told Jed I would be no more than a half hour! However, he was going to wait for me in the tavern opposite, so perhaps he hasn't missed me all that much.' She pulled Charity into her arms and hugged her. 'Eeh, but it's good to see you, Charity. I'm right glad you've been successful. I shall not come again—oh, it is not the ticket money, Jedediah is very good and denies me nothing, but he is a strict churchman, you see, and although Mr Weston is no longer parson Jed won't want to incur his displeasure by too much frivolity. Besides, his brother is the constable in Beringham, so there is another reason he wouldn't want to cross your father.'

'Yes, I see.' Charity kissed her cheek. 'Then I shall not visit you if you think it will cause you harm.'

'Aye, well, maybe one day, when Phineas Weston is no longer magistrate,' said Jenny. She grinned. 'After all, the old devil can't live for ever.'

When she was alone, Charity sat for a long time at her dressing table, thinking over the visit. It had been good to see her friend and Jenny's description of her life, happily married and with a growing family, had stirred something inside Charity and made her all too aware of her single state. But it took only a moment for her to dismiss the vague discontent. Jenny might have a loving husband and a family, but she was living in Beringham under Phineas's tyranny, and when Charity compared that with her own freedom and independence, she knew she had no desire to change places with her friend.

'Be honest with yourself,' she told her reflection, 'You have no idea what you are looking for, but if it is a man, he will have to be very special to make you give up the freedom you currently enjoy.'

It was the last night of *The Provok'd Husband* and such was its success that Hywel Jenkin had hired the Assembly Rooms for the reception once the performance ended. Charity removed her paint and powder and allowed Betty to help her into the midnight-blue silk she had chosen to wear. It was important that she should look her best, for she knew Hywel would be using the occasion to raise funds for the theatre and to secure more patrons.

By the time she had helped her maid to pack away all her costumes, the rest of the company had already left for the reception. It was but a short walk from the theatre to the Assembly Rooms on the High Street and in any other town she had played, Charity would have been happy to walk the short distance alone through streets that were still busy. However, since her meeting with Phineas she had taken to asking Betty to accompany her whenever she walked out. They were just stepping out of the stage door when Charity heard her name. She looked around.

'Mr Durden.' She was inordinately pleased

to see him and it was all she could do not to simper when he gave a little bow.

Stop it, Charity. He is only a man after all.

'I am on my way to the Assembly Rooms, ma'am. If that is your destination, perhaps I may escort you?'

A smile burst from her at his invitation, even while she was admonishing herself for blushing like any schoolgirl.

'Why—why, yes, sir, thank you.'

'Will you send your maid home?'

'Mrs Harrup is my dresser as well as my maid. Mr Jenkin has hired a room and refreshments for all the backstage staff, too.'

And if they had not, Charity would still have insisted that Betty walk behind.... Wouldn't she?

Charity took his arm and allowed him to escort her away from the theatre. A biting wind whistled through the streets and there was a threat of snow in the air. She pulled her cloak a little closer about her.

'Are you cold, madam?'

Ross laid his hand over hers, where it rested on his sleeve. His touch was oddly comforting.

'No.'

'But your gloves are so thin.' His grip tightened on her fingers until she could feel the warmth of him. She glanced at his hands. They were large and capable, encased in York tan gloves. Surely their warmth could not penetrate through that and the kidskin that covered her own hands? Yet heat was spreading through her whole body as she walked beside Ross Durden. She was aware of a temptation to press even closer to his side, but she resisted and tried to strengthen her resolve by reminding herself it was not part of her plan to ally herself with any man. However, walking in silence beside him was awkward so she searched her mind for something to say.

'I understand you were a sailor, Mr Durden.'

'I was.'

'But you gave it up to run Wheelston.'

'I had no choice.' His tone brought her eyes flying to his face. In the sudden flare of the street lamp she thought he looked put out, as if he regretted his words, and her suspicions were confirmed when he said more gently, 'There was no one else to take over when my mother died.'

'And do you miss the sea?'

She felt his dark eyes turned upon her.

'Would you miss acting, Mrs Weston, if you were obliged to give it up?'

She considered for a moment.

'I enjoy it, certainly, but I could live without

it. However, I would be loath to give up the independence I have now.'

'Ah, independence. Surely if you have sufficient wealth, independence is guaranteed.'

'For a man, perhaps, but for a woman, an unmarried woman, there are always the constraints of decorum and propriety.'

'The solution must be to marry, then.'

Charity shook her head.

'Not at all. I have no intention of handing over control of my life and my fortune to any man.'

Charity pressed her lips together, startled by her own vehemence, which more than matched the bitterness she had heard in his voice. She hoped he would not question her, and it was with some relief she noticed they had reached the Assembly Rooms. She carefully removed her fingers from his arm and preceded him up the stairs.

The rooms were already crowded, and within moments of entering Charity was at the centre of a laughing, chattering crowd. She looked up at Ross, directing a look of smiling apology at him. He merely nodded and moved off, leaving her free to give her attention to her friends and acquaintances, but she felt vaguely dissatisfied. Not that she wanted Ross Durden to cling to her side all evening, but she would have liked him to show a little more disappointment at having her snatched away from him so quickly. She shrugged off the thought and scolded herself for becoming far too conceited.

Mrs Tremayne was approaching and Charity summoned up a smile of welcome. The widow was one of the theatre's richest patronesses, but even if she had been a pauper Charity liked to think she would not have treated her any differently.

'My dear, did I see you come in on young Durden's arm?' The widow's rather sharp countenance was flushed with heat from the crowded room. 'Quite a surprise to see him here tonight, but I would put you on your guard where that young man is concerned, if no one has already done so.'

Charity blinked. 'No, ma'am, they have not.'

'Well, you will soon discover he has very few friends in Allingford.' The older woman leaned closer. '*Such* an ungovernable temper.' She looked up as the rustle of silk heralded Lady Beverley's approach. 'Will you not agree with me, my lady?'

'Agree with what, madam?'

'That Mr Durden's intemperate nature makes him a man best avoided.'

'Any man may lose his temper if the provocation is great enough,' returned the magistrate's wife in her usual cheerful manner. 'I have never experienced his ill temper, although I do agree the young man did not behave very well, leaving his poor mother to manage Wheelston without any help. However, we do not fall out with him over it—after all, he is owner of a substantial property and Sir Mark is always anxious to get on with his neighbours wherever he can.' She smiled at Charity. 'I always make a point of inviting Mr Durden to our little soirées, but he never comes. In fact, he rarely visits Allingford.'

'Then you have not seen him this evening? He is here,' declared Mrs Tremayne. 'He came in with Mrs Weston on his arm.'

'Did he now?' Lady Beverley's brows went up. 'Well, well, that is unusual. And he escorted you, Mrs Weston? How interesting.'

'It is nothing, ma'am,' said Charity, hoping she was not blushing. 'I met Mr Durden on the street and he accompanied me for the last few yards, that is all.'

'Very gallant of him,' returned Lady Beverley. 'But it is hardly surprising that he should take the opportunity—why, any gentleman would do so.'

'But Mrs Weston should be on her guard,' Mrs Tremayne persisted.

'Well, now you have warned her I am sure

she can be.' Lady Beverley tucked her hand in Charity's arm. 'Now, if you will excuse me, ma'am, I am going to steal Mrs Weston from you. Sir Mark has brought guests who are mad to meet her.' With another smile she carried Charity off, saying with a twinkle, 'That is not exactly the truth, but I know how Mrs Tremayne rattles on and I so want you to tell me all about your next production…'

'In a moment.' Charity led her to a quiet corner. 'I recall at our first meeting you said Mr Durden's was a taciturn nature, but that it was—how did you phrase it?—understandable in the circumstances.'

'Heavens, did I? Fancy you remembering that.'

'As an actor I am obliged to remember a great deal,' replied Charity, not to be distracted. 'What did you mean, ma'am? What circumstances?'

The lady glanced across the room to where Ross was standing alone by a window.

'The family at Wheelston always kept themselves apart, my dear. Ross Durden was sent to naval college as a boy, so here in Allingford we knew very little of him, save for his occasional visits to Wheelston. Of course, when he *remained* at sea after his father died, that did cause some talk.'

'So is it people's disapproval that has made him taciturn?' Charity shook her head, her eyes narrowing with suspicion. 'I can see from your look that there is more to it than that.'

Lady Beverley gave a nervous little laugh, 'My dear, I vow you are like a terrier with a bone, worrying away at me like this! It would be wrong of me to speculate and I do so hate gossipmongers—'

'Come now, ma'am. If you are going to allow people like Mrs Tremayne to warn me against the gentleman, then you must give me a reason.'

Lady Beverley looked at her desperately, but seeing that Charity would not be moved, she capitulated, saying with a sigh, 'When Mrs Durden became ill Wheelston gradually fell into disrepair. Creditors went unpaid and the staff were turned off, all save Mrs Durden's nurse companion. There was some talk at the time that she and Mr Durden were engaged to be married, but that might have been pure gossip, for the young lady was rarely seen in Allingford. Certainly she stayed until the old lady died, although she told Dr Jarvis—in the strictest confidence, of course—that she was only staying on out of Christian goodness. She said Mr Durden had instructed that the rents must be put up to help pay for the upkeep of the house. Well, there was only one way *that* could end: the tenants couldn't pay and were forced to move out. Wheelston was in a very poor way when old Mrs Durden died.' She gave a little sigh, her kindly, cheerful countenance unusually sober. 'Her nurse companion left before the funeral— Well, what else could she do, if there was no money to pay her salary? By the time Mr Durden came home again his mama was buried and the house and estate had been closed up for several months.

'Perhaps he *was* to blame for the parlous state of affairs—there is no doubt that it could have been avoided if he had left the navy sooner and taken charge of Wheelston—but I saw him soon after he returned and I believe he was very much shocked by what he found, so perhaps he had not realised...'

'So everyone condemns him because he let his estate fall to pieces?' Charity asked, incredulous. 'Surely he is not the only landowner to be guilty of such negligence—'

'Oh, no, my dear, it is much worse than that.' Lady Beverley pulled her closer. 'He went off in search of his mother's companion and they rowed terribly, so much so that he was charged with blasphemy.' Lady Beverley sighed again. 'I suppose he lost his temper. Being a sailor I have no doubt that he was brought up to be familiar with all the most outrageous curses and oaths!'

'And do you think they had really been engaged to be married?'

Lady Beverley spread her hands. 'It was a rumour, never confirmed. But even if she jilted him, nothing can excuse him ripping up at her so brutally. However, he has been severely punished for it. The conviction for blasphemy barred him from holding any military appointment and he was stripped of his captaincy. He could not return to sea and he has been living at Wheelston ever since, doing his best to build the place up again.'

'So that was what he meant.'

Lady Beverley looked puzzled. 'I beg your pardon, my dear?'

'I asked Mr Durden why he had not gone back to sea and he said he'd had no choice. Poor man.'

'Yes, but if he had not lost his temper and said such vile things then he would not have found himself in that position. And he has shown no contrition, no remorse for his error. That is why Mrs Tremayne was giving you the hint, my dear, and she is right to urge caution. If the man cannot control his temper, it would be very unwise for you to become too friendly with him.'

'I have not met Mr Durden often, but I had not thought him hot-headed,' said Charity slowly. 'And blasphemy is such an—an *archaic* charge. What he said must have been very bad, otherwise I am sure Sir Mark would have sent him away to cool down—'

'Oh, my dear, the case did not come up before my husband! If only it had, then the outcome might have been very different. No, Mr Durden was charged in Beringham. You see, the young woman was married to the magistrate by then and Mr Weston is the last man to forgive a blasphemer.'

Charity blinked at her. 'She is m-married to Phineas Weston?'

'Why, yes! Apparently, soon after she left Wheelston she inherited a small fortune from an aunt, which made her a very eligible match. I suppose poor Mr Durden was distraught that she hadn't married *him*, for that would have solved all his financial problems. No, no, it was Phineas Weston who charged him with blasphemy. That might have gained Mr Durden some sympathy in Allingford, had he not chosen to keep himself so aloof.' She laughed. 'Such a pity that you should have chosen to style yourself as Mrs Weston, my dear. It is not at all a popular name around here, you know.'

The familiar chill crept over Charity. Her father was still wrecking lives, although now he was using the law as well as the Bible to jus-

tify himself. Her eyes strayed back to Ross. No
wonder he rarely smiled, if he had been robbed
of a promising career by a few ill-chosen words,
uttered under severe provocation.

She tried to put the matter from her mind
as she worked her way around the room, chat-
ting to the rich patrons she already knew and
charming the new ones that Hywel introduced
to her. There was no opportunity to speak to
Ross again, but she was very aware of him in
the room. He spoke to very few people and
spent most of his time standing at the side of
the room. He was a man apart.

She blocked the thought. If she did not take
care, she would be feeling sorry for the gentleman, and that would never do. Her father
had frequently flown into a rage at the slightest provocation and she had suffered the consequences. She had no intention of allowing her
sympathies to lead her into any kind of liaison
with a penniless hothead.

Her smile never faltered, and she continued
to chatter and laugh as if she had not a care in
the world, yet Charity was exceedingly tired.
She longed to send for Betty and to take her
leave. However, there were still a number of
people seeking her out and it was nearly an
hour before she could go in search of Hywel

Jenkin. She found him talking to a little group that included Ross Durden as well as Sir Mark and Lady Beverley. Charity hesitated, wondering if she should wait until Hywel was alone, but the hour was advanced and she was longing to go home.

Hywel smiled as she came up beside him.

'Ah, and here is the leading light of our group of players!'

'I wonder how you manage it, Mrs Weston,' declared Sir Mark. 'To be performing night after night and then to stay up to all hours, entertaining us with your sparkling wit and conversation. It must be very fatiguing.'

'One grows accustomed.' Charity included them all in her smile, her eyes sliding away from Ross Durden's dark, intense gaze.

However, it seemed he was determined to gain her attention, for he asked her quietly, 'And when is your next performance, Mrs Weston?'

His deep voice was like warm velvet on her skin. Ideas and half-formed sentences chased around in her head. She had heeded the warnings to avoid Ross Durden, but now realised that she had spent the entire evening thinking of him, wanting to impress him by saying something witty and clever. Now when she had her chance, she could not even open her lips! She was relieved when Hywel answered.

'The first week in April, sir. We are presenting *The Clandestine Marriage*.'

'Ah, that is a particular favourite of mine!' exclaimed Lady Beverley. 'And Mrs Weston is to play Fanny, am I correct? Of course I am, for who else could play the beautiful young heroine? But April? Why, that is weeks away. How are we to entertain ourselves until then?'

'We must allow our players a little break before we begin rehearsals,' Hywel responded. 'They need a holiday.'

Charity met his smiling gaze and chuckled.

'We need our sleep, too, so I will bid you all *adieu*.'

Lady Beverley put out her hand.

'Before you go, Mrs Weston, pray tell me you will come to my little soirée on Tuesday next? Just a few friends, you know, and you need do nothing but come and enjoy yourself.' She continued with an arch smile, 'Now, I will not take a refusal, since Mr Jenkin has just told us you will not be playing.'

'Then I shall do my best to attend, ma'am.'

Laughing, Charity took her leave and went off to find her maid. She half expected Ross to offer to escort her home and knew a moment's disappointment when he did not come after her.

All the better for you, my girl, she told herself crossly. *That gentleman is taking up far too much of your thoughts!*

The weather had remained cold, but now it took an icy turn and Charity was glad to stay indoors, although not for long. It took her no more than a couple days to catch up on her correspondence and to set the little house in order, and after that she began to miss her usual busy schedule. With the theatre closed and rehearsals for *The Clandestine Marriage* not yet started, Hywel and Will Stamp had gone off to enjoy a little hunting in the West Riding, and many of the other actors had taken the opportunity to visit family or friends. Charity would not have minded being alone in Allingford, had not a fall of snow on the icy roads made it too treacherous to hire the gig and go out exploring.

By Tuesday, the day of Lady Beverley's evening party, Charity was longing for company and an evening of pleasure and entertainment, but those thoughts were driven from her mind when Betty came in with her morning hot chocolate. One look at the maid's flushed cheeks and heavy eyes was enough to have Charity scrambling out of bed and ordering her to go and lie down immediately.

'Aye, that I will, Miss Charity, just as soon as—'

'As soon as nothing,' said Charity firmly,

taking the cup from her hands. 'You will go to bed this minute and I shall bring you a soothing tisane to help you sleep. No, do not argue with me, if you please. You will recover very much quicker if you do as I say.'

She shooed her maid away and put on her wrap. Thankfully Thomas, her manservant, had kept the fire burning in the kitchen, so it did not take her long to boil a little water to steep the mixture of elderflower, peppermint and yarrow that she had found in Betty's herb store.

Looking after her maid and keeping house filled Charity's day, but come the evening the novelty of it all was wearing thin and she was looking forward to spending the evening with Sir Mark and Lady Beverley. She changed her homely woollen gown and apron for her cotton-lined taffeta. The deep, rich red of her gown would stand out amongst the cream and white muslins that were so very fashionable, but it had the advantage of buttoning down the front, which made it much easier for her to get on without Betty's help. She put up her hair and took out the garnet parure that matched her gown. The set comprised a necklace, earrings and a jewelled pin that she fixed amongst her golden curls.

Charity regarded herself in the mirror. Was it too grandiose for a country soirée? Perhaps. A mischievous smile tugged at her lips. She was an actress and a little ostentation was expected of her. Satisfied that she would not disappoint, she put on her pattens, wrapped herself in her fur-lined travelling cloak and set off the short distance to Beverley House.

Sir Mark and Lady Beverley lived in a fine new town house overlooking the market square. It was only five minutes' walk away, but Charity was thankful to reach her destination. A thin covering of snow glittered in the light from the streetlamps and an icy wind was blowing, so cold it burned her cheeks. A glance in a mirror in the hall of Beverley House relieved her mind of its biggest fear, that her nose might be glowing to rival the stones of her parure.

She was glad she had come. The welcome was warm and she found herself in good company—her hostess had invited those friends from the theatre who had remained in Allingford, as well as a number of local writers and artists. If Charity noticed that a certain dark, taciturn gentleman was not present, she gave no sign and managed to look unconcerned when someone mentioned his name to their hostess.

'Mr Durden? No, he is not here tonight.' Lady Beverley gave a little laugh and her twinkling eyes rested upon Charity. 'It seems that even the company of our celebrated actress could not persuade him out of his reclusive ways, for I made a particular point of telling him that you would be here, my dear.'

Charity smiled, murmured something appropriate and moved away to join her colleagues from the theatre. She was soon caught up in a lively discussion about plays, and their actor/manager's plans for the remainder of the season. All too soon the clock was chiming eleven, the hour she had set herself for going home.

'Will you not stay longer?' Lady Beverley urged her. 'I have had so little chance to talk to you. If you are worried about walking home alone, I can always send for the carriage.'

'Thank you, ma'am, I would not dream of troubling you to fetch out your carriage for such a short journey. It is but a step and I am perfectly content to walk. And at this hour there will be plenty of people on the streets.'

'But it would be no trouble and the night is yet young. Do stay, Mrs Weston. I am sure one of our friends here would escort you back to your house—'

Charity was touched by her hostess's concern, but she was adamant.

'You are very kind, but my maid is ill and I do not want to leave her alone for too long.'

Seeing she could not be persuaded to stay, Lady Beverley waited for her to collect her cloak and accompanied her to the door, sending her off with the promise that she and Sir Mark would attend the first night of the new play.

Warmed by such an abundance of goodwill, Charity put up her hood and set off for North Street. It was snowing and she walked briskly, keeping her cloak pulled close about her. The streets were quieter than she had expected, but she guessed very few people would linger out of doors on such a chilly night. She turned the corner into North Street and into the biting wind, so she lowered her head and pulled her hood farther over her face to keep the icy flakes from her face. She had glimpsed a travelling coach standing at the roadside a little way ahead of her and she felt sorry for the coachman huddled in his greatcoat, and for the horses as the heavy flakes began to settle over the equipage. They would all be glad to get home tonight.

As she walked past the carriage she heard the creak of the door opening but took no notice until a pair of strong arms seized her and a gloved hand covered her mouth. She was lifted off her feet and bundled unceremoniously into the carriage.

Chapter Five

Charity struggled hard against her captor. With the door closed and the blinds drawn it was black as pitch inside the carriage, and she felt an uncontrollable panic rising within her as it jolted into motion. Her first thought was that she had been abducted by her father, until she heard herself addressed by a cheerful and decidedly Irish voice.

'Whist now, me pretty wildcat, just stop yer spittin' and scratchin' and I'll let you go.'

She was unaccountably relieved—her situation might be dire, but nothing outweighed the terror that her father instilled in her, despite her years away from him. She stopped struggling and felt those strong arms release their iron grip. There was a deep chuckle and the suffocating hand was removed from her face.

'There now, that's—' The words ended in a

smothered exclamation as she threw herself in
the direction of the door and began to scrabble
at the panelling, trying to find the handle. 'Hell
and confound it, woman, *will* you be still!'

She was hauled back onto the seat and a
vice-like grip clamped her against a large solid
body. She could see nothing in the darkness,
but she forced herself to be calm and use her
other senses to get her bearings. The man holding her must be big, because she was considered tall, yet her cheek was pressed against his
shoulder. The scratch of the material against her
face and the smell of the damp wool suggested
he was wearing a heavy greatcoat. There was
something else, a faint trace of the clean, spicy
scent that reminded her of a stolen kiss. Just
the thought of it sent a hot blush through her
whole body and added a very different alarm
to her fears. The blackness was unnerving, so
she forced out an angry question.

'Are you kidnapping me?'

'Faith, what else would I be doing with such
a termagant?'

She tried unsuccessfully to shrug off his re-
straining arm, saying irritably, 'The darkness
is making me feel sick. Can you not put up the
blinds?'

'Aye, if we are clear of Allingford.'

Still holding her to him, he reached across

to the windows and released the blinds. It was snowing harder and the flakes were sticking to the glass, but at least the darkness was relieved a little.

'Where are you taking me?'

'Faith, now, you don't think I'd be telling ye that!' Again that deep throaty chuckle. She turned her head to peer up at the man, but it was impossible to see anything other than a black shape against the grey of the window. A black shape defined by wide shoulders and the points of a tricorn hat.

'So it is you again,' she declared. 'The one they call the Dark Rider.'

He grinned, his teeth gleaming white in the gloom.

'Aye, that I am.'

Charity wondered if he would kiss her. She was a little alarmed to realise that part of her wanted him to do so. Quickly she looked away. He could not see her face in the dim light so it was nonsense to believe he might read her thoughts, but she would take no chances. She summoned up her most haughty, scathing tone.

'Are you such a hopeless highway robber that you have turned to abduction now?'

'Not at all, 'tis another means to the same end.'

There was something in his voice that stirred

a thought, a memory, but it was too fleeting to hold.

'You will catch cold this time,' she told him. 'I have no rich friends—not even a wealthy lover to pay a ransom.'

The iron arm around her tightened a little.

'Ah, your lover is a poor man, then, Mrs Weston?'

There was a warm, teasing note in his voice, but it only made her shiver—would it be better or worse for her if he knew she had never had a lover, that despite her appellation and her profession she had never given herself to any man? She had heard that some rogues could not resist a virgin. She would prevaricate.

She responded coldly, 'I do not have a lover at the moment.'

'Surely you don't expect me to believe that— or d'you mean there's not one special man?'

'Dear heaven,' she cried indignantly, remembering her father's scathing words, 'why must all men assume that because I am an actress I am profligate—?'

She broke off, choked by rage and frustration.

His hold on her relaxed and after a pause he said gently, 'Then I'll be beggin' your pardon, Mrs Weston, I did not mean to insult you. I perceive I was in error.'

'A common mistake,' she retorted bitterly, 'and one made by better men than you!'

They travelled in silence for a while, but when the carriage slowed he tightened his grip on her arm as he pulled the muffler from his neck.

'We'll be reaching our destination soon, I'm thinking, so if you'll forgive me, Mrs Weston—'

She held him off, saying in some alarm, 'What are you going to do?'

'Blindfold you. 'Tis best if you don't know where you are.'

The Irish brogue had lessened and something in his tone again touched a chord in her memory. If only she could remember! He pushed back her hood, then gripped her shoulders and turned her away. The next moment the woollen muffler covered her eyes. She flinched as she was once more plunged into blind darkness and had to fight down a whimper, determined not to show fear before this horrid creature.

'Is this really necessary?' It took all her training to keep a quiver of uncertainty from her voice. 'Just how far do you expect me to travel like this?'

'To be sure, 'tis not far, but I can't take a chance on you seeing where you are, in case you try to cut and run.'

Cut and run. An Irish seaman, perhaps? It

was a nautical expression and one she had heard recently, in Allingford...

'I know you!' She reached up to snatch the blindfold from her face. 'You are Ross Durden!'

She ended on a gasp, wondering belatedly if she had been wise to speak out. The silence within the rocking, jolting carriage seemed to stretch on for ever, but at last he laughed.

'I knew I should have stayed away from you. I have held up dozens of local people and none has yet made the connection. What gave me away?'

The lilting brogue was gone, but his tone remained relaxed, easy, as if they were enjoying an everyday conversation. She did her best to reply in kind.

'That term, cut and run. But I was already suspicious because of your voice, the timbre of it and a certain inflection that I had heard before when I visited you at Wheelston.'

'I see. Well, then, there is no point in blindfolding you.'

She looked towards the window.

'Your precautions would have been quite unnecessary,' she told him. 'I cannot see a thing through this snow-covered glass.'

'I didn't know it was going to snow so hard,' he said reasonably. 'And there is some good news for you. Now I need not put you in the cellar.'

'Cellar?'

'Why, yes. I couldn't risk you looking out of the window and recognising Wheelston, so I had decided you must be kept below ground.'

The very thought of it made her shudder, but she refused to show fear.

'And where did you acquire this equipage—is that stolen, too?'

'As a matter of fact, the carriage has been languishing in a corner of the Wheelston stables for years. You may have noticed the horses are not the fine, high-stepping cattle one sees on gentlemen's carriages. These two are more used to pulling a farm cart.'

The carriage slowed and turned, and when it bumped and swayed she guessed they were on the neglected drive leading to Wheelston. At last they came to a halt and the coachman climbed down to open the door. She assumed from his small stature that the figure huddled beneath the hat and snow-covered greatcoat was Jed, the stable hand she had seen on her previous visit. Her mind was racing. If there were only two of them, perhaps she might have a chance of escape. She put up her hood as her companion jumped out, but when he turned and held his hand to her she said icily, 'Thank you, I am quite capable of alighting on my own.'

Charity stepped down. The snow was already ankle deep and beginning to drift. Soon the roads would be impassable.

'Oh.' She turned back to peer into the dark interior of the carriage. 'My reticule, I must have dropped it. Can you see it, Mr Durden?'

As soon as he leaned into the carriage she took to her heels. Jed's shout of alarm spurred her on and she had almost reached the open gates before Ross Durden caught up with her and grasped her shoulder.

'Oh, no, you don't!'

Charity tried to fight but her tormentor put an end to her struggles by sweeping her up into his arms and marching back to the house.

'Put me down, you monster!' She had only one arm free, but she brought up her hand to slap him hard across the face. His step did not falter and he did not loosen his grip. With his hat shadowing his face she could not even tell if he had flinched under her assault. The carriage moved off towards the stables, so she knew she had only Ross Durden to deal with, but his size and weight made him a formidable opponent and the ease with which he was carrying her told Charity that he was no weakling. As he pushed open the door she reached up beneath her hood and pulled the jewelled pin from her hair. It was nowhere near as long as a hatpin, but it was the only weapon she had and she would use it.

She was unprepared for the sudden way he dropped her onto her feet, but as soon as she regained her balance she flew at him, aiming the sharp point of the pin directly at his face. His hands shot up and grasped her wrists, twisting her arms behind her back. The jewelled pin fell from her fingers and clattered onto the floor.

'Enough, madam, or I shall forget I am a gentleman!'

She was pinioned against him, every ragged breath forcing her against his chest, which was surely heaving more violently than his recent exertions warranted. An inner voice urged caution, but Charity was in no mood to heed it. She stared up boldly into his shadowed face.

'Gentleman? Ha! You are a rogue, an abductor, a—a thief!' When he did not reply, she drew in another breath and added at her most scathing, 'An unconscionable wretch!'

He did not move, his hold on her did not slacken and his very silence began to unnerve her. She strained to pierce the gloom that hid his countenance, but with only one lamp burning in the hall the shadow cast by his hat was too deep. The darkness was drawing her in.

She found herself leaning against Ross, raising her face, running the tip of her tongue over her parted lips.

Stop it—you are inviting him to kiss you!

This was not her, it was some wild, abandoned creature he had roused, something inside her that she had not even realised existed until she had met the Dark Rider. There was a tug of attraction in her bones so strong she could not control it and she knew, she just *knew* he could feel it, too. The thought both thrilled and frightened her. It was in the very stillness that surrounded them; the air crackled with it. She watched, transfixed, as his head slowly dipped closer. He would kiss her; she knew it. There was an inevitability about it that defied reason. He still held her captive with her wrists behind her back, pressing her against him, and despite the layers of clothing between them she could feel his body, hard and tense. Like a predator, ready to pounce.

A sudden gust of wind blew in, enveloping them with an icy blast, and the open door creaked on its hinges. The effect upon Ross was like a douche of cold water. He jerked his head up and tore his eyes away from that tantalising, upturned face, so pale in the lamplight. By God, did she not know how bewitching she was?

Cautiously he freed one of her wrists and stepped away from her to close the door. He half expected her to attack him again, yet when he turned back she had not moved, but stood as if rooted to the spot. The angry challenging look had gone and she now looked dazed and forlorn. He quelled the sympathy that began to unfurl inside him. He scooped the hairpin from the floor and put it in his pocket before releasing her other wrist.

'Despite what you think of me, I was born a gentleman,' he said curtly. 'You can remove your pattens now, madam. You will not need them in the house.'

She did not move. He gestured towards a bench, and like one in a dream she sat down and began to take off her outer shoes. By heaven, she had taken the wind out of his sails, first by seeing through his disguise and then by simply standing before him looking so damned alluring! His body had reacted violently to having her stand so close, but it was not just the physical arousal, the longing to possess her body. He had felt her heart beating against his chest, as if it was some small, wild bird fighting for its freedom, and it had awoken in him a fierce desire to cherish and protect her, to lay his life at her feet.

Great heavens, he was no Sir Galahad, and she was no gentle damsel in distress. She was a weapon he needed to use against his enemy. He must never forget that. Ross picked up a bedroom candle from the hall table and lit it from the lamp. He would not abandon his plan, but he knew he would have to work damned hard to keep it on course.

Charity took her time to remove her pattens, thankful for a few moments to make sense of all that was happening to her. Ross Durden was a very dangerous man, not only because he was holding her captive, but because of the way he made her feel. She had never experienced such a strong attraction to anyone before. Her body ached for him, all the more so, she thought, because she had never wanted any man before.

Very much the attraction of a moth for a flame.

Whatever it was, it could be her undoing if she stayed here. She straightened, casting a surreptitious glance towards her captor. He was waiting for her at the foot of the stairs, the lit candle in his hand illuminating his lean face, showing her the dark, brooding eyes, the hawk-like nose and the grim set of his mouth. She had never seen a more stern and unyielding countenance, but it did not deter her. Nor did it lessen her desire one jot. She closed her eyes for a moment as the irony of the situation struck her, that at seven-and-twenty she should be so unaccountably attracted to the most unsuitable man she had ever met.

What was she thinking of; what did her attraction matter? She was already doomed, for she knew his identity. He could never set her free now. She must stay alert and look for an opportunity to escape.

'If you are ready, Mrs Weston, I will show you to your room.'

She approached cautiously and maintained as much distance as possible between them as they made their way up the stairs. He threw open the door to a small bedroom on the first floor. A full hod of coal rested on the hearth, but no fire burned there and the room was only marginally warmer than the carriage.

'So this is to be my prison.'

'Hopefully not for very long.' He used his candle to light several more around the room. 'I will have Jed come up and light the fire as soon as he has stabled the horses, and I am sure we can even find a warming pan for the bed.'

She dropped a mock curtsy.

'La, I thank you, sir.'

He showed his teeth at that.

'Just remember, I could have put you in the cellar.'

He went out, locking the door behind him, and she was alone.

Charity paced the little chamber, keeping her travelling cloak pulled firmly about her. The room was sparsely furnished with a large chest of drawers and a small cupboard beside the heavy, old-fashioned bed that had its full complement of pillows and blankets, but lacked curtains. There was a carpet on the floor and a washstand in the corner, although the jug was empty. She went to the door. It was a solid structure fitted with a heavy lock. She gave the handle a cursory tug, but it did not budge. She sat on the edge of the bed to consider her situation. It must be midnight, or even later, but she had left Betty sleeping in her bed and had told Thomas not to wait up. It was unlikely anyone would miss her until the morning.

She was surprisingly calm and wondered how this could be. She was locked in a room, miles from Allingford, the prisoner of a man who purported to be a gentleman, but whom she knew as a highwayman.

A man who had the power of life or death over her.

She should be shaking with fear, but perhaps, after more than a decade in the theatre, she was accustomed to crises and drama. Besides, the memory of those stolen kisses would not go away and she just could not make herself believe that the man who had delivered them could be all bad. But it made no sense: reason told her Ross Durden was dangerous and she should be terrified.

She heard the key grate in the lock and Jed appeared, his arms full of wood. She jumped off the bed, wondering if she might make a dash for the stairs, but even as the thought crossed her mind Ross Durden came in and closed the door behind him.

'I thought I should come, too, in case you tried to escape while Jed was lighting the fire for you.'

He spoke pleasantly, but his eyes were black and hard as jet. There was no mistaking the implacable look in them. He was not a man to be persuaded by tears or tantrums. With a scorching glance Charity hunched her shoulders and walked across to the window, where she stood staring out into the night. There was little enough to see save the feathery flakes that were being blown almost horizontal by the howling wind.

'Would you like some supper?'

She wanted to swear at him and tell him she

would have none of his food, but that would be foolish. She must not anger him unduly. He continued.

'There is ham, or a game pie, or you may have a hot meal, although that will take a little longer, possibly up to an hour.'

She took a final look out of the window before turning to face him.

'I can wait. It is such a cold night—I would like something hot.'

'Very well.' He glanced at Jed, who was dusting his hands off as he watched the flames lick around the kindling and small logs he had piled into the hearth. 'Put a little coal on top of that, Jed, and you can come back later to build it up.'

'There is no need,' Charity said quickly. 'I am perfectly capable of looking after a fire.'

He met her defiant look with one of mild amusement.

'I am sure you are, Mrs Weston. Very well, Jed, come along. We shall leave the lady to her own devices for a while.'

'Supper will be an hour, you said?' She shrugged when her question caused him to stop and turn at the door. 'I only ask so that I know how long I must amuse myself.'

Oh, good heavens, why had she said that? She had left herself open for him to make the most audacious reply. As an actress she was used to it and could turn aside impudent comments with a smile and a light word. But that was in the theatre. Here she was a prisoner and at the mercy of her captor. But who was the real Ross Durden, the wicked highwayman or the sober gentleman farmer? She waited uneasily for his reply.

Ross gazed at the woman across the room. Her head was up and she was giving him back look for look. She had courage, he had to admit that, but he saw the wariness behind her bold stare. She must be frightened, to be alone and helpless. Again he had to stifle the urge to comfort her.

'An hour,' he affirmed. 'The fire in the kitchen has only just been rekindled. It will take some time to prepare a meal for you, but I will do my best to make it sooner.'

'I would prefer you to make sure it is properly cooked!'

'P'raps the leddy 'ud like some ale while she's waiting,' suggested Jed from the doorway.

'I want nothing but my food,' she snapped with an imperious toss of her head. 'In an hour.'

With a shrug Ross went out and locked the door. He found himself smiling as he went back to the kitchen. He had expected questions, tears and even hysterics. He had been prepared to spend some time explaining that he merely needed to keep her here for a while. But his *guest* showed no sign of wanting his reassurance. Perhaps it was no bad thing that she had discovered his identity. She would know he meant her no harm. He shrugged off his coat and hung it up on one of the hooks by the kitchen door. Time for explanations later. First he must prepare a meal, and one that would satisfy the lady.

It was just under an hour later when Ross carried a heavy tray up the stairs. It was laden with hot dishes, and Jed was following with a similar tray bearing a glass of wine and a selection of sweetmeats from Mrs Cummings's jealously guarded store cupboard. When he reached the locked room, Ross put the tray down upon a side table and drew the key from his pocket. Before he opened the door he knocked softly.

There was no reply, but that did not surprise him. The lady was most likely still in high dudgeon. He turned the handle, but the door opened no more than an inch before stopping. Ross cast a quizzical, laughing glance back at Jed.

'Damn, she's set up a barricade.'

He put his shoulder to the door and pushed, hard. Whatever she had put against the door was heavy and protested with a low rumble like thunder as it was forced back across the floorboards. As soon as the opening was wide enough Ross slipped through, tensed and ready to fend off any attack.

None came. The chest of drawers had been pushed against the door and the room was empty and cold—the small hod of coal still stood beside the hearth, Jed's fire had burnt itself out and the window was wide-open.

The drifts in the fields were deeper than Charity had anticipated and progress was slow. The snow had stopped and the sky was clearing. If she had known that would happen she would have waited to run away until later, when her captor and his servant were asleep, but her only thought had been to get away and quickly, before the snow became so thick that she would not be able to walk through it.

She had left the road at the very first gate into a field, hoping that her tracks would soon be obliterated as the wind whipped up the lying snow into fresh drifts. At least the rising moon provided her with sufficient light to see her way. The wind snatched at her cloak and hurled icy flakes into her face. When she had driven out this way in the gig she had passed several hamlets and hoped that she would find shelter at one of these before too long, although the lie of the land meant she could see nothing but a hedge some way ahead of her.

A white blanket disguised the uneven ground and she struggled to keep her balance as she sank into snow up to her knees. She was holding her hood closely about her face with one hand, the other trying to keep up her skirts, but it was impossible, and the edge of her travelling cloak was already caked and heavy with snow. Her feet were achingly cold and she felt every uneven bump in the ground through the thin kidskin soles of her slippers. She was not a great lover of breeches parts, where the role dictated she should dress up as a man, but now she thought fondly of the top boots and buckskins folded away in one of her trunks at the theatre. She also wished for her thick leather gloves— the silk ones she was wearing were soaked through and chilling her hands. A treacherous memory returned of Ross Durden covering one gloved hand with his own as he had escorted her to the Assembly Rooms. How long ago that seemed, and how naive she had been to think it a gesture of gallantry.

Tears started to her eyes, brought on by the fierce biting wind, she told herself as she prayed she might reach a dwelling, and soon, before she succumbed to the cold.

I could die out here.

The thought made her press on even harder. She had known the risks when she had climbed out of the window. She had decided then that the chances of surviving were greater out here than if she remained at Wheelston. The thought of Ross's sizzling kiss haunted her, but she was not such a fool as to think it meant anything to her captor. She might offer herself to him— that might buy her a little time—but the outcome would be the same. He could not risk her denouncing him as a highwayman. And since highway robbery was a hanging offence, what had he to lose by killing her?

Something, a sound, a vibration through the ground, caught her attention and she looked around to see a huge dark shape approaching. She knew it must be a horse and rider, but fright magnified the shape into a monster rearing up behind her, hunting her down. In a panic she began to run, but the flat expanse of snow ahead covered deep ruts and she quickly lost her footing. She fell headlong into the snow with a cry of frustration. Something cold and wet pushed into her face. The hot breath of a dog blasted against her frozen cheek.

'Back, Samson.'

Strong hands grabbed her shoulders and Ross hauled her none too gently to her feet.

'Let me go!'

'Don't be a fool.'

'I'll not go back with you. You cannot make me!'

'Oh, can't I?' The grip on her shoulders tightened. 'If you don't cease struggling, I'll knock you unconscious and put you over my saddle.'

Charity felt the tears welling up.

'You are a monster!'

'You have already told me that, but I am trying to save your life. Come along now, let's get back to the house. Once we are indoors you can vilify me as much as you wish.'

As he turned her she caught the icy blast of the wind in her face and reeled away. Ross pulled her against him. He gave a low whistle and the horse came closer.

'If I throw you up into the saddle, can you hold on?'

Charity forced her mind to work. 'N-no. I cannot bend my fingers.'

'We must keep you moving. Robin shall walk alongside and protect us from the worst of the wind.'

Charity allowed herself to lean against Ross and tried to match her steps to his as they trudged back through the snow. The dog, Samson, trotted ahead of them and seemed to have an instinct for finding the easiest path. With a strong arm helping her along and the great horse

sheltering them, the going was definitely easier, but every step was painful. It seemed such
a long way. Had she really come so far? As if
answering her unspoken question her companion muttered, 'We are nearly there.'

Then the house was in sight, a dense black
square against the night. The front door opened
as they approached, spilling golden lamplight
onto the snow-covered drive, and a figure appeared.

'I built up the fire in the bedchamber, like
you said, Cap'n.'

'Thank you, Jed. Stable Robin, if you please,
then make two hot drinks, as I instructed—only
no grog for the lady!'

Ross helped Charity across the threshold. He
kicked the door closed behind him and with a
curt command to Samson to go to his box, he
swept Charity into his arms.

Ross climbed the stairs, taking care not to get
his feet caught in the trailing skirts of her vo-
luminous cloak. She lay passively against him,
her head resting on his chest, golden curls tick-
ling his chin. He tried not to think about that,
nor the fragrance of her perfume, a light but
heady mix of flowers and citrus that assailed
his senses. It had been a long time since he had
held a woman in his arms and he could not recall ever carrying one up to a bedroom before.

In other circumstances he might have dropped a kiss upon that smooth brow or moved his hand to cover her breast that swelled just beyond his fingers. He dragged his mind away from the pleasant thought—the lady would not appreciate such gestures and right now his concern must be to make sure she did not suffer any ill effects from her imprudent escapade.

The door of the bedchamber was closed and he was obliged to set her upon her feet before he could open it. Gently he drew her inside. Jed had done a good job. A hearty fire now blazed in the hearth and the heavy curtains had been pulled across the windows, shutting out the night and adding considerably to the comfort of the little room. There was even a warming pan standing in one corner, ready to fill with coals later to warm the sheets before gently laying this beautiful creature in the bed. Once she had been undressed, of course. Most likely she was soaked through to her soft, ivory skin.... Ross felt himself growing hard at the thought of it.

He uttered up a silent prayer. This might be the place, but it was certainly *not* the time for such thoughts. He summoned up all the years of naval discipline to his aid.

'Well, now,' he said crisply, 'you must get out of those wet clothes.'

* * *

Dazed and exhausted, Charity pulled at the strings of her cloak and allowed it to slip unheeded to the floor. She was aware of Ross scooping it up and throwing it over a chair, together with his own greatcoat. Slowly she peeled off her long silk gloves. They were wet from the snow and she thought in a detached way that they were quite ruined.

'Now your gown and petticoats. Your skirts are saturated.'

She wrapped her arms across her chest, shaking her head.

'I have n-nothing to put on.'

'I'll fetch you something.'

He went out. Charity moved closer to the fire and sank down before it, shivering. The flames were hot on her face, but she was aware that her back was cold, as were her legs, wrapped up in damp skirts. She should do something, but it was as if the cold had numbed her brain. All she wanted to do was stay here before the fire.

'By heaven, haven't you undressed yet?'

The rough male voice roused her a little, but not enough to do more than shrug. With a sigh of exasperation he pulled her to her feet.

'Come here, let me help you.'

He dealt quickly with the buttons at the front of her gown. His hands were surprisingly deft and in a matter of moments he pushed the heavy material off her shoulders and it slid to the ground with a whisper. Next he untied the strings of her petticoats and she stood before him in only her stays and her shift.

'Well, thankfully your undergarments are dry,' he muttered.

The part of her brain that was still working told her she should be embarrassed, but she could not summon the energy. She noted dully that those dark eyes did not linger on her near nakedness. Instead he turned and picked up the wrap he had brought with him.

'I'm afraid it will be a little large,' he said, helping her to put it on. 'It is my banyan.' He wrapped it around her and tied the belt. He ran his hands up over the sleeves until they came to rest upon her shoulders. 'At least it will keep you warm.'

There was a knock at the door. He released her and turned away.

'The hot drinks you asked for, sir.'

'Thank you, Jed.'

'If there's nothin' else, Master, I'll be off to me bed. It's bin a long day.'

'No, nothing else, Jed. Goodnight.'

Charity took little notice of the voices at the door as she pushed up the sleeves, which extended a long way past her fingertips. She was feeling a little less numb now, but she was aware that her feet were aching with the cold and she realised that she was still wearing her wet shoes and stockings. She sat down and slipped off her shoes, but her aching fingers could not unfasten the knots of the garters that held up her stockings. As Ross came over she quickly pulled the wrap over her legs.

'What is it?'

She bit her lip.

'I c-cannot untie my…'

He dropped to his knees. 'Let me.'

'No!'

Her hands grasped at the wrap and held its folds tightly. He looked up, one brow rising slightly.

'Isn't it a little late for such modesty?'

'Where is your housekeeper? Perhaps she would…'

She faltered when his look told her he thought her a simpleton.

'I have given Mrs Cummings a few weeks off to visit her family in the south. Do you think I would be here now if she was in the house?' He continued, a note of exasperation creeping into his voice, 'If she *had* been here she would not have allowed the fire to go out in the kitchen and *I* would not have been obliged to prepare your meal for you, so we might have avoided this whole sorry business! Now, madam. Let me help you out of those wet stockings.'

She clutched the wrap about her tighter.

'No. I shall try again. Please turn away.'

With a shrug he rose and moved away. Charity opened the wrap and tried again to release the ribbons at her knees, but her fingers refused to work properly and her clumsy attempts only made the knots tighter. She gave a little mewl of frustration. Looking up, she found he was watching her.

'Would you like my help?'

'Yes.' He did not move and after a moment she added, through gritted teeth, 'If you please.'

He was not so ungentlemanly as to laugh, but there was a definite twinkle in his dark eyes when he knelt before her again.

She pushed aside the wrap to display one garter and after a quick glance he drew out his pocket knife and quickly sliced through the ribbon. The second garter suffered the same fate and she was able to remove her stockings, trying to maintain a sangfroid that suggested she was quite accustomed to undressing in front of strange men—or in front of any man. He handed her a cloth and she began to dry her legs and feet, rubbing hard to restore some warmth to the chilled limbs. The heat from the fire on her bare skin was very comforting, but as she was not alone she quickly covered her legs again with the colourful wrap.

'Here.'

A steaming tankard appeared before her. She looked at it suspiciously.

'What is it?'

'Honey, lemon and ginger. Or you could have mine, which has rum in it.'

'Thank you, no.' She wrapped her hands around the tankard and breathed in the comforting, sharp-sweet scent rising from the cup.

Gradually the hot drink and the warmth of the fire took effect. Her fingers and toes stopped aching and the chill tension in her back eased, restoring her spirits. Whatever terrors might lie ahead, for the moment she was warm and thankful to be indoors. She watched Ross Durden pull up a chair and sit down on the other side of the hearth, stretching out his long legs towards the fire. He stared silently into the flames, his countenance grim and forbidding.

'You should remove your boots,' she told him. 'They are sodden and it will do you no good at all to keep them on.' The severe look fled. He raised his brows and she added tartly, 'I am sure it is no odds to me if your feet rot away, only it is like to make you irritable, which would no doubt impinge upon my comfort!'

'I am not so impolite as to remove my boots in front of a lady.'

'Since you have forcibly abducted me and are holding me here against my will, I am surprised you would let such a little impropriety weigh with you.'

He laughed at that.

'You are right, of course. So if you will excuse me, madam.' He pulled off his boots and stood them to one side of the fire before stretching his stockinged feet towards the blaze. 'The difference between my footwear and yours, Mrs Weston, is that the damp has only penetrated my leather boots at the seams. Your flimsy shoes positively soaked up the wet.'

'They are dancing slippers, not designed for walking abroad in such weather as this.'

His face darkened again.

'No, it was foolhardy of you to go out. Crassly stupid.'

'If you had not imprisoned me here, I should not have been obliged to do so!'

'If I had known you would act so imprudently, I would have put you in the cellar, as I first intended,' he growled. 'You might well have been killed just climbing out of that window.'

'Nonsense, I tested the ivy first to make sure it was secure enough.'

'And what if your skirts had become entangled?'

'But they didn't.'

'And just how far did you expect to get in this weather? None but a fool would risk going out in this.'

She sat up very straight, angry colours flying in her cheeks.

'None but a fool would remain here to be murdered.'

His brows snapped together.

'What makes you think you are going to be murdered?'

'How can you do anything else, now I know your secret?'

He looked at her blankly for a moment, then closed his eyes and put back his head, giving an exasperated sigh.

'I thought that once you had guessed my identity you would know I meant you no harm.'

'Ha! You expect me to believe you will let me go free?'

'Yes, once you have fulfilled your purpose.'

Charity pulled the heavy wrap more closely about her before she asked the inevitable question.

'And what might that be?'

'To force your father to give me back what is mine.'

Chapter Six

Of all that had happened to Charity this night, these last words struck her as the most incredible. She stared at Ross, trying to discern some sign in his countenance that he was funning, but he looked very serious indeed.

She said cautiously, 'You think I am Phineas Weston's daughter?'

'I know it. I heard him say so.'

Charity bit her lip. It would do her no good to deny it, then.

'And you think he would *pay* for my freedom?'

'Of course.'

She drained the tankard, but even the warming properties of ginger could not dispel the familiar chill deep inside when she thought of her father.

'You are air dreaming. Phineas Weston has no interest in me.'

'We shall see.' He rose. 'We shall talk again in the morning. Would you like something to eat? I am afraid the hot food I prepared for you has spoiled from being left on the fire for so long. I suggest a little of the game pie.'

Charity shook her head, suddenly very tired.

'Thank you, no. Sleep is all I require at the moment.'

'You would be better to eat something.'

He went out and Charity leaned forward in her chair, her head dropping onto her knees. Insufferable man, to insist she eat when all she wanted to do was to sleep. It would serve him right if she pushed the chest of drawers against the door again and went to bed, but she was so tired that even the thought of it was too much and instead she remained hunched in her chair, her eyes closed, until she heard him return.

There was the scrape of a chair being dragged across the floor. She opened her eyes to find him sitting beside her, a platter on his knees containing a large wedge of raised pie. He cut off a sliver and handed it to her.

'Eat this.'

It was a command. Charity wanted to resist and upbraid him for his autocratic manner, but she was too tired to fight. Besides, she realised that she was indeed hungry. They ate in silence, Ross sharing out the pie. As soon as she had finished one piece he would hand her another, until all that was left on the plate were a few crumbs. He carried the platter to the chest of drawers and returned with two glasses of wine.

She took one and sipped it, watching him as he dropped back into his chair. He caught her eye and his brows went up. She responded to the question in his eyes.

'I am curious about you, Mr Durden. You are an enigma.' The food had put new heart into her and she was emboldened to ask, 'Which is the real Ross Durden, the sober gentleman or the reckless highway robber?'

'Which do you think?'

She considered. 'I would like to believe it was the gentleman,' she said at last. 'Although I do not like to think that you are really quite so sombre. You never laugh.'

'I find little to amuse me. Your father has seen to that.'

Her hands tightened on the glass. Somehow it did not surprise her that Phineas was involved in this. Dear heaven, would she never be free of him?

She said quietly, 'Will you tell me why?'

His mouth thinned. 'It need not concern you.'

'I think it must, since I am your hostage. I have a right—'

'Hostages have no rights, Mrs Weston.' He drained his glass and reached out to pluck her empty one from her hands. 'You should sleep now.'

His tone brooked no argument. She went to rise, but he stopped her with a hand on her shoulder. It was quite gentle, but there was sufficient strength for her to know it would be useless to resist him.

'First let me warm the sheets for you.'

He scooped hot coals from the fire into the warming pan and slipped it beneath the bedcovers. He looked up and caught her watching him.

'I hope this is the correct way to go about it. It is not something I have done before.'

Despite her exhaustion she felt a smile tugging at her lips. He was certainly an odd sort of villain.

'It looks correct to me.' She pushed herself to her feet. Heavens, how weary she was. 'I shall need to relieve myself before I retire....'

'We do not yet run to an indoor water closet here, Mrs Weston.'

His answer made her look towards the window, where despite the thick curtains the howling wind could still be heard.

'However, I would not ask you to step outside again tonight. There is a chamber pot in the cupboard beside the bed.'

'You appear to have thought of everything.'

'I hope so.' He emptied the coals back onto the fire and stood the warming pan on the hearth before picking up his boots. 'Oh, I ordered Jed to nail the window shut. My room is only next door and I am a very light sleeper, madam. You may be sure that I shall hear it if you attempt to break the glass and escape.'

She said, with a last tiny spurt of energy, 'Much as I object to being held prisoner, Mr Durden, you may be sure that the most pressing matter for me at this moment is sleep!'

With a short laugh he went out, and she heard the key turn in the lock, but this time it did not rouse her to fury and frustration. She was too exhausted for that. Besides, he had said he had no intention of hurting her and strangely enough she believed him, although she wondered what he would do when Phineas refused to pay a ransom for her. She gave her head a little shake; she was far too tired to think about that now.

She pottered around the room, collecting up her clothes and arranging them over the chairs before the fire so they would dry. Whatever was in store for her tomorrow, she would face it when it came, and did not intend to do so wearing Ross Durden's garishly coloured banyan.

Charity had no idea how long she slept, but when she heard the key in the lock she was instantly on the alert. The line of light around the edges of the thick window curtains told her it was morning, but she kept the bedclothes pulled tight to her chin as the door opened.

'Good morning. It is ten o'clock and time you were out of bed,' Ross Durden greeted her cheerfully as he strode across to the room and threw back the curtains. The dazzling light made her put one arm across her eyes and she heard him chuckle.

'It is a fine morning, but it snowed again in the night and is now knee-deep everywhere, so I would not advise you to go out of doors. I have brought you a jug of hot water so you may wash. Get dressed and come down to the kitchen. Breakfast is waiting for you.'

She bridled at his tone, but he did not notice, for he was reviving the fire that had burned itself down to a dull glow. She noted he was not wearing a jacket and the full sleeves of his white shirt billowed from the waistcoat, accentuating the width of his shoulders and tapered waist. Tight buckskins stretched over his hips and thighs. She found her mouth going dry at the sight of him hunkered down before the hearth, and an unfamiliar yearning gripped her. He exuded a disturbing amount of strength and energy, which in her present sleepy state put her at a disadvantage and made her assume a haughtiness that would have had her friends staring in astonishment.

'I am not accustomed to breaking my fast in the servants' quarters.'

That brought forth nothing more than another deep chuckle.

'Oh, you'll find no servants there, Mrs Weston. We must fend for ourselves. And you must dress yourself, too.' He picked up her stays and dangled them from one finger. 'Unless you would like me to help you....'

Colour flooded over her neck and face, not just from embarrassment but she was also aware of a delicious curl of desire winding through her at the thought of his doing just that.

'I shall manage perfectly well, thank you.'

'Good. Then I shall wait for you downstairs. When you reach the hall you will see the kitchen door behind the stairs.'

'What, you trust me not to run away?'

He was at the door, but her words made him stop.

'If you are not there in twenty minutes, I shall come in search of you. You would be very unwise to try running off. Your tracks would soon give you away. But I don't think you will put me to the trouble of coming after you again.'

He said no more, but the stern look in his eyes promised terrible retribution if she disobeyed him.

It took most of the allotted twenty minutes for Charity to make herself presentable. Her petticoats had dried overnight, although her gown was sadly watermarked, as were the satin dancing slippers. However, they were all she had to wear, so she wasted no time in regretting what could not be changed. She opened the bedroom door, but quickly retreated and only came out again once she had folded a blanket into a shawl to protect her against the icy air of the passage.

She was relieved to find the kitchen comfortably warm, and as she entered Samson came over to give her a friendly sniff, his black tail waving slowly. Absently she put a hand on his head before making her way towards the range, drawn by the cheerful glow of the coals.

Ross was filling the coffee pot from the kettle, but he looked round when Charity Weston entered the room. She had one of the blankets from the bed wrapped about her shoulders, the dull brown wool only enhancing the lustre of the golden curls that cascaded from a simple topknot. Her beauty was quite startling and his eyes were drawn to her lips. They were full and red, as if she had been nervously biting them. His heart lurched and he wished he was welcoming her here as his guest rather than his prisoner.

Pull yourself together, man!

Sternly quelling the urge to apologise, he greeted her cheerfully.

'So there you are. I'm afraid there is no bread as you might know it, for Mrs Cummings has not been here to make it. However, there are these.' He gestured towards the ceiling and a rack, which had a number of large, very thin oatcakes thrown over it. 'They are very fresh and still soft, which is the way I like them best. But even when they are crisp they are quite palatable, you know, spread with butter and jam.'

'I am not so high and mighty that I do not know that,' she replied warily. 'My mother used to make them. I suppose your servant prepared these.'

He held out a chair for her.

'No, madam, I did. I used to help Cook make them in this very kitchen when I was very young, and when I went to sea I took her recipe with me. It proved extremely popular to men accustomed to ship's biscuit.' He reached up and pulled down one of the oatcakes and put it on a plate before her. 'Here, try it and I will pour you some coffee.'

He pulled another oatcake off the rack for himself and sat down.

She said, as if making light conversation, 'There is no doubt that I will have been missed by now. I should like to let my friends know I am safe.'

'Impossible. You seem to have forgotten, Mrs Weston, that I have kidnapped you.'

'If you are truly a villain, why did you take such care of me last night?'

He tried not to think of the shock of finding her gone, the fear that had consumed him at the idea of her perishing in the snow. He had been horrified when she'd told him she had run away because she was afraid for her life. He was a villain, indeed, to put her through this. A villain with a conscience, but he could hardly tell her that.

'I need you in good health,' he said coolly.

'My friends at the theatre are not rich—'

'I am not interested in your friends. Only your father.'

'You really expect Phineas to pay for my safe release?'

'I do.'

'I am afraid you are very far out there,' she

said quietly. 'As far as Phineas is concerned, I am no longer his daughter.'

He observed her carefully. There was a tension in her voice, as if she was trying to conceal pain, but he was not fooled. She was an actress, and a good one.

'You will not make me believe that, madam.'

She put down her cup.

'I ran away from home at fourteen and became an actress. In his eyes I am nothing but a disgrace to his name.'

'But he would not want any harm to come to you.'

She closed her eyes for a moment, as if to push unpleasant memories away. Suddenly it was important to him to reassure her.

'Believe me, madam, I shall not harm you. I mean only to keep you here for a little while.'

'And if my father will not pay you?'

'He will pay.'

'You are wrong.'

He sat back and regarded her. Even in a crumpled evening gown and with her hair pinned up so carelessly, she was beautiful, fair as wax. Her eyes were the deep blue of a summer ocean and gazed out from a face that was quite perfect, from the wide brow and straight little nose to the delicate cheekbones and pretty chin that was now tilted up in a challenging manner.

It was inconceivable that any man, even Phineas Weston, would refuse to help this glorious creature. He shrugged and feigned indifference.

'Then we will have to wait and see who is right, won't we?'

'That could take some time, and I have nothing more than a comb with me.'

'After you have written a note to your father you can give me a list of what you consider necessary and I will see what I can do.'

Charity regarded him helplessly. He was like a block of granite, solid and unmoving. Perhaps he was telling the truth and he did not mean to harm her, but what choice would he have, once Phineas had proven himself equally resolute, as she knew he would?

She sat forward, saying quickly, 'If it is money you want, then I have my own fortune. Property, too, which I could—'

'I don't want your money,' he interrupted her harshly. 'My quarrel is not with you, it is with your father.' He pushed back his chair. 'Come along. If you have broken your fast, we will go to my study and you can write a note to him.'

* * *

'Ooh, how *dare* he do this to me!'

Charity gave a little huff of frustration as she paced up and down the bedchamber. Ross had locked her in her room and gone out, after extracting a promise from her that she would not try to escape.

Not that such a promise would have stopped her from making the attempt, but before leaving Wheelston he and Jed had hacked away the ivy that had climbed so usefully around the window, so that even if she had smashed the glass to escape she would risk breaking bones in the drop to the ground some twenty feet below. Not content with that, he had also taken away her cloak and her slippers, making the idea of walking miles for help through the snow even more uninviting.

After she had broken her fast Ross had insisted she write to her father. He had also agreed that she might write to Betty, but he had dictated the letter for her. It was a simple note, saying that she had met some old friends at the Beverleys and gone off for supper with them, only to find herself cut off by the snow and invited to stay on for a few days. All perfectly reasonable, she had to admit, and Betty would not doubt the truth of it, at least for a few days.

Given that she was suffering from a heavy cold, her maid might even be glad of the respite.

The sun had set and the temperature was dropping rapidly. Charity went back to the fire and threw on the last of the coal. She was angry, but even more than that she was bored by her inactivity. She had just drawn the curtains and lit the candles around the room when she heard the sound of footsteps approaching. Relief that she was no longer alone in the house was subsumed by anger at her captor. There was a particularly ugly pair of porcelain dogs adorning the mantelshelf and she picked one up, preparing to hurl it at Ross's head when he came into the room. However, the voice that requested admission was that of his servant.

'The master sent me up with the things you asked fer,' said Jed, coming in with a selection of packages, which he placed on the bed. 'Cap'n Durden says that there is hot soup in the kitchen, if you'd like to come down and join him. When yer ready, that is.'

Having delivered his parcels and his message, Jed retired. Thwarted of venting her anger upon Ross Durden, Charity put the ornament back in its place and contented herself with ripping open the packages he had sent up.

She had to admit he had exceeded her expectations. Her list had been for a few basic requirements such as a toothbrush and a shawl, but not only had he purchased a fine hairbrush and a nightgown, he had also procured a woollen kirtle and bodice for her, together with a fine lawn chemise, a muslin neckerchief and a pair of serviceable shoes. There was also a package containing new silk stockings and a pair of scarlet-ribbon garters, but however grateful she might be for those she was not going to tell him so!

Attired in her new garments and feeling very much as if she was playing the role of a country maid, Charity made her way downstairs to the kitchen, where an appetising aroma wafted out to greet her as she opened the door.

'Where is Jed?' she asked Ross, who was engaged in cutting thick slices from a loaf of bread.

'He has rooms above the stables and prefers to take his meals there.'

'Oh.' Charity moved towards the table, most of her anger evaporating. It was impossible to be cross with a man who was preparing food for her. One who had purchased goods for her comfort.

'Thank you for the clothes. I never expected—'

'I went into York,' he said shortly. 'The mail

had gone through, so the main road was passable, and you can get most things there, such as fresh-baked bread.'

He held up the loaf for a moment before he went back to cutting slices from it, the candlelight glinting on the knife blade.

'I could do that for you,' she offered.

He glanced at her, a glimmer of amusement in his hard eyes.

'So you can stab me? I think not.'

She blushed and put up her hand to acknowledge that his comment was not too far from the truth.

'I would not stab you. At least, not if you agreed to let me go.'

'I cannot do that.'

She sat down at the table.

'You delivered my letters?'

'Yes. Or rather, I had them delivered. No one will know from whence they came.'

'How soon do you expect to hear from my father?'

'Within a day or two.'

'You will be disappointed.'

'We shall see.'

His calm assurance was infuriating. Charity looked across the table at her captor. His clothes were plain, but although the black curly hair had been somewhat tamed by a good brushing, there was still something piratical about him. Perhaps it was the strong lines of his face, that determined cleft in his chin or the dark eyes beneath the equally dark brows. In her profession she met a great many men and had become adept at summing them up—a necessity if she was to keep the more amorous ones at bay—but Ross Durden intrigued her. She tried to draw him out, but every attempt failed. Even complimenting him upon the excellence of the soup received only a nod of acknowledgement. When he escorted her back to her bedchamber at the end of the meal, she was no nearer to understanding him.

The next three days followed the same pattern, and Charity was increasingly frustrated by the inactivity. Each morning after breakfast she was locked in her room, provided with sufficient coal for the day and books to entertain her, and when Ross returned she was allowed downstairs to join him for dinner. He was invariably dour and taciturn, yet upon occasion she saw the glint in his eyes that reminded her of the roguish highwayman.

The fourth morning saw a further fall of snow, but it did not prevent Ross from sending Jed out to saddle up his horse.

'You are going out again?' Charity asked him as she helped to clear away the breakfast dishes.

'Yes. Into Beringham, to see if Phineas has left a sign that he is ready to meet me.' He gestured towards the door. 'It is time for you to return to your room—'

'Oh, please do not lock me up again!' She turned towards him, impulsively clutching his shirtsleeve.

Something flared in his dark eyes, a sudden gleam that affected her like a lightning bolt running through her, from her head right down to her toes. She was shockingly aware of him, conscious of the fact that they were alone in the room—in the house. They were so close that the slightest movement would bring their bodies together and that would ignite a fire in her that could not be controlled.

Quickly Charity stepped back, crossing her arms, not so much in defence but to stop herself reaching out to him. She dragged her eyes away from his face, embarrassed lest he should think she was trying to buy her freedom by offering herself to him.

He cleared his throat.

'I am sorry if you dislike being locked up—'

'It is not that, it is the idleness—I am so *bored*! I will not run away, you have my word

I will not step outside the door, but please, let me move freely about the house.'

She bowed her head, ashamed of her weakness. She hated to appear so *feeble*. Yes, that was it—she felt powerless. No doubt that was the reason her body reacted so violently whenever Ross was near. He exuded strength and it drew her to him. If only she had a little more freedom, a little more to do each day, she would be better able to combat this dangerous attraction. However, a quick peep up at him showed that he was frowning, his countenance so forbidding that her spirits sank. Sighing, she was about to turn away when he spoke at last.

'Very well, if you give me your word that you will not leave the building. Jed is working around the house today and I shall leave Samson outside; he will soon give voice if he sees you.'

'Oh, *thank* you.' Her smile of relief only earned her another black frown.

'Do not try any of your tricks, madam. I shall leave orders with Jed that if you try to escape he is to bring you back and lock you in the cellar. And do not be fooled by his slight appearance, he is as strong as whip leather and will not hesitate to use force if it is required.'

His warning was unnecessary. Charity had decided against trying to escape again while the snow lay so deep on the ground. Instead, once she was alone, she set off to explore the house. She was well acquainted with the kitchen and the small chamber that had been allotted to her, but she was curious to see the other rooms. Despite the overcast sky, the snow reflected a considerable amount of light into the hall and for the first time she could appreciate the elaborate carving on the staircase and the panelled walls. There was a large drawing room on one side of the hall with a bay window overlooking the drive. A spinet stood in one corner, but when she tried it the keys stuck, swollen by the damp. Behind the drawing room was a smaller parlour that had at some time been decorated as a lady's sitting room, and on the other side of the hall was the dining room and Ross's study with its mahogany desk, where she had written the letters he had dictated to her. The rooms were handsome and well appointed and she noted that they bore evidence of having been regularly dusted, but there was an air of neglect about the place. Apart from the study, none of the other rooms appeared to have been used for many years.

Upstairs was much the same. Most of the chambers were empty or used to store unwanted furniture. She found a suite of rooms at one end of the building that she guessed were used by the housekeeper, Mrs Cummings, and the well-oiled door next to her own chamber led to the master bedroom. She hesitated, feeling very much like an intruder, but curiosity overcame her and she stepped into the room, reasoning that if Ross had not wanted her to enter he could easily have locked the door.

It was an elegant apartment with panelled walls and elaborate plasterwork to equal that of the reception rooms downstairs. A large bed stood opposite the windows, the bedcovers straightened, pillows plumped up and its scarlet hangings tied back. A large trunk stood in one corner of the room with a folded velvet jacket lying on its domed lid, and on the top of a bow-fronted chest of drawers a set of silver-backed brushes was laid out with mathematical precision. Shipshape. Even if she had not been told that Ross had been a naval officer, she would have guessed it from the neatness of this room. She walked over to the washstand. The bowl was clean and hanging from a rail at the side was a towel and razor strop. The razor itself was sitting on the edge of the washstand and she picked it up, pulling the shiny blade out of the ivory handle.

She remembered Ross refusing to let her have the bread knife. Here was a much more fearsome weapon, should she want it. However, she disliked violence and just the thought of it made her shudder. Quickly she closed up the razor and put it back on the washstand, then stood for a moment looking down at it, thinking again that Ross was an odd villain to allow her to roam freely through his house. Or perhaps he knew that such kindness would keep her there more surely than any chains. She left the room, closing the door carefully behind her. She would finish exploring and find something *useful* to do with the rest of the day.

When at last she made her way back to the kitchen she found Jed there. He looked up when he heard her and tugged at his forelock.

'I came in fer a bit o' that bread the master bought...'

'Please, help yourself,' she said. 'I am sorry—do you normally eat in here? I am intruding in your domain.'

'Nay, missus, I prefers to bait in th' stable, 'specially when the cap'n's got guests.'

A wry smile curled her lips. 'I am not really a *guest*, Jed.' The old man looked uncomfortable and Charity gave him her most charming smile, trying to put him at his ease. 'There is some soup on the fire. I left it warming through in case Mr Durden returned early. However, he has not come, so perhaps you would like to have it?' She gestured to the table. 'Please, do sit here and eat it. I should be glad of the company.'

Jed needed very little persuasion to stay in the warm kitchen, and Charity put a steaming bowl of soup before him. Cutting him a slice of bread took her thoughts back to the master of the house, and she asked if he had known Mister Durden long.

'All 'is life,' he replied between spoonfuls of soup. 'I came to Wheelston as a lad and worked here ever since.'

'I thought all the servants were given notice when Mrs Durden was ill.'

'Aye, all t'others were turned off, but I stayed on, despite that hell-hag—'

'Jed!'

'Not the mistress,' he explained hurriedly, seeing Charity's shocked face. 'That vixen 'as called herself companion. She let me stay on in the stables, doin' odd jobs. But I knowed what she was up to, despite 'er false smiles an' cheatin' ways. Bamboozled the old leddy right and proper, she did.' He scowled. 'And the master. I were the only one left when the cap'n came home, after the mistress had died. Nowhere else to go, see, and I didn't want no wages.'

'But Mr Durden pays you now?'

'Oh, aye. Insisted on paying me back wages,

too, which he needn't have done, but he's not one to do a man down.'

'He is a thief, Jed,' she said quietly. 'A highway robber.'

'Not he,' came the confident reply.

'But he is,' Charity insisted, leaning her hands on the table. 'I have seen it for myself. I was in one of the coaches he held up.'

'And what did he tek?' demanded the old man, fixing his bright, bird-like eyes upon her. 'Money? Jewels?'

She thought of the brooch he had returned to her, and the stolen kisses.

'The mailbag,' she said at last. 'He took the mailbag.'

'And left it at the roadside to be discovered the next day.'

'I do not know about that—'

'Well, I do. Cap'n Durden is as honest as the day. If he hadn't been—' He broke off, fastening his lips together as if to hold in secrets.

'Yes, Jed? What were you going to say?'

'Nowt. If you wants to know about t'master, then you must ask'n theesen.' He rose. 'Thank'ee for the bait, ma'am. Now, if ye'll excuse me, I'll get back to the yard.'

It was clear she had offended him and he would say no more, but what he had told her intrigued Charity. Ross Durden was in need of money, she knew that, so she could understand him turning to highway robbery, but why would he risk his life holding up mail coaches if he took nothing from them? His taciturn nature made it unlikely that he would ever tell her, yet he had granted her the liberty to roam about the old house, and that raised her spirits enough to think she might yet charm a little information from him.

The sun was setting by the time Ross reached Wheelston, and the temperature was dropping rapidly. His eyes scanned the surrounding fields, checking the vast expanse of smooth, white snow for footprints. He hoped that Charity had not made any attempt to run off. With Samson and Jed outside he doubted she would have got far, but it was more than that. She had given her word, and he was surprised how much he wanted to believe that he could trust her.

Ross left Robin in the stables and made his way into the house through the service door. He stopped in the passage and took off his greatcoat, shaking off the rapidly melting snowflakes before entering the kitchen.

The warmth hit him immediately, as did the savoury smell of cooking. Charity was stirring a large pan set upon the coals, but she looked round when he came in. He felt an overwhelming relief to see her there and could not prevent his lips curving upwards. Her answering smile lit up the room. The heat from the fire had brought a becoming flush to her cheeks, very like the delicate colour that had painted them this morning after she had clutched his arm, when he had wanted to drag her into his arms and kiss away all the hurt and anguish he was causing her. He thrust aside the thought, since it could lead nowhere. He had promised himself he would behave like a gentleman while she was in his house, but it was proving surprisingly difficult. Thank heaven she would not be here for very much longer.

'I hope you do not mind, but Jed killed one of the hens for me,' she told him. 'He said the bird was a poor layer and would not be missed. I searched the larder and found a little cream and some lemons, so I have made a chicken fricassee. And there is a potato pudding to serve with it.'

'You have been busy,' he remarked.

'I had to find something to do.' She bit her lip in the nervous little habit he was beginning to recognise. 'I hope you do not mind, but I also kindled a fire in the little parlour. I thought, perhaps, we might sit there after dinner.'

Charity waited for his response, half expecting him to refuse, to insist that she should return to her room upstairs. However, after a brief hesitation he shrugged.

'Why not? That is a good idea, especially since we have something to celebrate.' She raised her questioning eyes to his and he nodded. 'Your father has responded. I should explain that he has a much-coveted bust of Caesar in his hall—I know of it because I have spoken to people in Beringham who have seen it and heard him boasting of how much it cost him. You will recall, in the letter you wrote, I instructed him to move the bust to an upstairs window if he was ready to talk terms. Well, he has done so.' He paused. 'You do not look very happy about it, madam. It means you are a step nearer to being free.'

'Of course, I am quite delighted,' she said in a hollow voice.

'Good. Now I will go and change—a fricassee of chicken deserves that I should wash off the dirt from the road, I think!'

Charity watched him go. She had almost been enjoying herself, playing at housekeeping, but his news had changed all that and now she was chilled with apprehension. She had no idea what Ross would demand for her release, but she did not want to be beholden to her father. As she prepared the sauce for their dinner she tried to think why Phineas would have agreed to talk to Ross. Not to buy her freedom, she was sure of that.

Dinner was excellent and Charity accepted Ross's compliments with a nod and a little smile. She cleared the kitchen while Ross banked up the range for the night and went off to see to the fire in the parlour. When she joined him there a little later she found he had pulled two armchairs up to the hearth and set wine and glasses on a small side table.

'Madeira,' he explained, seeing her eyes resting on the decanter. 'I thought you might like it.'

'I would like to try it, thank you.' She sat down in one of the chairs and waited for him to serve her. The wine was warm and smooth with a rich, nutty flavour. She sipped it appreciatively. The atmosphere was relaxed, and a quick glance at her companion suggested that he, too, was at ease, his long legs stretched out towards the fire and crossed at the ankle. He was gazing into the flames and appeared lost in thought. She drew a breath.

'So my father has agreed to meet you.'

'Yes.'

'May I ask where and when?'

'It is better that you do not know the details.'

'Why not? I have already told you that I could pay you—'

'It is not just the money.'

There was bitterness in his voice and a note that warned her not to continue, but her curiosity was too great to give up now. She ran her tongue across her dry lips and pressed on.

'Mr Durden—the first night you brought me here, you said you wanted Phineas to return your property. What is it that he has taken from you?'

'My wife, for one thing.'

'Your *wife*?' Charity jerked upright, her eyes wide with surprise.

He laughed harshly. 'Do not look so shocked, madam. Perhaps I should have said my *intended* wife. Hannah—the present Mrs Weston—was my mother's companion.'

'Yes, I had heard that.'

'I met her when I was home on leave and we…became very close. Or at least I thought so.'

He fell silent, his brow dark and furrowed. Charity remembered that Jed had mentioned the companion and in the most unflattering terms. She said gently, 'Will you tell me?'

She thought at first he had not heard her, but then he exhaled softly, like a sigh.

'Six years ago my father died. I was in the West Indies at the time and it was several months before I could come home. My mother's health had never been good, but she wrote to tell me that she was coping well and had taken on a companion—Hannah—to help her. When I returned to Wheelston I discovered that my father had made some unwise investments just before he died and had left very little, apart from land. My mother was distraught. She did not want anyone to know of the change in her fortunes. I used my prize money to pay off the debts and left her with sufficient funds to tide her through until the next harvest, when the rents would come in. Mama and Hannah both insisted I should return to sea, because the on-going war meant there was every chance of more prize money. They convinced me they could run Wheelston. After all, we had tenants for the two adjoining farms and a good body of servants, so there was no physical work to be done. Hannah was the perfect companion, or appeared to be. My mother adored her and I—' His fingers tightened around his glass until the knuckles gleamed white. 'I thought we were doing the right thing. I was confident that I could make more money at sea than if I stayed at Wheelston.'

'And did you?' she asked, when he fell silent. 'Did you win more prize money?'

'Aye.' His hand resting on the arm of the chair clenched into a fist and his frown deepened into a scowl. 'I sent it all home, along with every penny I could spare.'

'What happened?'

'I heard little from Wheelston, but that did not worry me, correspondence between home and ships is generally very good, but there can be problems. There was the occasional letter from my mother, accompanied by a note from Hannah telling me that all was well. Then nothing.'

His chair scraped back as he got up abruptly and fetched the bottle from the side table. Charity allowed him to refill her glass and waited in silence for him to take his seat again and resume his story.

'My mother died in the spring of '05, but it was a full month before I heard. I received a letter from an old family friend in Allingford who sent his condolences and expressed regret—and some disapproval—that I had not seen fit to come home when she became so very ill. I requested immediate leave and sailed for England.'

He stopped, his gaze fixed on the fire. The

flames danced in his dark eyes like tiny red devils.

'I came back to find Wheelston a mere shell, the estate neglected and the tenant farmers gone.'

'Gone?'

'Yes. Their rents had been increased and when they could not pay they had been driven off the land.'

'Wait,' she said, frowning. 'You did not order the rents to be raised?'

'No, of course not. Is that what you were told?' His lip curled. 'I have never spoken of it to anyone in Allingford, so I assume they had that information from Hannah. I can only conclude that she was behind it all, squeezing every penny out of the estate and running it into the ground. I learned that my mother's funeral was a poor affair with her friends paying for her to be interred beside my father, but her name had not been added to the headstone. Only then did I realise the restraint in that friend's letter! Only a selfish, uncaring brute would leave his mother to struggle on in such circumstances. I came back to find bills outstanding with tradesmen in Allingford, and the stonemason would not engrave the headstone without being paid first. Of Hannah and my prize money there was no sign.'

'But how can that be?' asked Charity, frowning. 'Did the money never reach here?'

'Oh, yes, it reached here.' His mouth thinned to an angry line. 'I know the Prize Agents can be tardy in paying out, but that was the first thing I checked when I got into port. I have no doubt my money arrived, but not a penny of it was spent on Wheelston. When I had returned to sea that last time, Mama suggested Hannah should have access to the account, too, in case anything should happen. From the little information I could glean it seems my mother's health deteriorated rapidly after I left and Hannah took over the running of the estate—or, I should say, the ruining of it,' he ended bitterly. 'I also discovered that she left Wheelston before my mother was even buried, telling everyone that she had not been paid and could not afford to remain. A few months later she was Mrs Phineas Weston and the *Beringham Courant* reported that she brought with her a dowry of three thousand pounds.'

'*Three thousand—!*'

He looked across at her, his mouth twisting into an unpleasant smile.

'Her wages as companion to my mother were less than fifty pounds a year. So how do you think she came by such a sum, Mrs Weston? A sum that is almost exactly the amount I had sent home over the past three years?'

Chapter Seven

Charity stared. 'You think she stole the money?'

'I don't think, I know.'

'But surely—did no one question this at the time?'

'Why should they? No one knew of the prize money, save Hannah and my mother. When Hannah married Weston she told everyone she had come into an inheritance.' He pushed himself out of the chair and began to pace up and down the little room, the candles flickering as he passed them. 'The money I sent went into the family account in York. Enquiries showed that Hannah had made regular withdrawals from the account, but I swear none of it went into this house or the land. Instead everything of worth was sold, tenants' rents were raised until they could not afford to live in the farms any longer and servants turned off. Only Jed refused to leave. He was devoted to my mother and stayed on to do what he could.

'I went to see Dr Jarvis—he had been the family doctor since I was a boy—and he did not mince his words. Told me I was a damned scoundrel for going off and leaving my mother at Wheelston without the money to run the place. It is clear from what you say that that is pretty much what everyone in Allingford believes.'

'But surely you told him the truth?'

'I tried, but he thought I was merely making excuses. My mother had not told anyone of my efforts to repair the damage caused by my father's ill-judged investments. And there was no formal engagement between myself and Hannah. God knows I wanted to make it official, I suggested we should marry before I returned to sea, but Hannah would not. At the time she said she wanted to wait until my mother's health had improved, but looking back I think she was already weaving her plans. After all, why tie herself to me when I had already given her access to all the money I possessed?'

'So what did you do? Did you go to Sir Mark Beverley?'

'What was the point? I had no hard evidence. Hannah had made sure everyone in Allingford knew that she had done her best to keep

Wheelston running.' His lip curled. 'How fortunate for her that Phineas Weston needed a housekeeper in the same week that my mother died, and even more fortunate that shortly afterwards Hannah's aunt died and left her a fortune.'

'What did you do?'

'I decided I must talk to Hannah. She kept avoiding me, until at last I ran her down at a reception in Beringham. I challenged her, there and then. She denied that there had ever been a betrothal between us and said she had no idea what had happened to the money I sent home. Weston stepped in then and warned me off, as if I had been some errant schoolboy making mischief. That is when I lost my temper.' He dropped onto the chair again and rubbed a hand across his eyes. 'I am not sure now just what I said—having lived mostly at sea for more than ten years one learns to curse quite roundly and I have no doubt I gave vent to my feelings when Weston began to trot out those biblical texts and spewed forth all manner of self-righteous balderdash.'

Charity nodded slowly, understanding more than most what he had gone through, for she remembered her father holding forth on many occasions in that overbearing, bombastic manner that made one smart with rage and humiliation.

'Your anger was understandable, given the circumstances.'

'But it was my undoing. Hannah brought a charge of blasphemy and I was summoned to appear before Phineas the very next day. I could not recall exactly what I had said, but I am certain it was not blasphemous. However, several of Weston's cronies were at that reception and only too willing to testify otherwise. Even then Phineas had not finished with his plotting and planning. He offered to buy Wheelston from me, hinted that if I accepted his absurdly low price he would quash the charge. I swore at him then and told him in no uncertain terms what I thought of him and his wife.

'After that there was no going back. I was still raging when I was found guilty. I paid my fine and thought nothing more of it. I packed up my things and headed to Portsmouth, determined to go back to sea. It was high summer and everyone was preparing for a big offensive against Bonaparte. I was going to throw myself back into my life in the navy, to serve my country or perish in the trying. However, when I got to port I realised that Weston had outmanoeuvred me. He had written to the Admiralty.' He looked across at her. 'Anyone convicted of blasphemy cannot hold a civil or military office. I was no longer a captain and I received a stinging letter from Lord Barham, the First Lord himself, accusing me of bringing the navy into disrepute and informing me that he would not countenance my presence on any ship under his command, even as an ordinary seaman. My character was ruined, my career ended.' He exhaled slowly. 'And I was therefore prevented from playing my part at Trafalgar, one of the most important naval engagements of this damned war.'

Charity realised her hands were tightly clenched around the wine glass. A scheming woman had tricked Ross of his money, but it was her father who had deprived him of his career and his good name—everything he held most dear. Was it any wonder he wanted revenge upon Phineas? A chill ran through her. He might well think himself justified in taking revenge upon any member of the Weston family.

'I am surprised you did not return intent upon murder.'

'Oh, I did think of it, but I wanted more than that. I wanted justice. So I came back to Wheelston.' He looked around the room. 'The old place was still my home and I wanted to build it up again. It was difficult, for shopkeepers in Allingford and Beringham were cautious about extending me credit.'

'So you became the Dark Rider.'

'Yes. So far no one has guessed my identity, save you.' For the first time since they had sat down together some of the anger left him. 'Everyone is looking for an Irishman on a black horse. I thought I had disguised my voice quite well.'

A wry smile tugged at one side of her mouth.

'You must remember, Mr Durden, I am an actress and used to playing a part. And the black horse?'

He grinned. 'More theatricals. It is Robin, wearing a little make-up. I black out the blaze on his nose and his white feet. It has been very successful thus far. And I am achieving my aim. The tenant farmers are reinstated and little by little I am beginning to turn the place around, with a few—ah—donations.'

'Would that be from the likes of Mr Hutton and—' she searched her memory '—Absalom somebody?'

'Keldy.' Ross laughed. 'Aye, they are two of Weston's closest cronies and were only too pleased to bear witness to my misdemeanour when Hannah brought in the charges against me, along with Sir James Fryton, a miserly baronet who lives in Beringham. I have no doubt he was persuaded to back up Hannah's story by the promise of a fat purse. They have all fallen foul of the Dark Rider and have forfeited a few hundred guineas between them. Weston himself is proving more difficult, since he travels with an armed guard. I have caught him twice so far, during his frequent trips to Filey—'

'Filey!' Charity looked up. 'Why should he go there?'

'Why should he not?'

She rubbed her arms. 'He had the living there for a short time when I was very young, but it is a small fishing village and his congregation was not particularly interested in his preachings of hellfire and damnation. It was a very poor living, too, and when my mother died he married again, used his new wife's money to better himself and buy the living at Saltby.'

'Perhaps he has friends still in Filey.'

'My father has no friends,' she said shortly. After a short silence she added, 'My mother is buried at Filey.'

'Perhaps he visits her grave.'

'Not unless he has changed out of all recognition.'

Charity could not keep the bitterness from her voice. She had driven to Filey and visited the little graveyard during her stay in Scarborough, and thought now of the neglected plot with its simple headstone. There was no sign that anyone had been there for years. She gave herself a little shake.

'I beg your pardon, we are digressing. You were saying you took a purse or two from Phineas?'

'Aye, but only small amounts.'

'And my father has no notion he is your target?'

'None at all. My attacks are random enough not to rouse any suspicion, but I only take from those who were instrumental in my conviction.'

'It is still highway robbery,' Charity reminded him. 'Is it worth the risk?'

'What have I got to lose?' He picked up the decanter and refilled their glasses. 'That was why I held up the Scarborough mail. I was visiting an old friend and I left Robin at the stables adjoining the booking office. Out of habit I checked the waybill for the next coach leaving the Bell and saw a Mrs Weston. I thought it might be Hannah.'

'But surely that was unlikely, since she is now rich enough to have her own carriage.'

'I wondered perhaps if she was up to something without her husband's knowledge.' He added roughly, 'I was not sure *what* I thought— that she had left him, perhaps. That she had realised just what sort of man he was.'

Charity wondered if he was still in love with

the woman who had betrayed him, if he still hoped she might return to him.

'Instead you found it was me.'

'Yes.'

'Why...?' She hesitated. 'When you knew my name, you could have taken my purse.'

He shook his head. 'I believed it was a stage name, a mere coincidence. I did not think anyone as lovely as you could be related to Phineas Weston.'

Her eyes flew to his face. The words had been matter of fact, indifferent, but they made her heart hammer dreadfully against her ribs. She should be used to compliments, there had been occasions when she was positively showered with them, so why should this one affect her so? Ross was not looking at her, but staring into the fire. He was not even aware of what he had said. She had an irrational desire to laugh, but stifled it and forced herself to think of his predicament, not hers.

'You said there are tenants in the farms again—surely that will bring in an income?'

'The farms were empty for two whole seasons; the continuity is broken. There is an old adage that it takes three years before one can live off the land—corn seed must be bought two years before one wants to eat the bread, beef is at least two years a-growing, and a ewe must suckle and graze her lambs well into a second year before the farmer can have his mutton. I sought out the old tenants and asked them to return, but they have no money for seed or stock and cannot pay me until the land is yielding them a living. Much of the money I have taken from Weston and his cronies has gone to setting them up.'

'I am sure those gentlemen would think their money wisely invested.'

Her irony was not missed and the harsh look fled as he grinned at her.

'And *I* am sure they would prefer to use it for their own pleasure!'

'And the woman who took your money in the first place,' she asked him. 'What of the new Mrs Weston?'

He shrugged. 'Weston is welcome to her. I want only my prize money. Which is where you fit into my plans.' He rose, saying in the cheerful, jaunty voice of the Dark Rider, 'Faith, m'dear, 'tis near midnight. Time for me to lock you up again, my fair captive.'

She sighed, wishing he had not reminded her of her situation. He pulled her to her feet and she stood before him, fixing her eyes on his face as she challenged him once more.

'But how can you let me go, even if my father pays the ransom? I know who you are.'

'And would you tell him?'

They were standing very close. With every breath the muslin scarf that covered her breasts came within an inch of his waistcoat, yet she could not step back. It was as if some cord was between them, drawing them ever closer.

She said unhappily, 'My father would force me to do so. He has that power.' She gripped his jacket. 'Don't trust him, I pray you! Do not give him an excuse in law to question me. Let me go now, let me escape and go back to Allingford. I swear I will tell no one your identity—I will even pay you the ransom. What are you going to ask of Phineas, the full three thousand pounds? It will take me some time, but—'

'No!' His face darkened and he reached up to pull her hands away. 'I have told you, it is Phineas who must pay for this. No one else.' He turned and, keeping a vice-like grip upon one wrist, he almost dragged her out of the room and up the stairs, the companionship they had shared forgotten. When they reached her bed-chamber he thrust a bedroom candle into her hands and with a brusque goodnight he shut her in and locked the door.

Charity sank down on the edge of the bed. She could not blame him for his actions, but she was at a loss to see how he could continue to live at Wheelston even if Phineas did pay her ransom. Once she was free her father would pursue her. He would use every means at his disposal to force from her the identity of her captor. The county boundary would be no protection; he would summon her to appear before him. A shudder ran through her—most likely he would interrogate her in private, and she knew from bitter experience how impossible it was to hold out against him. Once he knew Ross's identity he would use the full force of the law against him. Ross might have his prize money, but he would not be able to live in peace and enjoy it.

The problem went round and round in Charity's head as she made her preparations for sleep, but as she could find no solution, save to run away again, she went to bed feeling more depressed than ever.

The York to Pickering road ran through Stockton Forest, and a wise coachman would always whip up his horses to get through the woodland with the least possible delay. The driver sitting on the fringed hammer cloth of the smart travelling carriage on that icy morning was no exception. As soon as the trees were in sight he flicked his whip over the four beautifully stepping bays and exhorted them to 'Run, damn it!'

The trees sheltered the road somewhat, so the heavy snow was not quite so deep here and a carriage could make good progress. They thundered on, the trees rising straight and leafless on each side with their branches overhanging the road, like the columns and roof beams of some great cathedral. There was only one more bend and then they would be able to see the open road ahead of them. The coachman slowed a little and drove his team around the slight curve, only to find the track blocked by an untidy pile of branches and dead wood. Swearing loudly, he hauled on the reins and brought the team to a plunging halt.

'Oho, trouble here, me lad,' he muttered to the guard beside him. 'Keep yer eyes peeled.' Even as he spoke a masked horseman appeared between the trees and he commanded sternly, 'Right, Joe, let 'im have it!'

The guard pulled the trigger, but instead of the loud reverberation there was only the click of the hammer on an empty chamber. An angry bellow came from the carriage below them.

'What is it? What's afoot?'

'Highway robbery, Mr Weston,' the coachman called down to his master, adding bitterly, 'and Joe forgot to load the shotgun.'

'I did not! I—'

A loud, cheerful voice interrupted him.

'Whist now, gentlemen, will ye cease yer quarrelling? Don't be blamin' yer man, there, for he did check his pops right enough and they was loaded, but that was before you both took yourselves indoors to break your fast, which was when I removed the bullets—and I also removed 'em from that little pop gun you keeps in the carriage, too, Magistrate, in case you was thinkin' to shoot me with it.'

'The Dark Rider,' muttered the coachman. 'I thought we was safe from 'im this far west.'

'Ah, well, now, it's mistaken you were, but just you keep still up there and you'll be safe enough.' The horseman rode closer, grinning at the angry red face glaring at him from inside the carriage.

'Well, get on with it, you scoundrel. What do you want?'

'To parley, Mr Weston. Will ye not step into the trees with me? Your men can busy themselves clearing the path while we talk.'

'Parley?' roared the magistrate. 'I have nothing to say to you, sirrah.'

'Have ye not? After you moved that precious marble bust into the window yesterday, an' all.'

Phineas stared at him in silence for a long moment.

'Oh, so you are the blackguard who sent me that note, are you? Very well, I suppose we must talk.' He climbed down from the coach, cursing as he sank ankle deep into the snow, completely swamping his buckled shoes.

'Come over here where we'll not be overheard,' the masked man ordered, dismounting. 'And tell yer lackeys not to think o' followin' us. I'll put a bullet through the first one to try.'

Through the slits of his mask Ross watched as Phineas Weston approached, stepping gingerly through the snow, grumbling all the time.

'Damned inconvenient place to meet.'

'Sure, and you'd prefer an inn, I suppose,' replied Ross cheerfully. 'Where you could set a trap for me.'

'Well, what do you want?'

'You know what I want. Payment for the safe return of your daughter.'

'And if I refuse?'

'Ye'd be foolish to do that, Mr Weston.'

Phineas gave a harsh laugh.

'Why? What interest do I have in that daughter of Satan?'

The viciousness of the reply surprised Ross, but he said merely, 'Why, man, she's yer own flesh and blood. And a damned fine actress, too.'

'Damned fine whore more like,' snarled Weston, his callous words making Ross long to strike him. 'No, you keep her, sir, with my compliments.'

Ross caught his breath. Was Charity right after all? Did this man have no paternal feelings whatsoever? He pretended to consider the matter.

'Mebbe I *will* keep her. She's a handsome wench and would warm my bed at night. But what happens when I make it known that you turned yer back on her? Your own daughter.'

'Who's to say she is my daughter? I have never owned it.'

Ross shook his head.

'Tush now, are you denying all those rumours? And you, such a God-fearing Christian. There's many will be shocked to hear of it, I'm sure. Ah, well, if that's the way it is, we've nothing else to say to each other—'

'Wait.' Phineas frowned and began to pace up and down. 'You are right, damn you. She has built up a following for herself. I hear they come from as far afield as York to see her. It would ruin my reputation if 'twas known I'd refused to help, for all the girl's a damned nuisance.' He stopped and shot a fierce glaring look at Ross. 'So what's your price?'

'Two thousand guineas.'

'*What?* Out of the question.'

'Fustian,' retorted Ross. 'You paid as much

for that little filly you had running at York races last year.'

Phineas shook his head. 'No, it's too much. After all, I have no interest in the jade. I'll not acknowledge her, whatever the rumours. She's a disgrace to me, to my name. An abomination.'

'She's your daughter.'

Phineas gave a savage laugh. 'She's the devil's spawn, flaunting herself in public as she does. No, sir, "if thine eye offend thee, pluck it out". Do away with her, with my blessing.'

'Holy Mother, but it's an unnatural father you are!' exclaimed Ross, forcing himself to laugh. 'But if that's your final word, we'll see what her friends at the theatre will pay—'

He whistled for Robin to come to him, but through the slits of the mask he was watching Phineas, who was scowling and rubbing his chin.

'No, wait,' said the magistrate, an arrested look in his eye. 'Perhaps *you* are God's instrument in this,' he mused, 'sent to rid me of this troublesome wench.' He straightened and looked at Ross. 'Very well, I *will* give you two thousand guineas. Only I don't want her alive.'

Ross clenched his jaw to prevent an exclamation of abhorrence.

'Go on.'

Phineas's eyes were gleaming. He continued

in a conspiratorial manner, 'Get her to write me another letter—I presume she did pen the last one? I wouldn't recognise her hand, but no doubt her friends in the theatre would do so and we must make it credible. Put in your demands. I'll agree to pay you the two thousand guineas, but then there must be some sort of…accident. Leave the body on the Beringham side of the county border and I will make sure the perpetrator of this heinous crime is never discovered.'

Ross felt the bile rising in his throat and he could not prevent his mouth twisting in a way that Phineas rightly interpreted as repugnance. The magistrate's own lip curled.

'Why so squeamish, man? What difference is it to you what happens to her? She is a beauty, I'll grant you that, so do with her as you wish while we play out this charade, but you'll not get a penny from me if she remains alive.'

Ross forced another laugh. 'By our Lady, 'tis an ingenious plan you've thought up there. But how d'you square it with your conscience, being a preacher man, an' all?'

'The Lord is a vengeful and an angry God, and some souls are too far sunk into wickedness to be saved.' Phineas raised his arms and cried to the sky, '"O daughter of Babylon, who are to be destroyed!"' He brought his savage gaze back to Ross. 'My daughter proved herself past praying for when she defied me and ran away thirteen years ago. I cast her off then, but now she has come back to mock me. Her presence in Allingford is a constant taunt, an affront to God. In you He has shown me a way to do His justice. So do we have a bargain?'

Ross shrugged.

'Why not?' He swung himself into the saddle. 'I'll contact you shortly to let you know where to leave the money.'

'Remember,' said Phineas, 'there will be no payment if she lives.'

With a final nod Ross turned his horse and rode away.

That had not gone the way he had intended. Not at all.

Charity awoke to a feeling of foreboding. No one had knocked and called her down to breakfast. She dressed quickly and tried the door. It was not locked, so she dragged a shawl around her shoulders and made her way through the unheated passages to the kitchen. The house had an empty, hollow feel to it; no one answered her call. When she saw Jed in the yard she went out to speak to him. Samson was at the door and barked as she stepped outside, but he did not prevent her from following Jed into the stables.

'Where is Mr Durden?'

'He ain't come home yet, ma'am.'

She spotted the tin of blacking on the bench beside Robin's empty stall.

'Is he— Has he gone out as the Dark Rider?'

Jed nodded. 'Set off before dawn, he did. Said he knew Weston had business that would mean 'im putting up in York last night and was going to catch 'im on the way home.'

Charity put her hands to her cheeks. She recalled Ross telling her that Phineas always travelled with an armed guard. What if he had been wounded, or worse? He might even now be languishing in York gaol. Or he might have succeeded and negotiated her release. The thought was even more chilling. How much would Phineas be willing to pay, and what would he demand from her in return?

'Don't you be worryin' about the master,' said Jed, misinterpreting her anxiety. 'He'll be back soon enough.'

'I wasn't worrying about Mr Durden.' At least, not much.

Jed frowned. 'I hope you ain't planning to run off again, ma'am, 'cos I have orders....'

Charity thought of the snow, still knee-deep all around the house.

'No, I have learned my lesson there. I shall wait indoors for Mr Durden's return.'

With a nod she went back to the house. The

fire in the kitchen was burning well, so she made coffee for herself, then rummaged in the larder for something to eat.

Once she had broken her fast she felt a little better, and the future did not seem quite so bleak. If Ross had succeeded, she hoped she could persuade him to take her back to the theatre. She would be safe there, at least until she could make her plans and disappear again. It was not ideal, but she was determined she would not allow herself to fall into Phineas's clutches.

The hall clock was striking midday when Ross at last came in. Charity was reading in the kitchen, her chair pulled close to the range for warmth. She jumped when the door opened.

'Oh! I did not hear you. I—'

He interrupted her without apology.

'Jed is preparing the carriage now. Collect your things and he will take you back to Allingford.'

'What has happened?' she demanded, alarmed by the urgency in his tone. 'Why must I hurry?'

Ross stepped up to the table and began to pull off his gloves.

'Phineas will not pay,' he said shortly. 'I am letting you go.'

She frowned.

'I don't understand.'

'What is so difficult about that?' His response was almost a snarl. 'Jed is going to take you home as soon as you are ready. Excuse me. I have a great deal to do.'

He strode out and she followed him across the hall to the study.

'But what about you?'

'That need not concern you.' He was pulling papers from his desk, paying her very little heed.

'But...Wheelston?'

'Once it is known that I am the Dark Rider, Wheelston will be forfeit to the Crown. The tenants should be able to start paying their rents next Lady Day, so I hope they will be allowed to remain.'

She pulled the shawl a little tighter around her.

'Has my father discovered your identity?'

'Not yet.'

'Then you think *I* will reveal it?'

He looked up.

'You told me yourself he would force it out of you. I would rather he did not have to. I would not have you suffer for my sake.'

She shook her head slowly.

'It need not be like that. Phineas cannot question me if he has no legal reason to do so. We

will convince him I was never here, adhere to
the story I have already told my maid. He will
think the Dark Rider was trying to dupe him.
You do not need to give up all this, we can keep
it a secret. You may trust me.'

He gave a savage laugh.

'The last time I trusted a woman—'

'I am not like Hannah!'

'Even if I believed that, Phineas would drag
the truth from you.'

'Not if he thinks the Dark Rider was lying,
that there was no kidnap. After all, what proof
did you give him?'

'He had your letter.' He stopped, his brow
furrowed. 'Although he did admit he could not
recognise your handwriting.'

She bit her lip. 'Please, listen to me. No one
need know I have been here, I can deny I wrote
the letter to Phineas. Let Jed take me back when
it is dark so that no one will recognise the carriage. I will say it was the snow that has kept me
away from Allingford longer than I intended—
no one will question that.'

'Do you think Phineas will not do so?'

'He has no jurisdiction in Allingford.'

'I am aware of that, but he is a dangerous
man.'

Her fingers crept up to the curl resting on
her shoulder.

'Do you think I do not know that? However, he cannot touch me if I stay in Allingford, with my friends. Once it is seen that I am safe and unharmed, he will think someone played a trick upon him.' She could see that he was wavering and she added softly, 'I will not betray you. You have my word.'

'Why should you do this for me?'

She blushed. Why indeed?

'Let us say I am atoning for past mistakes. And besides, you have been wronged by my father.'

He met her eyes for a moment, his own dark with suspicion. At last he said, 'The carriage will be at the door in a moment. You should get ready.'

'You will not quit Wheelston? I assure you there is no need to do so on my account.' When he did not reply she put a hand on his arm. 'Please, Ross, do not judge all women by the standards of Hannah Weston.'

It was the first time she had called him by his name. She saw the flicker of surprise in his face, quickly suppressed. He covered her hand with his own and his touch shocked her. It burned her skin and her hand trembled, causing his fingers to tighten as if he thought she would pull away from him. Charity raised her eyes to his face and his fierce, burning glance set her heart racing, thudding so hard and so erratically that it was difficult to breathe.

The air around them had changed; it was suddenly heavy and oppressive, charged with anticipation. Ross was staring down at her as if he was seeing her for the first time. She forced her eyes away from that disturbing gaze, but they moved no further than his mouth. How was it she had not noticed before the sensual curve of his lips? Her fevered brain began to imagine how those same lips would feel on her skin, not just her mouth. She had read of such things, heard them discussed by her friends in the theatre and had always thought the idea of giving a man such licence quite abhorrent, but now, with Ross holding her hand she suddenly wanted nothing more than to have him explore her body. She felt that familiar ache between her thighs and a hungry longing possessed her. An invisible thread was drawing her closer. She was a moth to his flame; if they came together she would disintegrate, but she didn't care....

A hasty step, a sharp knock on the door and Jed appeared.

'The carriage is ready, Master. I don't want to be keeping the horses standin' in this weather.'

The spell was broken. With a start Char-

ity stepped back and Ross made no attempt to
stop her when she pulled her hand free, but he
kept his eyes on her face while he addressed
his servant.

'There has been a change of plan, Jed. Mrs
Weston will go home after dark, so you may
take the horses back to the stables until later.'

She felt a rush of pleasure and when they
were alone again she waited, her body tingling
with a need she did not fully understand. Would
he reach for her now, drag her into his arms and
kiss her until she forgot the world? Her skin
was on fire from her toes to the very top of her
head. She was almost quivering with anticipation, wanting to hurl herself across the short
distance between them and cover his face with
kisses, but something held her back, a deeply
inculcated belief that he would be repulsed by
such behaviour.

*Face the facts, Charity Weston. You are the
daughter of his enemy. He wants nothing to
do with you—however differently you may feel
about him.*

He had sent Jed away because he had agreed
to her plan, not for any wish to make love to
her. His continued silence only reinforced this
conclusion and after a moment she said, with a
reasonable assumption of calm, 'You are going

to stay. I am glad of it and you have my word I will not betray you.'

'As to that, madam, only time will tell.'

And with that, he turned on his heel and strode out of the room.

Chapter Eight

'**W**here in hell's name have you been? You have missed the first rehearsals!'

Hywel Jenkin's blunt welcome made Charity smile, despite the faint persistent ache of unhappiness she had felt since leaving Wheelston. She knew that behind the bluff and bluster Hywel would have been concerned at her absence, as was her maid. Betty had interrogated her quite rigorously when she had returned to the house the previous night, wanting to know who were these friends in York and why they had not been mentioned before. In the end Charity had been obliged to give her a gentle reprimand.

'I am very sorry, Miss Charity, I am sure,' returned Betty, with a disapproving sniff that gave the lie to her apology. 'It just seems odd that I've been with you all these years and never heard of this Mrs Rawlinson, and neither has

Mr Jenkin,' she added, unable to disguise a note of triumph at being able to support her argument.

'That is because he would have known her unmarried name. It was only by the veriest good luck that we recognised each other at Lady Beverley's the other evening. We had so much to catch up on I was only too happy to return to York with her that night, but of course once the snow set in I was obliged to impose upon her hospitality for a little longer.'

'Hmm.' Betty sniffed again. 'Well, p'raps if you'd let me know how long you was staying away I wouldn't have been so worried about you.'

It had taken Charity some time to smooth her maid's ruffled feathers and she had come to the theatre prepared to do the same with Hywel. She had dashed off a note to him as soon as she had returned to North Street, telling him she would be there for the rehearsal the following morning, but she had expected a rare trimming, as she told him now.

'And you would deserve it, madam. Why, I have already had the handbills printed. I should have been in the devil of a fix if you had not come back. Where have you been, you minx? Who is this Mrs Rawlinson in York?'

Charity only shook her head, saying mischievously, 'I shall not tell you, my friend, you would not approve!' Seeing he was still looking angry, she said quickly, 'Nay, Hywel, it was very bad of me to miss rehearsals and I beg your pardon, truly. But I promise you I shall work very hard now.' She met his frowning look with a coaxing smile and after a short struggle with his temper he laughed.

'Away with you, baggage! You always could wind me around your little finger. Just make sure you are word perfect for opening night!'

She blew him a kiss as she went off to the stage, saying saucily, 'Pho, that is more than a week away. You often expect us to know our lines in a couple days!'

'The new play opens tonight.'

Jed made the remark as he helped his master unsaddle Robin. It was not yet dawn and they were working by lamplight in the Wheelston stables. When Ross did not reply he continued, 'When I were collectin' a ham from Farmer Greenwood yesterday he said his wife couldn't get tickets for this evening—sold out, they are, with people coming from York and beyond to see Mrs Weston play.'

Ross maintained his silence as he washed the blacking off Robin's long nose. Much as he wanted to see Charity, he would not be going to

the theatre. He would not be going into Allingford, or to any place where he might meet Charity Weston. She had kept her word—not the
slightest whisper had reached him that anyone
suspected the reclusive owner of Wheelston to
be the happy-go-lucky highwayman known as
the Dark Rider. He had no idea how Phineas
Weston had reacted to his daughter's return to
the stage. When business had taken him to Beringham he had listened to the gossip in the town
and spent an hour or so in the market tavern, but
although there were plenty of complaints by the
locals about their magistrate and his puritanical
ways, there was nothing to suggest that Phineas
was any more unreasonable than usual. It was
as if the kidnap had never happened.

Ross knew he should be relieved. He had
escaped very lightly from that escapade. Except that meeting Charity, having her staying
here, in his house, had shown him how bleak
his existence had become. He glanced across
the stable to the shadowy lump that was his
greatcoat thrown over a saddle peg with the
mailbag resting on top. He had spotted a letter
addressed to Phineas Weston, so he would look
at that before he broke his fast—he had become
an expert at opening and resealing those letters so that it was almost impossible to see that
they had been tampered with. However, he had

all but given up hope of finding something in-criminating in Weston's correspondence, and he was more cheered by the thought of the heavy purse he had taken from Sir James Fryton that night. The sight of the corpulent rascal's fear-ful expression when confronted by a masked highwayman had brought Ross some satisfac-tion, especially when he recalled how confident Fryton had been at his trial. He had cheerfully perjured himself, along with Keldy and Hutton, when they had upheld every one of Hannah's allegations, knowing full well that a charge of blasphemy would ruin him. He had no doubt that Phineas had rewarded them well for their collaboration, so he had no qualms about re-lieving them of the odd purse now and again to redress the balance.

But enough. He would think no more of that cursed trial. Or of Charity Weston. He must concentrate on the future, such as it was, and what he would do with that fat purse. With spring coming on he could use the money to buy cattle to graze the long meadow, now that it was stock-proof again, and he would be able to take on a couple men to work the Home Farm.

'So you ain't going to see Mrs Weston in her play, then?'

Jed's single-mindedness grated on his nerves, but he knew that the old man had taken a lik-

ing to Charity Weston during the few days she
had been at Wheelston. And why not, with her
golden beauty and a kind nature to match, she
would win the coldest heart—

Angrily Ross wrenched his thoughts away
from her.

'No, I am not going to see the play.' He gave
Robin's nose a final wipe and dropped the cloth
back into the bucket. 'There, you can clean up
his forelegs, Jed. I have other work to do.'

Gathering up his greatcoat, he strode away
from the barn and Jed's incessant questions.

The Clandestine Marriage played to full
houses, but although Charity peeped through
the curtains every evening she could never find
the one face in the audience she wished to see.
Since Jed had dropped her in North Street there
had been no word from Ross. It was for the
best, she told herself. There must be no chance
of anyone discovering the scandal. Her friends
and fellow actors were already suspicious of
her story, thinking that she had gone off on
some romantic assignation, and it could prove
dangerous if anyone should make a connection
between her and Ross Durden. Yet she could
not help wondering about him, and when she
attended the reception in the green room after

the last performance of the play, she struggled against the temptation to ask about him.

And failed.

'I thought that dour farmer might have been here tonight,' she remarked casually, her smile indicating that her only interest in the man was as a figure of fun. 'What was his name now? Mr...Durden, I think.'

She was at the centre of a large group that included Hywel Jenkin, Mrs Tremayne and Sir Mark and Lady Beverley. It was Sir Mark who responded.

'Too busy with his estate business, I shouldn't wonder. I saw him at the cattle market last week with the new man he has taken on.'

'If he is at last beginning to turn Wheelston around, then I am very pleased for him,' said Lady Beverley. 'I hope we shall see him in society a little more.'

'I think we shall,' opined her husband. 'You will find the people of Allingford much more willing to forgive Durden if he has money in his pocket.'

'But do not look for him here,' declared Mrs Tremayne. 'His sort are not theatre lovers, Mrs Weston. They come once, to see a new phenomenon, then never set foot inside the place again.'

Hywel threw up his hands, laughing.

'My dear ma'am, is that how you style our brightest star, a phenomenon?'

'Well, yes, Mr Jenkin, I do. You yourself told me that she is the most popular player you have ever had in this theatre.'

'And the crowds coming in from all over give us proof of that at every performance,' put in Sir Mark. 'Mrs Weston has put Allingford firmly on the map.'

'My dear sir, you are making our young friend blush,' exclaimed Lady Beverley, patting Charity's arm. 'Not that it isn't all too true, my dear.'

'That may be so, but 'tis dangerous talk, madam,' retorted Hywel with mock severity. 'So I shall take Mrs Weston away before she is so puffed up in her own conceit that she decides Drury Lane is the only venue for her talents. They are right, though, my dear,' he continued, when he had drawn her away. 'You should consider going back to town. You would cause a sensation—'

'I have no wish to cause a sensation, thank you. I am very happy playing here, at least for the moment.'

'That sounds ominous. Do you want to move on?'

'No-o, I am as happy here as anywhere.'

'My dear girl, are you deep in melancholy? It certainly sounds like it.'

She laughed, trying to shake off her gloomy mood. 'I beg your pardon, Hywel, I am a little restless at the moment, but it will pass, I am sure. Why, what would I do if I was to give up acting?'

'Settle down, perhaps. Start a family—' He grinned. 'Faith, I'd marry you myself, if I was twenty years younger!'

'La, thank you, Hywel! I do not want to marry an actor—we are all far too vain to make comfortable partners! I think I should like an honest, respectable husband. But respectable men do not marry actresses.'

'They do if the actress is rich enough!'

She shook her head. 'I am contrary enough to want a man to marry me for myself, not my money.'

'And he must be a paragon of virtue? I do not think such a man exists, my dear.'

A sudden vision of Ross filled her mind.

'No, I have certainly never met such a one.'

She ended on a sigh and Hywel looked at her closely.

'How jaded you sound, my dear. Perhaps you have been working too hard. I could find some-one else—'

'No, I am contracted to play for you until June

and I shall do so, especially since you promise me we will be doing one of Mr Dryden's plays.' She saw he was looking stern and clasped his arm. 'Pray, do not be anxious for me, Hywel. You know I am happiest when I am working.'

'Very well, but after that you will take a rest. Mayhap I will close the theatre for a couple months and we will embark upon a grand tour.'

She laughed. 'With Europe under Bonaparte's heel? Where do you propose that we go?'

'Worthing, perhaps, or Brighton. Or the Lakes? All that wild, dramatic scenery.'

'Yes, perhaps the Lakes.'

'Good. Then it is settled. And once you are rested,' Hywel continued, pulling her hand through his arm, 'you will sign with me for next season—let us go and tell your admirers the good news!'

Hywel led her around the room, making sure that Charity spoke to all the richer patrons, then introducing her to others who he hoped would soon join their ranks.

'And these gentlemen are come all the way from Beringham to watch the play tonight.' He stopped before them. 'Mrs Weston, if I might present to you Sir James Fryton and Mr Keldy.'

Not by the flicker of an eyebrow did Charity indicate that she knew those names, but she looked closely at the gentlemen as they bowed

to her. Both were well-dressed country gentlemen, ruddy-faced and round-bellied. They were
smiling now, but there was something forced
about their genial expressions that put her on
her guard.

'Delighted to meet you, m'dear,' murmured
Sir James, lifting his quizzing glass to exam-
ine her.

'And I,' declared Mr Keldy, his whiskery
jowls quivering as he smiled. 'A masterly performance, madam, and worth the drive from
Beringham.'

'I understand there is no theatre there,' she
remarked, watching them carefully. 'Nor much
of any type of entertainment.'

'Oh, we manage.' Sir James gave a hearty
laugh.

'Is this your first time at the theatre, Mr
Keldy?'

'Oh, no, no, Sir James and I have seen most
of your performances, ma'am. We came at
first out of curiosity—your name, you see,'
he continued, when she merely looked at him.
'Weston. The same as our local justice.'

Beside her Hywel was on the alert. Both men
were watching Charity closely. Knowing they
were friends of her father, she suspected they
had been sent here to report back to him. But
would he have told them she was his daughter?

Charity thought not. Phineas was too ashamed of the connection to make it known.

Hywel said quickly, 'Many actresses take a stage name, gentlemen.'

She gave a carefree laugh.

'We do indeed. And the reports I have heard of your Mr Weston is that he is no friend of the theatre. So you see, we could not be more different.'

'Of course, of course,' chuckled Keldy, looking relieved. 'Nothing but a hum. I knew it all along.'

'You were fortunate that the snow did not disrupt your production,' purred Sir James. 'I understand *you*, Mrs Weston, were prevented from attending the first rehearsals.'

She had been expecting this and had her answer and her smile ready.

'Why, yes, so foolish of me. I went off to spend a night with friends in York and then could not get back.'

'How frustrating for you.' Sir James gave an artificial titter. 'And so worrying for your many admirers—why, there was even a rumour in Beringham that you had been abducted.'

She opened her eyes.

'Abducted?' Charity's own laugh sounded perfectly natural and full of amusement. 'How absurd. Such drama because I missed two rehearsals.' She bent a quizzical look upon them. 'I hope you did not think anything wanting in my performance?'

Both men quickly disclaimed and after a few more words Charity moved on.

'Friends of your father, I take it?' murmured Hywel, when they were out of earshot.

'Yes. Sent here to spy upon me.'

'But why should they think you had been kidnapped?'

She spread her hands. 'Oh, you know how these silly rumours will spread.'

'Could it be that he has some paternal concerns for you after all this time?' She threw him a look of disdain and he added quickly, 'Surely it is not impossible that he has had a change of heart—'

'Phineas has no heart,' she retorted. 'The rumours will be an annoyance and he is afraid I shall publicly confirm them.'

They moved on around the rooms and Charity strove to put both her father and Ross from her mind while she mingled with the crowd. It was late in the evening when she noted the visitors who lived on the Beringham road gathered about Sir Mark, discussing the latest attack on the highway. Charity moved closer.

'The Scarborough mail was attacked again

only last week,' announced one worried gentleman.

'But on the other side of the county border,' explained Sir Mark patiently. 'I have to defer to Justice Weston to deal with that.'

'Are we sure it was the same man?' asked another.

'Undoubtedly.' The first nodded. 'The description was unmistakable. Big fellow with an Irish accent.'

'And he took a purse off me a couple weeks' back,' added Sir James Fryton, unable to contain himself. 'Damned scoundrel.'

'I hear Weston has put up a reward,' put in Lady Beverley.

Mr Keldy nodded. 'Aye. A hundred guineas. And he is organising patrols to hunt the fellow down. It will only be a matter of time before we catch him.'

'Well, that will be good news,' said Sir Mark. 'We cannot have such disruption on the King's highway.' He looked about him, smiling benignly. 'However, I have had no reports of the fellow being seen this side of Beringham, so you need none of you be anxious about your journey home this evening.' He caught sight of Charity standing on the edge of the group. 'And of course those of us who live in Allingford have nothing to fear at all.'

Charity returned his smile. *If only they knew!*

She turned away, stifling a sigh. If only she could see Ross, but it was too dangerous, and she would never forgive herself if he was caught because of her. Ross might consider that his cause was just, but if he was arrested he would be hanged like a common felon. So she must keep her distance, act as if they had never been more than casual acquaintances. She tried hard to put the man from her thoughts, but that was not easy when his absence was like a constant, physical ache deep inside.

A dozen times a day Charity found herself thinking of Ross, wondering what he was doing, hoping he was safe, and a dozen times a day she told herself to forget him. There could be no future with such a man, but somehow he had become lodged in her heart and no amount of reason could remove him.

Charity was glad that there was no break in her work. They were opening with *The School for Scandal* in two days, and rehearsals would soon begin for *All for Love*. This was the first time the company had performed the tragedy, so backcloths had to be painted and costumes selected. Many of the cast wanted hoops and wigs, but Charity argued that since the play was about the Egyptian queen Cleopatra they should wear a more ancient costume. Hywel supported her, citing the example of the great Mrs Siddons.

'We should dress you all in the Greek style,' he suggested. 'For the ladies there will be sandals—no stockings—and muslin draperies. Except for Mrs Weston. For you, my dear, it should be gold tissue, as befits a queen. I will send for the cloth now, if your dresser can make it up.'

'I can make up anything my mistress requires,' affirmed Betty, on her mettle.

'Then that is settled. We will work on the designs tomorrow. The handbills will say that we are presenting an authentic history. And besides,' he added, rubbing his hands together, 'the gentlemen will go wild to see the actresses so scantily clad.'

'Nay, since the fashion now is for these skimpy muslins they'll be as properly dressed as the audience,' declared Betty, raising a laugh from everyone.

The weeks passed in a hectic round of activity, and if Charity was not able to forget Ross, she was at least able to put him to the back of her mind during the day. At night it was a different matter and she was prey to strange dreams, dreams where she was naked in Ross's arms and he was kissing her, rousing in her such a need that she would wake, crying for she knew not what.

She would recover, she told herself. She was attracted to Ross Durden because he was so different from any other man she knew—dangerous, but kind, too, in his own way—and she had glimpsed a touch of humour in him, a seductive glimmer that had her believing it was more than a mere physical attraction. But it could not be, so she would be wise to forget him.

May brought warmer weather and the opening of Mr Dryden's play, which was well received. Charity threw herself into the role of Cleopatra. After the recent comedies she found the tragedy much more taxing and returned to her dressing room each night emotionally drained. However, the audiences were appreciative and she raised no demur when Hywel announced they would give another eight performances. Betty was not so sanguine and made no attempt to hide her disapproval.

'He shouldn't have done it,' she grumbled, helping Charity into her wrap at the end of another tiring performance. 'It's dead on your feet you are, ma'am, and no mistake.'

'I am not sleeping well,' admitted Charity. 'But that has nothing to do with the play. Indeed, I like being busy.'

'But 'tis the summer, Miss Charity, and you

need a rest, I can see that. Perhaps a little sea bathing. I hear that's very good for one.'

'Then mayhap we will go back to Scarborough when this play is finished and take the waters.' Charity sat in front of her mirror and began to remove her headdress. 'Betty, would you call upon Mr Jenkin and give him my apologies? He is taking everyone to supper this evening, but I think I should go home to my bed.'

'Aye, I will.' Betty nodded. 'Not that it's like you to be retiring straight after a performance. Just goes to show—'

She caught her mistress's eye in the mirror and was silenced. With her lips pressed firmly together she went out of the room.

Charity gave a sigh of relief. She was very fond of Betty; she had been her maid and her dresser for many years and consequently was not afraid to offer her opinions. She thought Charity was working too hard and she said so. However, Charity knew it wasn't the work that was tiring her, it was the sleepless nights, thinking of Ross Durden. She worried about him, wondering each morning if he had been riding out that night, if he had been caught. The fact that her father was in part responsible for Ross's situation did nothing to help. She found herself wishing that the kidnap plot had been successful and that Ross had obtained the justice he was seeking. That would have meant her leaving Allingford, disappearing lest her father beat the truth out of her about the Dark Rider's true identity. It would have brought her no nearer to Ross, of course, but sometimes she thought the price would have been worth it, if it meant Ross could give up his dangerous double life.

I love him.

The words hovering around her consciousness for so long now rang in her head, as clearly as if she had spoken aloud. Brushing out her curls, she thought it ironic that after more than a decade in the theatre, when many men, rich and poor, rakes and nobles, married or single, had offered to lay everything they possessed at her feet, she should fall in love with someone so ineligible, a man who had not courted her or made her promises of undying devotion—in fact, he was so intent upon rebuilding his estates and seeking justice from her father he had no time for her at all.

'It is a very sad state of affairs,' she told her reflection. 'You have fallen for the one man whom you cannot have.'

She heard a knock on the door and immediately straightened, hope rushing through her. Had he come at last? She turned to face the door, but as it opened the smile of welcome died on her lips.

Phineas came into the room, his wife hanging on his arm.

'No doubt you are wondering why we are here,' said Hannah with a glitteringly false smile.

'Not to compliment me upon my performance, I suspect.' Charity's cool response made the other woman's eyes snap dangerously.

'I have persuaded your father that he should talk to you.' Hannah came farther into the room, her eyes taking in the colourful chaos of their surroundings. Brightly hued gowns hung on a row of pegs on one wall, while garishly patterned scarves were thrown over the dressing screen, jostling for space with cream and white muslins. Charity hoped Hannah was suitably incensed by the decadence of the opulent robe of gold tissue that she had just removed and which was now draped suggestively over the daybed in the corner. She eyed her visitors coldly.

'We have nothing to say to each other.'

'Word is out that you are my daughter,' said Phineas.

'Mere rumours. You may be sure that I have not told anyone, not even those friends of yours you sent to question on me.'

'Perhaps *you* have not spoken of the matter,' said Hannah. 'Nevertheless it is now generally understood that Phineas is your father.' She spread her hands and gave a humourless smile. 'Your fame is widespread, my dear.'

'Perhaps it was that damned highwayman,' snarled Phineas. He came closer, bending to thrust his face close to hers. 'Did you not tell him your little secret? Did you not hatch that kidnap plot together?'

Charity forced herself not to lean away.

'I have no idea what you are talking about.'

'The Dark Rider,' he continued, his mouth contorted with anger. 'Is he not your lover?'

Her heart gave a little leap of fright, but she reminded herself he had no proof. As long as she remained strong and convincing he would have to believe her. A puzzled frown creased her brow.

'The Dark Rider,' she repeated slowly. 'Ah, yes. I remember that was what they called the man who held up our coach when I first came to Allingford. He stole a kiss—dear me, it would appear that little incident has been magnified out of all proportion.'

She saw the doubt in his eyes and allowed herself a smile.

'You should check your facts before throwing out such accusations, sir.'

'Now, now, Phineas.' Hannah pulled him away. 'You know we agreed the kidnap threat was all a sham. The fellow backed down quickly enough when you called his bluff.'

'Kidnap?' enquired Charity, looking bemused. 'Who was kidnapped?'

'Don't give me that innocent look, girl. I know your tricks!'

'Phineas, this is not how we meant to go on,' said Hannah sharply. 'We came to talk sensibly with your daughter.'

'Daughter!' Phineas looked at Charity with undisguised loathing. 'Do you think I want it known that a child of mine is no better than a common whore?'

Charity drew herself up. 'How dare you come in here and insult me.'

'Insult? It is no more than the truth. You parade yourself on stage, sell yourself—'

'I am an actress, sir, nothing more, nothing less.'

'Would you have me believe you are a virgin still?' He spat out the words. 'I have seen you on the stage. No one could think you an innocent who has seen how you flaunt yourself. And this latest role, an Egyptian queen—pah! A painted Jezebel making love to men, all in full view of your audience—you could not be so convincing if you were not experienced in such matters.'

She rose, keeping one hand on the dressing

table to steady herself. She was blazingly angry, but the old terror was fighting to get out as she looked into her father's livid countenance. She was a woman now, not a girl. He could not harm her; he could not take off his belt and thrash her here in her own dressing room.

No matter how many times she repeated the words in her head, the familiar fears were just under the surface and it was a struggle to keep them down.

'You have said quite enough,' she told him. 'You should go now.'

'My dear, pray do not be too hasty.'

Hannah addressed her, a patronising smile stretching her mouth while her eyes remained cold. Charity wondered how Ross could ever have loved this woman.

Hannah continued. 'We do not want to quarrel, Charity, dear, but you must see that the situation is impossible. Your father is a respected man—'

'Not in Allingford!'

'A respected man,' repeated Hannah, ignoring Charity's interruption. 'It does his reputation no good to have you here, blatantly flaunting yourself.'

'That, madam, is nothing to do with me. I have a job to do—'

'But you should not do it here,' Hannah retorted, her temper snapping. 'You must see how...how *degrading* it is for your father to have you plying your trade in the next town.'

'It is a respectable trade. I am not ashamed of it.'

'But it would be better if you plied it elsewhere.'

'Better for whom?' Charity asked her, noting the flush of angry colour building on the woman's cheeks.

'This is getting us nowhere,' exclaimed Phineas. He turned his venomous gaze upon Charity. 'I know why you are here. You wish to humiliate me. You know that I am opposed to all forms of play-acting—'

'But your wife seemed to enjoy *The Provok'd Husband*. Is that not so, ma'am?'

'Yes, I— No.' Hannah shot a nervous glance at Phineas. 'One cannot help but be swept up in the moment....'

'Aye, that is how the devil works, drawing in respectable people until they cannot see the damage such evil is doing to their souls.'

'Nonsense,' retorted Charity. 'You hate to see anyone enjoying themselves, it is as simple as that. This is a legally licensed theatre, we are breaking no laws and I intend to remain here until *I* judge it is time to leave.' She pointed to the door. 'I have had a tiring day and I would be obliged if you would both go. Now.'

Hannah's eyes narrowed, but she turned on her heel and walked to the door.

'Come, Phineas, I see that you were right about her. She is sinfully stubborn.'

Phineas glared at Charity.

'Be warned, madam, you would be wise to go far away from here. If you will not leave willingly, then you must be removed.'

She put up her brows. 'And just how do you plan to do that? You have no jurisdiction here.'

'I shall be watching you.' He leaned towards her again, hissing, 'And I don't believe you know nothing about that highwayman. I'd be willing to wager you are his whore, otherwise, when his plan failed, why did he not have the stomach for mine? I'll catch the scoundrel, you mark my words, and when I do he will hang and, if I can prove you are in league with him, you will hang, too!'

He stormed out, banging the door behind him, and Charity sank back down onto her seat. She closed her eyes, concentrating on breathing in and out as if steadying her nerves for a performance, although in truth she had just given the performance of a lifetime. The door opened again and she heard Hywel's anxious voice.

'I have just seen Weston and his wife leaving. Smudgeon told me they slipped in when the boy was minding the door. Are you all right, Charity?'

'Yes.' She opened her eyes and looked at him. 'Yes.' She sat up a little straighter. 'I braved his wrath, listened to his empty threats and I did not crumble.'

He frowned.

'Weston did not bully you into leaving Allingford?'

'He tried, but no.' A smile was growing inside her. 'No, he will never bully me again.'

Despite her newfound confidence, she was happy for Hywel to make it known to all his staff that Mr and Mrs Weston should not be allowed backstage in future. She also found her father's remarks about Ross troubled her. What did he mean when he said Ross had no stomach for his plan? Just what had Phineas suggested to Ross and why had he not told her?

The question nagged at her, but she was no nearer an answer two weeks on, as she prepared for the last performance of *All for Love*. She left her dressing room and went up onto the stage, trying to clear her mind ready for the play, and it was out of habit that she peeped through the curtains. The auditorium was packed and noisy and she was not expecting to see Ross, so her heart gave a little jolt when she saw him. Perhaps it was his stillness, standing at the end of one of the benches while all around him people pushed and jostled. He looked solemn, grim even, and her heart went out to him. She hurried back to the dressing room where Betty was busy mending one of her gowns.

'Betty, love, pray leave that and take a note out to the audience for me.' She pulled a piece of paper towards her and picked up a pencil. There was no time to hunt around for pen and ink. 'You will find Mr Durden in the theatre. Do you not know him? He is a tall gentleman, plainly dressed, and he wears his own hair, dark and naturally curling. Rather unruly, in fact.' Had she said too much? 'Seek him out, if you please, and make sure he gets this note.'

'Now, madam—!'

'Do not argue, Betty, there is no time—there is my call. I must go on stage.' Charity folded the note and handed it to her maid. 'Do this for me, dearest Betty, and I shall be for ever in your debt!'

The cheers and whoops of appreciation rang around the theatre. Charity made her curtsy, saluted Will, her leading man, then turned again to face the audience. She could not help herself, she peered into the pit. It was impossible to see clearly past the flaring limelight, but she remembered roughly where she had seen Ross, so she concentrated on that area. Surely it was his tall figure she could see at the end of one of the benches? She sank down into another curtsy and as she rose she pressed her hands to her lips, then extended them towards the darkness—and the place she believed Ross to be sitting.

There, she had done what she could to convey to him how much she wanted to see him. Will and the other actors were milling around on the stage behind the curtain. She stopped momentarily to congratulate them, then returned to her dressing room, immediately demanding of Betty if her note had been delivered.

'Aye, ma'am, I gave it him, but he looked so fierce when I spoke to him that I fear he was offended.'

'Then you must go and look out for him,' said Charity, pushing her towards the door. 'Bring him here directly and do not let Elias Smudgeon turn him away!'

'But what about your dress? You cannot get out of it alone—'

'You shall help me later. It is important that you find Mr Durden before he leaves the theatre.' She hustled Betty out of the door and shut it behind her, uttering up a prayer that Ross would not go home without seeing her.

I only want to ask him what Phineas suggested to him, she argued as she removed her headdress and wiped the heavy make-up from her face. *There is nothing wanton or lustful about that. I merely need to know what my father is up to.*

She brushed out her hair, trying not to think of the passing time, desperately hoping that he would not refuse to see her. At last she was rewarded by the sound of footsteps in the corridor. She snatched open the door and almost sighed with relief when she saw Ross standing there. He filled the doorway, his eyes glittering with a fierce light that burned into her.

'I was afraid you would not come.' She reached out and caught his hand, drawing him into the room.

'I should not have done so.'

Charity barely registered the curt tone, thinking only how much she had longed to hear his voice. Her eyes scanned his face, noting the clenched jaw, the tensed muscles around his mouth. His whole being radiated tightly controlled energy like a wild animal ready to spring. With the open door behind him she feared he might even now leave her. She was still holding his hand and with great daring she raised it to her lips.

'I have looked out for you every night—'

She heard him groan, felt the slight movement as he kicked the door shut.

'You should have looked in vain!' He dragged her into his arms. With a sob she turned her face up, inviting his kiss. 'Oh, my dear, golden girl,' he muttered as he covered her face with kisses. 'Did you know you were looking directly at me at the end of the play, when you blew that kiss into the audience?'

'I was not sure, but I hoped—'

Her breathless words were cut short as he kissed her again. He drove his hands into her hair, holding her firmly while he took her mouth and plundered it savagely. She responded with equal fervour, instinctively following his lead, tangling her tongue with his as her bones liquefied and the pent-up desire flowed through every part of her body. His hands roved over her, sliding down her back and over the soft swell of her buttocks to pull her closer. The gold tissue of her gown was lined with silk, but now it grated against her skin. Her breasts felt heavy and swollen, aching for his caress.

'No.' He forced out the word and raised his head. 'This is madness. Dangerous madness.

For God's sake, send me away now, sweetheart, before it is too late.'

She almost cried, bereft when he held her away from him. He was grasping her shoulders and she leaned her cheek against one hand, saying with a sigh, 'Oh, my dear, it is already too late for me.'

Keeping his gaze firmly upon her, he reached behind him and turned the key in the lock.

'If you are sure?'

She ran her tongue over her lips. They were swollen from his onslaught, but yearning for more. Whatever happened, if she never saw him again, she wanted this.

She said slowly, 'I have never been more certain of anything in my life.'

Her heart soared at the leap of triumph in his glance. He swooped down upon her again and she closed her eyes, felt his tongue slide like silk between her lips, his hands pushing the flimsy gown from her shoulders. There were no stays beneath, but the costume was shaped to cover her breasts like a skin and when it resisted his attempts to release her he ruthlessly tore the gold tissue away. Even as it shimmered to the ground he was lifting her out of it, carrying her to the daybed where he lay her gently down and fell to his knees beside her. Charity watched his face as he regarded her nakedness, exhilarated by the wonder in his eyes. He reached out to run his hands over her body, cupping her breasts, his thumbs circling the hard peaks until they were aching almost painfully. She arched against his hands and reached for him, trying to tear off his clothes. He released her just long enough to undress, then measured his length against hers on the narrow bed.

Shivering with anticipation, she held him and began to press eager if inexpert kisses upon his smooth, taut skin. He continued to caress her and when his gently questing hand slid to the join of her thighs she fell back with a gasp. His fingers moved into the satin softness and he stroked her slowly while his lips trailed over her face, across her throat then around to the delicate soft curl of her ear, and she almost swooned with the pleasure of the double onslaught upon her senses. Restlessly she moved beneath his touch, her body awakening to sensations she had never known existed. She began to run her own hands over the muscled contours of his body, revelling in the leashed power beneath her fingers. He shifted his position and began to kiss her mouth again, tangling his tongue with hers in a slow, sensuous dance that combined with his gentle, insistent caresses to carry her to new heights. She tensed, gasping as her muscles clenched around his fingers. She had no experience of such sensations, but her instinct was that there was something more, she wanted him joined with her, one flesh. She was burning, her body pliant and melting as he moved over her. She wrapped her legs around him and raised her hips. She wanted him to take her, to possess her completely. He slid into her, smooth and hard. She was so hot and slick that there was no pain and she cried out from the sheer joy of their union. He was moving inside her and she could feel the ripples of delight building. Without conscious thought she began to move with him as the wave of passion engulfed her. She was almost swooning when she heard his cry of triumph and delight and felt that final, hard thrust that sent her over the edge and falling, falling into oblivion.

Everything was quiet. From the lack of sound outside the dressing room Charity guessed that everyone had retired to the green room to celebrate the end of another successful run. Would they miss her? Perhaps, but she knew Betty would have noticed the locked door and hoped she would make her excuses. How long she had lain there in Ross's arms she did not know and did not care, but it must have been some time, because she felt the first chill of the air against her naked skin.

She shifted her position slightly and Ross stirred. His arms tightened around her again and he began to cover her face with kisses.

'It was madness to come here,' he muttered. 'I should have steered clear of Allingford, but I wanted to see you, just one more time.'

She held him close and nibbled his ear.

'If you had not come here, then I would have driven out to Wheelston. I had to see you.'

'No!' He raised himself on his elbows and frowned down at her. 'You must stay away. If anyone should suspect—'

'My father already does. Oh, he can prove nothing,' she added quickly, seeing his frown.

'Phineas Weston is a very dangerous man, Charity. You would be much safer if you went far away from here.'

'That is exactly what he said—'

'He's been here?'

'He came to my dressing room yesterday with his wife—'

'Hannah!' He rolled away and sat up. The chill suddenly seemed to enter Charity's bones.

'I beg your pardon, if it hurts you to hear of her—'

'No.' He turned back to her, cupping her face and gazing deep into her eyes. 'She has proven herself too scheming and devious for me to regard her with anything but contempt. She and

your father are well suited, but I would not have
her come within a mile of you!'

His concern warmed her and she thought for
a moment he was going to kiss her again, but
after a moment he moved away and began to
dress. Stifling a sigh, she got up and reached
for her wrap.

'I think she only wants me to leave Allingford. Phineas cannot control the rumours—even
people in Beringham are saying that I am his
daughter, and he wants me out of the way....'

Ross swung around, his black look alarming her. She recalled her father's words as he
was leaving, remembered belatedly that this
was the reason she had asked to see him. She
went to him.

'Ross, he said you had rejected his plan.
What plan? What did he say to you, at that last
meeting?'

He was not listening, his gaze fixed upon
the daybed.

'Is that...?' He tore his eyes away from the
dark, telltale stain on the couch and back to her
face. 'Charity, sweet heaven, don't tell me that
you are—were... That this was your first time.'

She frowned at him.

'Does it matter?'

'Does it—?' He closed his eyes, his lips moving but whether it was a silent prayer or a curse

she could not tell. He snatched up the rest of his clothes and began to throw them on. 'You told me you were not profligate, but I never thought— Never dreamed—'

'Ross.'

He took her arms, his fingers digging into the skin, the look in his eyes almost savage.

'Deflowering virgins is not something to be taken lightly.'

'No, of course not—'

He flung himself away and she watched, bewildered as he stood with his back to her, his shoulders heaving, as if in the throws of some deep emotion.

'Don't you realise I should marry you for this?'

She blinked at the repugnance in his voice. It sliced into her like a knife and she clasped her hands together tightly in an effort to stop herself from shaking. He ran a hand across his eyes.

'Do you not see how impossible this is? I cannot marry you, Charity.'

She rubbed her temples. After the euphoria of their lovemaking, how had they come to this?

'I have not asked it of you,' she said quietly.

He was almost dressed now and shrugging himself into his coat.

'I must go—'

She stepped in front of him and clutched his sleeves.

'No. What are you thinking? How can you leave me, after…after what we have just done?'

'Do not read too much into one tumble, my dear.'

She flinched at his cold drawl, but would not release her hold.

'No, I will not believe it meant so little to you.' The closed, shuttered look came over his face and she gave him a little shake. 'There is something you are not telling me, Ross. Have I not proven that you can trust me?'

'And have I not proven that you cannot trust *me*?' Gently but firmly he released himself from her grip. 'I am an outcast, Charity. I am tolerated here, but nothing more. I am welcomed by one or two of the most charitable families, but if they knew of my unlawful activities—! I cannot ask any woman to share such a life. Believe me, you should remove yourself from Allingford, away from your father. Away from me.'

'No!'

'Goodbye, Charity.'

'Ross—' She had to make one final attempt. She took a deep breath. 'Ross, don't go, please. I—I think I am in love with you.'

Something blazed in his eyes: delight, triumph, wonder. If he said he did not care for her now she would not believe him. She waited, hoping he would take her in his arms again. Instead he gave her a look of such tender sadness that she knew he was going to walk away.

'It will pass, my dear, believe me.'

'But why should it pass? Why should we not—?'

He put a finger on her lips.

'Charity, I am not for you. I have nothing— less than nothing, for if Phineas discovers I am the Dark Rider I shall certainly hang and any connection between us would leave you in a most perilous position.'

'Then give it up now! I have enough money for both of us—'

'Do you think your father would rest if you married me? Hannah would make sure he did not! I cannot protect you from them, Charity. You need to find yourself a rich, powerful lover to keep you safe.' He cupped her cheek, saying with a wry smile, 'With your beauty it should not be difficult.'

She wanted to tell him she did not want anyone else, but she knew he would not listen. She cursed that stubborn streak, even while she loved him for it.

'Ross—'

'No. I must go.' He pulled her close and

kissed her, hard, and while she was still recovering from the swooning power of that last embrace he left her.

Chapter Nine

Charity tossed and turned in her bed, going over and over that last meeting with Ross. After he had left the dressing room she had struggled not to cry. Betty had come in, her face and manner stiff with censure, but she had taken one look at her stricken mistress and held her peace. She had fussed around Charity like a mother hen, asking no questions and keeping up a flow of inconsequential chatter as she helped her mistress to dress and escorted her to the little house in North Street. Charity had retired immediately, pleading a headache, but her bed had not been the sanctuary she had hoped and now she lay, dry-eyed, staring into the darkness.

She did not regret giving herself to Ross. It had been her choice, her decision. She was no young debutante to be ruined by it. She had money of her own and even if a child should result from that one, glorious coupling it would be a child born of love and her money would ensure it did not suffer, even if Ross would not marry her.

She shifted uncomfortably, remembering the finality of that last kiss. She could not believe Ross had meant to hurt her. The brutal manner of his leaving had something to do with her father, she was sure of it. Something to do with the kidnap. What plan had Phineas suggested to Ross, and why would he not tell her?

She rose at her usual hour, little rested, but determined to find out the truth. While she breakfasted a message was sent to the stables, and she was soon trotting out of Allingford in a hired gig. The sun was shining; birds were singing from the hedgerows. It was impossible for Charity's spirits not to lift with such cheerful omens, yet when Wheelston came in sight she was aware of a frisson of anxiety. The building was as stark and forbidding as its owner. She drove directly to the stables, where Jed's welcoming grin gave her some encouragement. She handed over the reins to him and, upon enquiry, Jed told her the master was in the house.

Squaring her shoulders, Charity made her way to the kitchen. A grey-haired woman was kneading bread at the table, her white arms covered in flour to the elbows.

'And who might you be, walking in here bold as brass?' she demanded, startled.

Charity halted. She had forgotten the housekeeper.

'You must be Mrs Cummings.' She gave the woman her most charming smile. 'I do beg your pardon for coming in this way. I am Mrs Weston, from Allingford.'

'The actress?' The woman's brows shot up and for once Charity was thankful for her current popularity.

'Yes, and I am come to see Ro—Mr Durden.'

'Are you now? Well, the master went off to his study a few minutes ago. I'll go and see—'

'No, please, there is no need,' said Charity quickly. 'You are very busy and I know my way.'

Before the astonished woman could move, she swept across the room and out into the hall. As she closed the kitchen door behind her a laugh trembled upon her lips. Ross would have no easy task explaining this visit to his housekeeper!

In the study Ross was seated at his desk with his back to her, but he jumped up with an oath when he heard her quiet 'good morning'. The face he turned to her was pale and drawn, and there were dark circles beneath his eyes that suggested that he, too, had spent a sleepless night. The thought encouraged her, a little.

'What the devil are you doing here? How did you get in?'

'Through the kitchen,' she answered him, stripping off her gloves. 'I fear I have confirmed your housekeeper's worst fears about actresses. By the by, I cannot think she did not notice that you had a visitor while she was away—a female visitor. Did she quiz you about that?'

'She knows better than to ask,' he said shortly. 'I told you not to come. There is nothing here for you.'

His roughness flayed her and she responded bitterly.

'Don't worry, I have not come to weep all over you and demand recompense for my lost virtue.'

The harsh look fled.

'Charity, how can I—?'

'Stop!' She put up her hand, knowing if he showed her any sympathy her fragile control would crumble. 'There is no more to be said about that. I came here because I need to know the truth.'

She untied the strings of her cloak. Ross was still glaring at her and she feared he might yet manhandle her out of the house. She was relieved when he took the cloak and threw it over a chair.

'What happened when you met my father to demand a ransom?'

'I told you. He would not pay.' He would not meet her eyes.

'But there is more, isn't there? He proposed some other plan, did he not?' His silence and the grim set of his mouth sent a chill down her back. 'Did...did he suggest that you deliver me up to him?'

He strode towards the door. 'You should go now—'

'No. I am not leaving until you tell me what occurred. Do you think it too dreadful for me to contemplate?'

'He is your father.'

'Father?' Her lip curled in disdain. 'He lost the right to that title when I was still a babe.'

Ross was at the door, but he turned back to her, a frowning question in his eyes. She shook her head, quick, jerky movements that showed how tense she was.

'It was n-not so very bad, really. Not compared to the beatings and being locked in the c-cupboard and s-seeing him destroy my mother and my stepmother, bit by bit, with his petty tyranny.'

Her voice shook and the effort she was making not to break down tore at his heart. He said softly, 'Tell me.'

She did not answer immediately but chewed her lip, a darkling, faraway look on her face, as if she was recalling some unpleasant memory. At last she raised her chin, resolutely meeting his eyes.

'He cut off my hair. Mama used to call it my crowning glory. She would spend hours, when I was a child, brushing it until it shone. She said it was a gift from God.'

Ross looked at the honey-pale locks that gleamed beneath the frivolous little bonnet, framing her face like a gilded halo. He remembered them fanned out loose and abandoned over the pillow of the daybed, or running heavy as silk between his fingers. His skin tingled at the memory, but the sensation turned to a shiver as he stood, silent and unmoving while the words tumbled out of her.

'It was summer, such a hot day, and I thought nothing of letting the sun dry my hair, but Phineas said I was being provocative. Shamelessly immoral.' She wrapped her arms across her breasts, as if suddenly aware of him. 'I was fourteen years old and just beginning to think that I might one day find a man—a kind, gentle man who would want me for a wife. Someone to look after me.' She dropped her head.

'There were plenty of men at the sheep washing that day, but not one of them was prepared to stand up against Phineas. He...he made them hold me down while he cut my hair off with the sheep shears.'

Ross clenched his fists and raged silently at Phineas Weston. How could anyone, especially a man of God, humiliate a child in such a way? She had even then needed someone to protect her.

Charity pulled out a handkerchief and blew her nose. A prosaic gesture that made her seem even more vulnerable, but when she spoke again her voice was stronger.

'I vowed then that Phineas would never touch me again. I did not go home—my stepmother was by then such a browbeaten, timid woman and so in thrall to her husband that I knew I could never persuade her to come away with me. I just walked, away from Saltby and Beringham and all the places I had known. Heaven knows what would have become of me if I had not met Hywel Jenkin and his travelling players. He bade me join them, asked no questions of my appearance or my history until I was ready to tell him. I changed my name to Agnes Bennet and found I had a natural talent for the stage: I began by playing boy's roles, for which my short hair was no impediment, and through

Hywel's kindness and care I learned all the arts of the theatre. He encouraged me to go to London, to seek my fortune in Drury Lane.' She smiled. 'I did very well there.'

'So why did you leave?'

She gazed at him for a long moment, as if trying to decide how much to divulge.

'I behaved very badly,' she said at last. 'I persuaded a young man to fall in love with me.'

He paused and waited patiently for her to speak again.

'Gideon. He was very sweet.' The faraway look in her eye and gentle smile sent jealousy pounding through Ross like a battering ram.

'Then to bewitch him would not have been difficult, given your charms.'

Her eyes flew to his face when he spoke so roughly, and he saw the pain in them. She said quietly, 'It was all a charade, and I am not proud of it. There was a crowd of young bucks who came regularly to the theatre. I was flattered by their attentions and when they asked me—paid me very well—to participate in a practical joke I agreed. I was to captivate a young man and trick him into thinking he was marrying me, when in fact his bride was someone completely different. It was a very mean-spirited thing to do, and all for a jest.'

'Then why did you take part?'

'At first I thought there would be no harm in it. They were all rich young men, spoiled and impetuous. It was to be a prank, a joke. But Gideon was not like the others. He was kind, thoughtful and so charming that I was soon regretting I had agreed to trick him.' She would not meet his eyes and a blush of shame mantled her cheek. 'Unfortunately by then it was too late. I had put myself in the power of a very unpleasant character. At first I had been flattered by his attentions, but… He was a bully, no different from my father, in many ways.' She shuddered. 'I was fortunate that I managed to keep him at arm's length as long as I did. He was very cruel—it was his own cousin that he coerced into taking my place as Gideon's bride.'

'And the trick succeeded?'

She nodded.

'It was only by the greatest good fortune that disaster was avoided. I can take no credit for it. I knew Gideon's affection for me was infatuation, that he would recover, and, thankfully, he fell in love with his young bride. It was seeing them together that made me realise what I wanted from my life. A home, good, loyal friends, perhaps even a husband of my own.

'I knew then I should break free from the hateful man who sought to control me, and I did. I left London five years ago and vowed never to return.' A flicker of mischief curved her lips. 'At least, not as Agnes Bennet. Perhaps one day I shall return under my own name.'

'And did you mind, seeing the young man—Gideon—fall in love with another woman?'

'Not in the least. I was only thankful that I had not caused him irrevocable harm.'

Ross's jealousy subsided and his heart swelled as he realised how hard this confession was for her. She wanted no secrets between them: she was laying her soul bare, the ultimate expression of her faith in him.

'Why did you come to Allingford?' he asked her gently.

She gave an expressive little shrug. 'I was tired of touring, of never having a home of my own. I wanted to settle down, to find my real place in the world.'

'Perhaps that place is with Jenkin,' said Ross, determined to remove even that one, lingering doubt. 'He has done a good job of protecting you thus far.'

'He has been like a father to me, so much more so than my own unnatural parent. But I fear Phineas has not done with me yet.' She met his eyes with a steady, demanding look. 'That is why I must know what he planned for me, Ross. How can I protect myself if I do not know the truth?'

Blue eyes met black and held, a clashing of wills, both determined. Ross realised she had a right to know.

'He...suggested...' He stopped, eventually saying through clenched teeth, 'He did not want your safe return.'

She looked at him for a moment, uncomprehending, then with a little cry she dropped onto a chair.

'Oh, dear heaven. Does he hate me so much that he would leave me to my fate?' She gave a bitter little laugh. 'Why should I be surprised? He drove my mother to her grave, and my stepmama, spewing texts from the Bible to justify his vicious actions. I warned you he would not lift a finger to help me.'

'True.' Ross walked across to the window and stood looking out. 'But it is worse than that. He offered to pay the ransom, as long as I saw to it that you were not found alive.' He turned and came to stand over her, fixing her with his brooding gaze. 'Now do you see just how dangerous it is for you to stay in Allingford? Phineas will seize any chance to destroy you, and we know now he would go so far as to pay someone else to do it for him.' He raised his eyes to the ceiling and exhaled swiftly. 'And he calls himself a man of God.'

'He is a grasping, greedy hypocrite, and always has been.' She wrapped her arms around herself again. 'I will not run away. I have spent the past thirteen years as a fugitive, living under a false name, afraid that my father might one day catch up with me. But I am tired of living a lie. For years I have had nightmares about Phineas—I will not live that way any longer.' Suddenly the fight went out of her and her shoulders slumped. 'Perhaps I should not have come to Allingford, so close to my old home, but it felt right; Hywel, the theatre and my friends there—I thought I could ignore my father and that he could ignore me. If he was still parson at Saltby then perhaps that would have been possible, but he has wealth now, and power, and his self-importance is such that he will seek to destroy what he cannot control.'

Ross's heart went out to her, this golden girl with the tortured eyes. He wanted to take her in his arms and promise to look after her, but that was not possible; he could only make things more dangerous. Instead he pulled up a chair and sat down beside her.

'I have been trying to find a weakness, a way to discredit Weston, but he is shrewd and careful. Perhaps I should put a bullet in him.'

'But you are not a murderer, Ross.'

'Not for my own sake, but for yours—'

Charity's initial horror at learning that her

father wanted her dead was fading and she was ever more grateful to Ross for refusing to countenance his plan. She reached out to touch his hand and was heartened when he did not pull away.

'I would not have you commit such a heinous crime for me.' She jumped up, exclaiming, 'Oh, I will *not* give in! There must be some other way to bring him down.' She began to pace the room, her brow furrowed. 'I remember when Hywel told me how rich Phineas had become I wondered how that could be.'

'Well, he has three thousand of my prize money for a start.'

She shook her head. 'He came into funds before that. Hywel Jenkin said he gave up the living at Saltby and bought his big house in Beringham about five years ago. I remember the Saltby parish—it was not a rich living and the previous one was even poorer. Mama had no money of her own and although my stepmama had a modest dowry, even with the shrewdest of investments that would not be enough to buy a grand house, let alone to live in such luxury as Hywel described to me.'

'Gambling, perhaps?'

Her lip curled. 'Phineas thinks gambling even more of an abomination than the theatre.

No, I could more readily believe he is involved in some dark deed.'

'That is what I thought, too,' said Ross. 'Which is why I have been checking the mail-bags to see if there are any letters for him, anything that might give me some clue.' Her look of horror made his lip curl. 'Since I am already holding up the mail coach it seemed a logical step.'

'And have you ever found anything?'

'Nothing of any use, a few letters to other clergymen, more to his brother.'

Charity said absently, 'Phineas does not have a brother.'

'Of course he does—one Joseph Weston, who is presently living in Yarmouth….' Ross's words trailed off.

'My father is an only child,' stated Charity, her face set hard. 'It is recorded in the front of the family Bible. Believe me, I opened that book very often, since he made me copy out so many texts from it.' She rolled her shoulders, recalling the sting of his riding crop whenever she made an error. Forcing the memory away, she asked, 'What is so alarming about Yarmouth?'

'The naval dockyards,' he said slowly. 'And if I were First Lord of the Admiralty, it's Yarmouth I would use to launch an attack on Bonaparte's northern forces.'

'And what does this *brother* say—have you read any of his letters?'

'Of course,' said Ross, frowning. 'There is nothing in them but family matters.'

She gave a bitter laugh.

'My father was never one for family!'

'Perhaps he is mellowing with age.'

Charity thought of their last meeting and shook her head.

'I have not seen it. But perhaps I am wrong— after all, you have already told me he is making pilgrimages to Filey, too.'

'And Filey is on the coast.' Ross sat up. 'What if he is passing secrets to the French?'

Charity met and held his eyes.

'I would as lief believe that as think him mellowing.'

'There are rumours that Bonaparte is planning an alliance of sea power in the north.' He began to pace the room. 'Security must be tight at Yarmouth, so if I wanted to get information out of England, I would send it by a roundabout route—mayhap even to an innocuous little town like Beringham, then to the coast, somewhere small, where a fishing smack might cross to the Continent without notice.'

'Such as Filey.'

'Exactly. But why should Phineas help

Bonaparte? It seems incredible to me that any true Englishman would do so.'

'But Phineas might,' she said. 'He told me Bonaparte was the... How did he phrase it? "God's instrument...the scourge of the papists".' She clasped her hands tightly. 'If there is one thing my father hates above all else, it is the Church of Rome. He would consider himself justified in taking any action that helped to destroy it, even supporting the French.'

'Hell and damnation, then I have missed a trick!'

Ross's exclamation brought her eyes back to his face and he hastened to explain.

'I held up the mail last night and there was another letter for Weston from this "brother" of his. I did not even read it, just threw the mailbag back at them and let them continue.'

'Then it will have been delivered to him this morning.'

'Yes. Damnation, we must act quickly. I shall have to break in tonight and try to find it—'

'No. Let me go now and see what I can discover.'

He stared at her.

'Are you out of your mind? You cannot go to Beringham, it is far too dangerous.'

Her brows rose.

'It is market day, and if I know Phineas he will be holding a court. He would not miss the chance to fine his fellow men for their misdeeds. And even if he is at home I shall have my maid with me and make sure he knows that I have left word of where I am.' She smiled. 'I want to make peace with my new stepmama.'

'And what do you hope to achieve by that?'

'At best, to find that letter and at worst— I can at least describe to you the layout of the house.'

'No. I can as easily find my way tonight. I will not risk your safety.'

'Please, Ross, let me do this.' She held his gaze steadily. 'We will neither of us have any peace until he is brought down.'

It took some time to persuade Ross that she was determined, but at last he agreed, after she had told him that if he would not help her she would make the attempt alone. A swift plan was devised and she went back to Allingford to collect Betty.

As she drove back to North Street, Charity wondered just how much she should tell her maid. Betty had drawn her own conclusions about what had happened in the dressing room the previous evening, but she had maintained an affronted silence on the matter. However, if

Charity was going to enlist her aid in this latest escapade, she would have to tell her at least some of the truth.

'Ooh, Miss Charity, that is the most fantastical, madcap idea I have ever heard!'

Charity and her maid were in the gig and on their way to Beringham. Time was short so Charity had begged Betty to accompany her, promising to explain everything on the way.

'To break into a magistrate's house, to find a letter Mr Durden thinks might be there—'

Charity had said nothing about Ross's activities as the Dark Rider, only that he suspected Phineas of spying for the French. She had to admit the story did sound implausible.

'I will understand, Betty, if you do not wish to help us—'

'Of course I will help you, Miss Charity. From all you have told me of your father, you don't think I would let you go into his house alone? By heaven, you and Mr Durden are like a pair of star-crossed lovers from one of Mr Jenkin's plays!'

Charity threw her a wry glance. 'I suppose we are, only in this instance I have no idea what the ending will be!'

* * *

The afternoon was well advanced by the time they reached Beringham. Charity remembered the town from her childhood, but it had changed considerably in the thirteen years since she had run away. It was still a bustling market town, but she thought it compared unfavourably to Allingford. The town was less colourful, the people far more sober in their dress and countenance. One or two turned to stare as she drove through the High Street and Charity smiled and nodded, happy to acknowledge that she was the celebrated actress from the neighbouring town. She had to work hard not to search the crowds for a sight of Ross, but he had told her he would be close and the knowledge supported her as she raised her hand to knock on the door of Phineas Weston's grand town house.

'I don't like this, mistress, and so I tell you,' muttered Betty as they waited for the summons to be answered.

'No more do I,' murmured Charity through smiling lips. 'That is why I have brought you with me, for protection.'

They were shown inside through the ornate entrance hall and into an overfurnished drawing room. Charity adopted a stately pace and took the opportunity to note the layout of the hall—drawing room to the left, two closed doors to the right with the bust of Caesar in pride of place between them, sweeping staircase to the upper floors. She gestured to Betty to sit on the bench in the hall and wait for her.

She was left alone in the drawing room and immediately crossed to the double doors, peeping through into the dining room beyond. She had returned to the centre of the room by the time her hostess entered. Hannah was as over-decorated as her drawing room. Her yellow gown was in the latest mode, but bedecked with such an abundance of lace and ribbons that even when she stood still her gown fluttered and trembled of its own accord.

'My husband is not at home.'

Charity heard the cold tone. She answered pleasantly and with total insincerity, 'I am very sorry to hear that, but perhaps it is not such a bad thing. I came…' She paused, looked away, her whole demeanour one of shy uncertainty. 'I have been thinking about you since your visit to me.' Hannah's hostile look became tinged with bewilderment. Charity gave her a sad little smile. 'Having no family begins to weigh upon one after a while.'

'If I understand correctly, it was you who ran away,' replied Hannah. She did not invite Charity to sit down, but continued to watch her carefully.

'I was very young.' Charity gave a sigh. 'I realise now just how headstrong I was as a child. How headstrong I still am and prone to lose my temper all too quickly.' She fixed Hannah with her most bewitching smile. 'I hope you can forgive the hateful things I said to you the other day.'

'I think it is your father you need to see. To give him your apology.'

'You are very right, ma'am.'

'But he will not be home for some time.' Hannah moved towards the door. 'Perhaps you could come back....'

'Of course, but please, while I am here—' She broke off, limpid blue eyes fixed upon Hannah's face.

'Yes?'

'If I might see his Bible?'

Hannah's brows shot up. Whatever she had been expecting, thought Charity grimly, it had not been this!

'His Bible!'

Charity nodded, clasping her hands together before her in mute appeal.

'Yes, if you please. The big leather-bound one. He used to read it to me every night.' It was an effort not to shudder at the memory. 'I would draw such comfort from seeing it.'

Hannah stared at her for a long moment,

then with a shrug and a nod she went to the door. Charity followed her across the hall and through the second of the two doors. She found herself standing in a book-lined room with a large mahogany desk in the centre. Her father's study. Her memory had not failed her. All her childhood she remembered her father keeping the family Bible in his study.

Along with the worn leather riding crop he had used to beat her.

No time to let the past weigh down upon her now. She needed all her energies for the task ahead.

'Ah, here it is!' She hurried across to a lectern by the window, noting as she did so that the study was above the kitchens and overlooked a small service yard. It was surrounded by a brick wall with a door leading to a back lane. The door would be locked, but the wall, although high, would not be impossible for a man to climb over. She laid her hands on the tooled leather cover of the Bible, saying reverently, 'Father's most treasured possession.'

She opened it and stared at the flyleaf, momentarily forgetting her role.

'The Weston family record,' said Hannah crisply, following her gaze. 'Your name has been scratched out, but you will not wonder at that, when you consider the pain you have caused your father.'

Charity was gripping the lectern so hard that her knuckles had turned white, but she hoped the other woman would see that as a sign of grief and not the revulsion she actually felt to see the black scoring through her name, so heavy that it had scratched a hole in the page.

'You are quite right,' she answered quietly. 'I have a great deal to repent, I think.'

But not running away from Phineas Weston. Never that.

She said, her voice a nice mixture of timidity and hopefulness, 'Mrs Weston—Hannah—I wonder if you would let me…read a little from this holy book? I think it would help to—to soothe my soul.' Without waiting for a reply, she carefully turned over the pages. From the hall came the faint sounds of knocking at the door. 'Ah, Psalm Thirty-two, how appropriate.' She put up her head and declaimed, '"Blessed is he whose transgression is forgiven, whose sin is covered".'

She continued to recite, even when the footman appeared. He murmured something to his mistress, who listened in growing irritation. She looked up at Charity as if to say something, then changed her mind and followed the servant from the room, leaving the door open behind her. As soon as she was out of sight Charity moved across to the desk while the words continued to fall from her lips without pause.

When Hannah returned to the study some five minutes later Charity was sitting at the desk, her head resting in her hands.

'What in heaven's name do you think you are doing?'

Charity raised her head and wiped away the tears that trembled on the ends of her lashes.

'Oh, I beg your pardon, but I was so overcome by the occasion that my legs refused to support me.' She pushed herself to her feet. 'I have angered you, I should leave.'

'You should come back when Phineas is here to see you,' replied Hannah, clearly uncomfortable. 'I do not know what he would say if he knew you were here.'

'Do you not think he would welcome this sinner back into the fold?' Charity gave a sad little smile. 'Perhaps you are right, ma'am.' She went out into the hall, and Betty jumped to her feet at the sight of her mistress.

'Are you staying in Beringham?' asked Hannah as she showed her guest out. 'Can I send a servant to fetch you when Mr Weston comes home?'

'Alas, no. I will write to my father and we will appoint a mutually convenient time to meet.' Charity put out her hand, then withdrew it again, saying with an arch look, 'Ah, no. Perhaps we should not exchange such friendly gestures until we know my father's wishes upon the matter.' With a final, sad little smile Charity bid the astonished Hannah goodbye and sailed off down the street.

'Oh, lordy, I don't know when I have ever been so frightened,' muttered Betty, hurrying along behind her.

'I would have been a lot more frightened if Phineas had been present,' retorted Charity.

'Aren't we going to look for Mr Durden?' asked the maid as Charity turned into the inn yard to collect the gig.

'No. It is better if we are not seen together here. We meet at Wheelston, as agreed.'

Ross was waiting in the stables when the gig drove into the yard. He called to Jed to see to the horse and strode out to help Charity to alight.

'I was never more relieved than when I saw you leave Weston's house,' he told her, masking his concern with a tone of indifference.

'No more so than I,' she responded feelingly.

There was a hectic flush upon her cheeks and her eyes looked overbright. He wanted to fold her in his arms and tell her she was safe, but that could not be. If their suspicions were correct and they could prove Phineas to be a villain, then perhaps… He dare not even think so far ahead.

He suggested the maid should go into the kitchen, then turned back to Charity.

'Let us go into the house and you can tell me all about it. I left instructions for a fire to be kindled in my study, and refreshments to be waiting there for us—ratafia or brandy. I thought you might need something stronger than tea.'

They did not speak again until they reached his study. Ross went over to the side table, where decanters were set out in readiness, and as he filled two glasses he watched Charity from the corner of his eye. She paced about the little room, stripping off her gloves and then pulling them through her hands with quick, nervous gestures.

'My father has done very well for himself since I left home,' she said at last. 'His house is overstuffed with every fashionable thing! Even my new stepmama is dressed in the highest kick of fashion, and very unbecomingly, too!'

She broke off, sending him a glance full of apology but he shrugged.

'You may say what you like about Hannah. It

is a long time since I thought of her with anything other than abhorrence.'

'She is very pretty, but there is a hardness about her, a calculating look in her eye.'

'She is a good mate for your father, then.'

He was pleased to hear her laugh, so much more natural than the brittle smile she had given him upon her arrival.

'Yes, I think you are right. He will not be able to bully her as he did his other wives.'

'And you had the opportunity to see the layout of the house?'

Her answering look positively brimmed with mischief.

'Better than that. The diversion we planned worked very well. I was in the study when your messenger called, and Hannah was obliged to leave me alone for a while, but she thought I was reading from the Bible.' Again she laughed, the sound raising his spirits like sunshine. 'I gave a performance worthy of the great Sarah Siddons herself. I rattled off Psalm Thirty-two in the grand manner. I am not Phineas Weston's daughter for nothing, and the psalms were drummed into me from an early age. However, it is fortunate that my new stepmama is not so familiar with the Bible as Phineas, for I pretended it had opened fortuitously at the Psalms, when in fact I was looking at Deuteronomy!'

She sank down in a chair beside the fire and accepted a glass of ratafia. Ross frowned when he saw the way her hands were shaking.

'I should never have let you go there. It was not necessary—'

'Oh, but it was for me. How can I be free of my past until I have faced it?' Her smile widened. 'And I have the letter.'

'You stole it! But when Phineas discovers that—'

'No, no, I knew if I took it that Phineas would notice and be on his guard.' She laughed and pointed to her head. 'It is in here. I memorised it. Now bring me paper and a pen and I shall write it all down for you.'

Chapter Ten

The sun was high in the cloudless blue sky when Ross rode into Scarborough. The restless waves of the German Ocean danced and glittered in the distance, and brought back all the old longing for the naval career that had been snatched away from him. Regret, bitter as gall, rose in his throat, but he forced it down. No point in worrying about what was past. It was the future that concerned him now, a future that might—if everything worked out—include Charity Weston.

During his ride to the coast he had recalled their evening together, how he had watched her as she sat at his desk, furiously writing down the letter she had memorised. She'd been too engrossed to look up and catch him off guard. He'd made the most of the opportunity, taking in the full glory of that shining hair, the long curling lashes that swept down over her eyes, the straight little nose and determined chin.

He'd wanted to kiss every part of her beautiful face, but most of all he'd wanted to kiss her mouth, to taste her again as he had in her dressing room, when her inexpert but fervent response had fired him with desire. He'd known other women, but none had roused him in quite the same way. He had watched her as she bent over the paper, and had thought how comfortable it was to have her with him. If only he could keep her there.

But what did he have to offer, save a crumbling estate and a drawer full of debts? Even if he could prove that Phineas was a spy, his own circumstances would not change. He remembered turning his eyes to the smoke-grimed ceiling, thinking he must be the most ineligible bachelor in Allingford.

Then some slight sound had brought his attention back to the table to see Charity sitting back in her chair, a little smile playing about those luscious red lips.

'That is it. Complete, verbatim.'

She had covered two sheets of paper with elegant, sloping letters.

'Surely not. How can you recall everything in such detail?'

'It is a gift I have always had, to be able to

read something and remember it easily, and my years in the theatre have only made it stronger. Trust me, this is word for word what was said in the letter.'

Trust me. He stared out now across the sunlit waves, smiling at the memory of Charity sitting in his chair, at his desk. His glorious golden girl. A cloud blocked the sun and the sudden chill brought him back to reality. She was not his and never would be, not while her father held such power.

He stabled his horse and made his way to a neat little house in a quiet side street, where he was informed by a bobbing maid that Captain Armstrong had gone to the spa to take the waters and had not yet returned. The delay was frustrating, but Ross realised it could have been worse, since his friend might well have left Scarborough without informing him. He therefore went off to while away a couple hours in the company of the seamen at the harbour.

When he returned to the house some hours later the same little maid informed him that Captain Armstrong was expecting him. He was shown into a small but comfortable parlour, where he found his friend sitting in a chair beside the window.

'No, no, John, don't get up,' said Ross quickly, coming into the room.

'Don't think I could if I tried,' came the laughing reply. 'My energy is spent after going to the spa!'

'You are taking the waters, I believe,' said Ross, pulling up a chair. 'Is that aiding your recovery?'

'Aye, it's kill or cure, my friend. Have you seen the place? The spring is at the bottom of a cliff. It's ironic that one needs to be fit as a fiddle to get up and down all the damned steps! But enough of this—tedious stuff, to be talking of one's ailments. Tell me instead what brings you back to Scarborough again so soon.'

'A serious matter, John. You've stood by me since I left the navy in disgrace, so I wanted your opinion.' Ross frowned. 'All the way here I have been wondering how much to tell you,' he said heavily. 'It will make no sense unless you know the whole—'

'Wait.' John stopped him with an imperious hand. 'Is this going to take long? Hmm, and if it is serious, too, then we will need to refresh ourselves. Will brandy suit you, or would you prefer grog?'

Having called to his maidservant to bring in the brandy bottle, the captain poured a generous helping into two glasses and handed one to Ross, commanding him sternly to tell him everything and look lively about it.

'So there you have it,' said Ross, some time later. 'You may brand me for a villain, John, but my deeds pale into nothing compared to what I believe Weston is involved in.'

'I'll brand thee a fool,' growled the captain. 'Taking to highway robbery is the road to the gallows, nothing more, but I admit this Weston sounds a nasty piece. Never did like preachers using the Lord's word to justify their bullying ways. But you say he's been corresponding with someone in Yarmouth?'

'Aye, someone purporting to be his brother, although Char—Mrs Weston says her father is an only child.' Ross drew a folded paper from his coat and held it out. 'This is the copy she made of the last letter we know of, the one that arrived for Weston two days ago.'

He waited in silence while his friend took out his spectacles and read the document.

'And you think this is all coded references to the military preparations?'

'Isn't it obvious?' replied Ross. 'Weston has no Cousin George and the family he says are gathering in Yarmouth could well refer to soldiers and ships.' He saw the frowning look in his friend's eyes and gave a snort of impatience.

'Come, John, any naval man worthy of the name would know that Yarmouth is the ideal place from which to launch an attack upon Bonaparte's northern fleet. And look at the names he cites—he says Richard and Robert are in town. Captains Dacres and Stopford, perhaps? And he says Uncle Sam is expected any day—that could be Commodore Sir Samuel Hood. And his very last line—he says James is expected to organise the festivities and he will advise him of the arrangements! If that isn't a reference to Admiral James Gambier and the date he plans to sail, I don't know what is.'

John returned his frowning gaze to the paper.

'It *could* be so and you make a good case for it, Ross, but—'

He broke off, shaking his head, and Ross said sharply, 'Well? Out with it, man.'

John took off his spectacles and fixed Ross with a solemn gaze.

'This is not proof, Ross, it is no more than hearsay, since it was written out by Weston's daughter. Have you considered that this young lady—if she is so estranged from her father as you suggest—might be seeking to punish him? She may have made it all up—'

'No, never!'

'Let us say she embellished it, then. Do you

truly believe that she read this letter only once and remembered it all so perfectly?'

'Remembering lines is her trade.'

John sat back in his chair, smiling slightly.

'I know. I saw her when she played in Scarborough last year and was captivated. She is certainly a beauty, Ross, but for all that, can you trust her?'

'With my life, sir.'

The two men stared at each other while the longcase clock in the corner ticked slowly. At last John Armstrong nodded and looked back at the letter.

'I had word from London only yesterday that Bonaparte crushed the Russians in a sea battle at Friedland. The Czar must now sue for peace, of course. We did send a fleet to hit the French lines of communication, but we were too late, dammit, and Bonaparte will use the fact that we did not come to the aid of our allies to blacken our name. Perhaps I should not be sharing this with you, but I've no doubt it will be in all the newspapers in a day or two.' He tapped the paper in his hand. 'The reference here to his previous correspondence and "Cousin George" sending some of the family ahead of him two weeks ago might refer to the contingent that set sail from Yarmouth in mid-June—the timing is certainly correct.' He paused again, frowning over the letter. 'Very well. Leave this with me. I shall take it to those who will know better than I if there is something amiss here.'

'Would you like *me* to—?'

'No, no, my boy, just because I haven't yet regained my sea legs doesn't mean I can't travel at speed.' John heaved himself out of his chair. 'Now, if you will excuse me, I must make my arrangements. You take yourself back to Wheelston and sit tight.' He held out his hand, gripping Ross's fingers tightly and giving him a faint smile. 'Pity you are no longer in the navy, Durden. Your talents are sadly missed.'

Charity could find no rest. She prowled around the little house in North Street, jumping at every noise outside the door, hoping it might be Ross.

'Although why you should expect him I don't know,' she told her reflection when she went upstairs to change her gown. 'He said he would not come, not yet.'

But remembering that last, lingering look he had given her when she had left Wheelston, she hoped—prayed—that he would not be able to stay away.

She was engaged to dine with Hywel that night at Beverley House, where her hostess had promised her a quiet evening.

'Just the four of us,' said Lady Beverley, when she welcomed Charity into the drawing room. 'I hope you do not mind.'

'No, indeed, ma'am,' Charity assured her, relieved that she would not be expected to converse with dozens of people when her mind wanted to dwell only upon one dark individual.

'And we shall not be keeping late hours,' added Hywel. 'Mrs Weston must be at her best for her benefit evening at the end of the week.'

'Ah, yes, of course,' murmured Sir Mark. 'What is it you are doing again?'

'We are replaying *The Rivals*,' said Hywel. 'We opened the season with it.'

'Ah, yes, of course, of course. Lady Beverley and I will be there to see it, will we not, my love? I have no doubt the house will be packed for Mrs Weston's last performance of the season.'

'We shall see.' Charity smiled. 'At this time of the year no doubt many people will have moved away for the summer.'

'Not from Allingford,' said Lady Beverley comfortably. 'In town, perhaps, there is some reason for moving out of the heat, but not here. We are all very happy to stay at home, save for those who are gone to try a little sea bathing.'

They went into dinner and Charity made an effort to converse freely, although part of her mind was constantly thinking of Ross, remembering that parting kiss and wondering how soon he would return to her. She managed to keep up her cheerful pretence until the end of the evening, when the tea tray was brought in, but being allowed a few moments to herself, her mind wandered off again.

It had been very late by the time she finished writing out the contents of the letter for Ross, but he had refused to let her stay in his house until the morning.

'I would not be able to keep away from you,' he'd told her, the look in his eyes sending a delicious shiver running down her spine.

She had dared to tell him that she would not wish him to do so, but although he had laughed at that and kissed her, he'd been adamant.

'You must go back to Allingford and act as if you had not seen me. Every time we meet increases the chances of discovery.'

'We could go away from here, far away, where it would not matter—'

'No.' Ross held her away from him. 'I will not do that to you. You said yourself you were tired of being a fugitive, always looking over your shoulder.'

'Rather that than I should lose you for ever,' she had begged him, but she did not care. When she'd put her hand up to his cheek he had covered it with his own, pulling it down to his mouth to press a kiss into the palm.

'There,' he had said, folding her fingers over the spot where she could still feel the burn of his lips. 'Hold that for me until I can come to you again.'

'What are you going to do?'

'Take this letter to a friend who will know how to use it against Phineas.'

'And if it isn't enough?' She'd clung to him. 'Will you give up your quest for justice and come away with me?'

'Perhaps, but let us hope this letter will do the trick. It may take me a while to discover how best to proceed and it will be safer if we do not meet again until I know how the land lies. Now, let us find your maid. You must go home.'

He had escorted them to the front door, but when Betty walked out to the gig he had pulled Charity back into the shadows and wrapped her in his arms, kissing her long and deep. Charity had responded, holding him close, but when he'd raised his head she had not pulled him down again, accepting that they must part, at least for now.

'Well, Mrs Weston, what is your opinion?'

Charity stared blankly at Sir Mark. She had no idea what he had just said to her. She smiled sweetly and was about to beg his pardon when they were interrupted by a knock on the door and the butler walked in. He approached his master and held out a silver tray, upon which lay a sealed paper.

'What's this?' demanded Sir Mark testily. He fixed his eyeglass in place and picked up the letter. 'Hmm, now who is sending me messages at this time o'night?'

Lady Beverley handed a cup to Charity, saying with her easy smile, 'Being a magistrate's wife, one grows accustomed to a constant flow of letters that cut up one's peace.'

'But not this time,' declared Sir Mark. He held the paper out to Hywel. 'Good news, I think. We may feel more comfortable when we travel in future.'

Lady Beverley looked up. 'Oh, why is that, my love? What does it say, Mr Jenkin?'

'It is a note from Mr Weston.' Hywel flicked a quick glance at Charity. 'It seems he has caught the Dark Rider.'

'And you will never guess who it is,' added Sir Mark, his bright eyes twinkling. 'Mr Ross Durden, no less!'

It was all Charity could do not to drop the fine porcelain cup when Sir Mark made that announcement. Years of acting and self-control came to her aid. She sank down in her seat, praying that her hands would not shake and make the cup rattle in its saucer.

'Good heavens,' she said lightly. 'Does he give any details?'

Hywel handed the paper back to Sir Mark, who shrugged.

'Merely to say the fellow is safely in the lock-up. I suppose Weston will deal with him to-morrow.'

'D-deal with him?' Charity could control her expression to appear mildly interested, but she could not stop her heart thudding so heavily the blood drummed in her ears.

'Weston will question him and then, no doubt, he will be transferred to York for trial.'

'Well, that is good news, indeed,' declared Lady Beverley. 'Though I would never have guessed Mr Durden would be the highwayman. All reports I heard said the robber was an Irishman. However, the news may well encourage more people to travel from Beringham for your benefit performance, Charity.'

The conversation moved back to the theatre and Charity took her part, although she could never afterwards remember what was said. She was desperate to get away and when at last it was time to leave she made no objection when Lady Beverley offered the use of her carriage.

She did not think her legs would support her for much longer.

'I am very sorry that note arrived from your father,' said Hywel, as they rattled through the empty streets. 'I could see that the mere mention of his name upset you.'

'It was most unwelcome,' she responded, with perfect sincerity. 'I only hope our hostess did not notice.'

'Oh, I think not. Lady Beverley is kindness itself, but not the most acute of observers.'

Charity forced a little laugh and engaged him in idle chitchat until the carriage pulled up at her door. With a smile and a cheerful word of farewell she went inside, but as soon as the door was closed she sank down onto the nearest chair, shaking. She wanted to burst into tears but she fought against it. Crying would not help Ross now. She must act.

Ross woke to the sound of a distant cock crow, but did not move immediately. He tried to work out why he was not in his own bed. An attack, riders coming at him in the dusk, blows. Opening his eyes, he found himself staring up at bare stone walls and a square of light where the sun struggled through the grimy glass of the single barred window, high up in one of the walls. His hands were manacled and he sat up carefully, flinching at the pain of his bruised and aching limbs. Raising his arms, he put a hand to his temple and touched his hair. It was sticky with blood.

He heard footsteps and the rasp of bolts being drawn back, but his head was throbbing and the sudden squeal of metal hinges made him wince. He opened his eyes, expecting to see his gaoler. Instead he saw Charity standing in the doorway.

'Oh, dear heaven, what have you done to him?' she demanded in outraged accents.

The man standing behind her shifted uncomfortably.

'He was brought in like that, Mrs Weston.'

'And you have done nothing to ease his suffering?'

'It ain't my job to—'

'It is your Christian duty,' she told him roundly. 'And this—this *hovel* is not even provided with a jug of water. You will fetch one immediately, if you please. And a cloth, that I may clean up his wounds.'

The constable goggled at her. 'But I can't—'

'You *can* and you will, Constable. If you have nothing to hand, then Mrs Rigg will assuredly provide you with what you need. And do not worry about your prisoner escaping. You may lock me in here with him while you are gone.'

It was a masterly and assured performance,

and at any other time Ross would have appreciated it greatly, but for now he was merely thankful when the constable withdrew, shutting the door behind him and returning the lock-up to the gloomy half-light that did not make his eyes hurt.

'You should not have come here,' he managed.

'How could I not, once I knew?' She put down her basket on the stone bench and drew out a flask. 'I have brought you a little wine and bread. Will Stamp has been locked up several times after a—what do you gentlemen call it?—after a spree and he always complains about the lack of food and drink.'

'I cannot say I had noticed until now,' said Ross, but took the flask and drank deeply before tearing off a piece of the bread she held out to him.

'How did you know of this?' he asked her.

'I heard last night that you had been arrested.'

'Arrested?' He laughed, wincing as the pain lanced through the bruises on his face. 'I was waylaid on my way back to Wheelston. I know I had crossed the county border, but once they had overpowered me they dragged me here—I take it I am in the Beringham lock-up?'

'Yes.' She sat down beside him. 'My friend Jenny is the constable's sister-in-law.'

'And does the constable know whose daughter you are?'

'There are rumours, of course, but no, he thinks not. You see, he interviewed me when the Scarborough mail was held up and asked me then if I was the magistrate's daughter. I told him it was a stage name.' She clasped her hands in her lap. 'Jenny knows, of course, because we grew up together, but she has told no one. However, she did persuade her brother-in-law to let me in.'

'I would she had not done so,' he retorted bitterly, then reached across to grip her hand. 'Not for my sake, love, but for your own. It can only do you harm to ally yourself with me—' He broke off as the constable returned with a small jug of water and a rough cloth folded over his arm.

Charity immediately picked up her basket. 'Put it here. Since there is no furniture, I take it this stone bench must be bed, chair and table for your prisoner.'

'Well, madam, it ain't supposed to be cosy.'

Only Ross saw Charity's eyes flash with anger at the constable's surly response. She said cheerfully, 'No, indeed, Mr Rigg, I quite understand that. But do you think you could allow me a little more time with Mr Durden?'

'I don't think I should. Justice Weston wouldn't like it.'

'I doubt if he would like you letting me in here at all,' replied Charity in the voice of sweet reason. 'However, he need not find out. You know we were very careful to make sure no one saw me come in here. And there is no need for you to neglect your other duties. You have seen that there is nothing more dangerous in my basket than a little food and drink, so you may safely leave me here.'

The constable blinked, clearly dazzled by her smile.

'I told you, Mrs Weston, he's due up before the Justice at noon—'

'Then I shall help him make himself more presentable. What harm can there be in that?'

Ross held his breath—surely this staid officer of the law would not be swayed by her charms?—but to his amazement the constable retired, saying he would give her an hour, no more. When they were alone he uttered a short bark of laughter.

'By heaven, how did you manage that?'

'Flattery, a few kind words and a little money,' she said, dipping the corner of the cloth into the jug. 'Not that I attempted to bribe him, but I did leave a small purse with his sister-in-law.'

She put her fingers beneath his chin and gently turned his head to the light so that she could bathe away the dried blood on his face.

'Are there any other injuries?' she asked, her voice trembling a little. 'Did they hurt you very much?'

'They were not gentle, but then, I did not give in without a fight.' He touched her arm as she drew in a sharp, hissing breath, as much to prove to himself that she was real as to reassure her. 'It is not so very bad. Apart from the cut on my head I am merely bruised, I think.'

'I was afraid when Sir Mark told us you were caught. I thought perhaps Phineas—'

'I have not yet seen him, although I have no doubt it was he who arranged my capture.'

'Sir Mark said the message came from Phineas, so he was most certainly involved. There.' She stepped away. 'I have cleaned up your head as best I can, but I can do nothing about the dark stubble or the fearful mark on your cheek.'

'Do I look very dreadful?' he asked her.

The pain in her eyes told him the answer, but she replied with admirable calm. 'Quite frightful. You would attract far too much attention if you left here in such a state. However, with your hat pulled low and once we have brushed the dirt from your coat I think you will look tidy enough for us to make the attempt.'

'What?'

'When the constable returns we must, er, *persuade* him to let you go.' She reached into the pocket of her travelling cloak and pulled out a pistol. 'That is why I brought this. Thankfully Constable Rigg was so embarrassed when I told him to check the basket that he did not ask to search my person.'

'Is it loaded?'

'No.' She handed it to him. 'It is one we use on stage and does not work, but I hope it will do the trick.'

'And just what had you in mind?'

She took a deep breath. 'When Rigg comes back we will take him prisoner. I will fetch my carriage, which is waiting at the inn in the square, and when we drive slowly by the lock-up you will run out and—'

'Pure folly,' exclaimed Ross, getting to his feet. He held up his manacled hands. 'How far do you expect me to get like this?'

'I have no idea, but I have money. I thought we could bribe a blacksmith to remove your chains, and then we might head towards Scotland…'

'No!' He threw down the pistol and grabbed her arms. 'My darling girl, we would be caught within days, and if we were not, we would be outlaws, never able to rest—is that what you want?'

'If it is the only way to be with you, then yes.'

His heart lurched as he saw the tears in her eyes. He dragged her to him and kissed her roughly, but the way she clung to him only convinced him that he must get her away from there. Steeling himself, he broke off his kiss.

'I cannot be party to this madness. When Rigg comes back you must go and do not come near me again until this is all over.' He added, with far more confidence than he felt, 'We were fortunate I was attacked on my return from Scarborough and not on my way there. The letter you wrote out for me is now on its way to the Admiralty. I am convinced there is enough substance to our suspicions for them to act. The net will soon close upon Phineas Weston.'

'But not soon enough, Ross. Phineas will see you hanged at the first opportunity, we both know that.'

'I only know that you are in danger every moment you stay here with me.' He cupped her face. 'Oh, my love, do you think I could ever forgive myself if I thought I had brought about your downfall? I love you too much to allow that. Go back to the theatre, my dear, enjoy your success there and forget me.'

'Never.' She stared up at him, her eyes deep blue pools of tears. 'I cannot leave you, Ross, I cannot forget. I love you, there is no life for me without you.'

'There is, there must be,' he said fiercely. 'I—'

He broke off. There was the rumble of voices and heavy footsteps coming closer. He felt Charity tremble, heard her whisper one word. 'Phineas!'

Swiftly he put her away from him and threw himself down on the bench, stuffing the pistol into his jacket pocket.

'Follow my lead,' he commanded tersely. 'You must get out of here and live for me!'

Charity had no time to reply. The door was flung open and Phineas strode in, followed by two gentlemen whom she recognised as Hutton and Keldy. From their damaged faces she surmised they had been involved in Ross's capture. The constable came in behind them all, looking forlorn and anxious.

'So—' Phineas's cruel, sneering smile swept over her '—am I interrupting a touching scene?' He indicated the men behind him. 'I set my people to watch the lock-up, knowing you would turn up.' He snarled at Charity, 'How much did you slip Rigg here to let you in?'

'Not a penny,' she answered coolly. 'I

appealed to his better nature. Is that not so, Mr Rigg?'

The constable gave a nod, the look on his face a mixture of fright and relief.

'Mrs Weston is living up to her name,' drawled Ross, slowly sitting up. He indicated the basket. 'She is bringing a little charity to a condemned man.'

'Comforting you, is she, Durden? The actress giving succour to her lover.'

'Sir Mark Beverley asked her to come.' Ross uttered the lie with all the assured confidence of a leading man. 'You had best be careful, Weston. The lady has powerful friends in Allingford.'

He spoke quietly, but there was just enough conviction in his voice to make Hutton and Keldy take a step back. Phineas frowned, his eyes narrowing.

'Not powerful enough to save you, Durden,' he said silkily. 'A search has been made of your house—'

'I hope you haven't alarmed my housekeeper.'

'Of course not. My people treated her with the utmost respect.'

A faint smile lifted one side of Ross's mouth. 'I don't doubt it, especially when she told you she was once cook to Sir Mark and Lady Beverley, and continues on good terms with them.'

'My people were well aware of their duty, being within Sir Mark's jurisdiction,' snapped Phineas. 'But nevertheless we found evidence that you are the highwayman—the black mask in your bedchamber, for example.'

Charity shot a glance at Ross. He was leaning back against the wall, apparently unperturbed by this revelation.

'Is that all you have on me, Phineas? The relic of some masked ball?'

'And the blacking in your stable. Your man has disappeared, but I don't doubt when we find him he will tell us he used it on that black nag of yours. You will hang for this, Durden. We will find witnesses to testify against you.'

'What, those two toadies behind you?' Ross curled his lip. 'Why not, they have already perjured themselves for you.'

Charity saw her father's face darken alarmingly, but Ross was not looking at Phineas. Instead he turned his head to address her.

'I think it is time for you to leave, madam, Sir Mark will be waiting for your report upon what you have found here. Pray thank Lady Beverley for her kindness in providing me with breakfast. You will not object if the lady leaves us, will you, Magistrate Weston?'

Charity met Ross's eyes, but his were hard, indifferent. He was dismissing her, trying to keep her safe from danger.

I love you too much to allow that.

In the dark nightmare of this whole situation his words were like a beacon, a warm, bright light she could not ignore.

Phineas was glaring, his jaw working as he tried to curb his temper.

'If Beverley is expecting you, then you had best go,' he barked.

Charity looked at the two men, her father with his barely controlled fury and Ross who was gazing through her as if she was a stranger. She knew how much her father would like to keep her there, under his control, but Ross had given her a way out.

If she wished to take it.

'Not just yet. There is something I should like to discuss with you, Magistrate. In private.'

She heard the violent hiss of Ross's breath.

'Madam, go. I have had enough of your prating sympathy. Return to Allingford, *immediately.*'

Charity forced herself to ignore him and the pain she knew lay behind his harsh words. She concentrated upon the arrested look in her father's eye.

'This is a *personal* matter, sir. It requires… discretion.'

'Very well, we will go to the house.' Phineas spoke over his shoulder to the men behind him. 'Keldy, Hutton, I will speak to you later. Constable, lock up the prisoner when we leave and make sure you do not allow him any more visitors, do you understand?'

'No!' Ross jumped up. 'One more word alone with the lady—I would send a message to Sir Mark—!'

'Too late,' declared Phineas. He paused, his cold eyes shifting between Ross and Charity, and a cruel smile lifted his lip. 'Much too late, I fear, Durden. I think the game is now going very much my way.' He turned to Charity. 'Madam, shall we go?'

She ignored his outstretched arm and walked out of the lock-up. It was an effort not to look back at Ross and it took every ounce of her resolve to make her feet walk across the square to the grand house that Phineas now owned. She felt very much as if she was walking into a lion's den.

Phineas ushered her into the drawing room, where Hannah was reclining on a couch, an open book in her hands.

'My dear, we have a visitor.'

Hannah sat up quickly, her eyes narrowing.

'So she did go to see him. Like a bitch in heat.'

Charity felt a sudden flash of anger and turned to Phineas. 'What I wish to discuss with you is best done in private.'

'What is this?' he demanded with feigned amazement. 'After you made such an effort to come and see my lady wife the other day, professing yourself repentant and wanting to make amends. Perhaps you would like to tell us what you were hoping to achieve by that?' Charity remained silent and he continued, 'But I have no secrets from my wife, especially in this matter. I think you are about to plead for Durden's life and, since his capture was in no small measure due to my dear lady, I think she has every right to hear you.'

'Oh, yes.' Hannah's malicious smile grew when she saw Charity's brows rise in surprise. 'I was in the audience at your last performance—dear Phineas is so busy these days that I had arranged the visit myself—and I would not have mentioned it to him, had I not seen something so alarming that I just could not keep it to myself.

'That kiss, my dear, when you were making your curtsy. I had seen Mr Durden in the audience, and it was quite clear to me that you were directing your salute to him and him alone.' She tittered. 'Heavens, my dear, as I said to your father when I returned, you might as well have pinned your heart to your sleeve!'

Charity drew herself up. 'And why should I not?'

'Because the fellow is a damned scoundrel,' retorted Phineas. 'When Hannah told me about your shameless behaviour I realised how it was. Why, I'd wager that your visit here to see Hannah was at his instigation, trying to find some way to get his money back, I don't doubt.'

'So you admit you took his prize money.' Charity fixed her eyes upon Hannah, thankful that they had no idea of the real reason for her visit.

'A lovesick fool and his money are soon parted,' Phineas sneered. 'And now we have him safely locked away. He will stand trial for highway robbery.'

Charity shook her head. 'You have no proof of any of this.'

'I shall find sufficient proof to hang the fellow, you mark my words.'

And he would, she knew it. What he could not prove he would fabricate and Ross would hang. She schooled her face to show none of the dismay she was feeling.

'Let me save you the trouble of perjuring

yourself and damning your soul,' she said, meeting his eyes with a steady gaze. 'I will make you a trade. Let Ross Durden go and I will return to the fold as your dutiful daughter.'

Hannah jumped to her feet, saying, 'What sort of bargain is that? Phineas could keep you here now and still hang Durden.'

Charity shot her a contemptuous glance. 'I came here at Sir Mark Beverley's behest.' She repeated Ross's lie. 'You could hold me here against my will, but would you want Sir Mark to come looking for me?'

'She is right, my dear wife. This must be carefully handled.'

Hannah came up to her husband, saying in a wheedling voice, 'But, Phineas, you promised me Ross Durden would hang.'

'So ruining his career by your trumped-up blasphemy charges was not enough for you.' Charity's lip curled. 'It appears Congreve is right: "Heaven has no rage like love to hatred turned, nor Hell a fury like a woman scorn'd".'

'I never loved him. He was a means to an end. I intended to better myself.'

'By stealing his money and running his estate into the ground.'

'Estate, hah! A crumbling ruin and a few poor farms. I knew I could do better than that!'

'So you married a ranting preacher turned magistrate.'

'Enough,' roared Phineas. 'This is getting us nowhere.'

Charity shrugged. 'Your wife insists you hang Ross Durden. Very well, try if you can do so. He is not without friends and this is no blasphemy case to rest upon the verdict of a magistrate and a couple dubious witnesses.' She turned to go. 'All pretence is at an end now. I am going back to Allingford, where I shall spare no pains in future to make it known you are my father—'

'Wait.' As she reached the door Phineas called to her, 'If I let Durden go, you would give up the stage and return here? You would announce that you repented of your wickedness?'

A cold iron hand squeezed her heart. This was the point of no return.

Chapter Eleven

'Put yer coat on, Mr Durden. Magistrate wants to see you.'

The constable stood by the open door, a second, burly individual at his shoulder, clearly on hand to prevent the prisoner escaping. Not that Ross had any such thought. Since Charity had walked out with Phineas he had been prey to the very worst apprehension and conjecture. She had gone off with the magistrate, determined to buy his freedom, and now he would discover just what price she was paying. The lock-up was cool, and as he stepped outside Ross paused for a moment, feeling the hot sun on his shoulders and blinking in the strong light.

He turned towards the inn where the magistrate held his court, and was surprised when the constable gripped his arm.

'Not that way. Justice Weston will see you in his house.'

* * *

Phineas was in the study, sitting behind his desk with Hannah and Charity occupying chairs on either side of him. Ross was not surprised to see Hannah was present, gloating over his disgrace, no doubt. However, he gave her no more than a cursory glance before turning his attention to Charity. She was very pale, but composed, and the fact that she would not look at him only increased his fears for her.

'Take off those chains, Constable,' Phineas ordered. 'You are free to go, Durden.'

'Not until I know the price of my freedom.' Ross did not move, save to rub his sore wrists once the manacles were removed.

Phineas scowled, but commanded the constable and his assistant to wait in the hall.

As the door closed Hannah said sweetly, 'Your lover has bought your freedom, Ross.'

'Then put me back in the lock-up. I will take my chances in court.'

'I'm afraid that is not possible,' replied Phineas. 'My…daughter has decided to repent her wicked ways, in return for your liberty.'

Ross fixed his eyes on Charity, sitting pale and silent, her eyes lowered.

'What have you done?' he asked her, his throat dry with fear. 'What have you promised them?'

Phineas rapped on the desk. 'Do you hear me, Durden? Your horse is even now being fetched to the back door and you are free to go.'

'Not that it will do you much good,' murmured Hannah. 'The charge still stands against you and you will be arrested if you are caught. And hanged, you may be sure of that.'

'However,' Phineas continued, 'I have agreed to give you twenty-four hours to make your arrangements and get out of the area.'

'At what price?' he demanded. 'For God's sake, tell me what she has agreed to.'

'Of course, you should know,' Hannah purred, like a cat over a bowl of cream. 'My stepdaughter has seen the error of her ways. She wants her father's forgiveness, isn't that so, my dear?' Charity said nothing and Hannah continued. 'She will give up the stage and make her life here with us. You used to tell me, Ross, that one volunteer is worth ten pressed men. Charity will become a servant to Phineas and me for seven years.'

'No!'

'But yes,' said Phineas, and Ross's fists clenched at his smug tone. 'And just to make sure she does not change her mind, she will sign a contract to that effect. I am sure that will be time enough for me to teach my errant daughter the ways of the Lord.'

'I'll be damned if I let that happen,' declared Ross. He held out his hand. 'Charity, come with me now. Let me take you back to Allingford—'

Phineas snarled. 'My daughter may leave this house, Durden, but if you try to accompany her I will have you shot as an escaped felon.'

'He will leave here alone.' Charity spoke softly, but with conviction, her words falling into the tense silence. 'I have given you my word, Phineas, and I will adhere to it, as long as you keep to your side of the bargain. Perhaps...' She rose. 'Perhaps you will allow me a few moments alone with Mr Durden.'

Hannah gave an exasperated cry. 'Ungrateful hussy, how much more do you expect your father to grant you?'

Charity turned on her. 'You will have seven years of my *gratitude*, madam. Is that not enough?'

'Still so proud, still so insolent,' declared Phineas, shaking his head. 'Say your goodbyes here and now, madam, or not at all.'

Ross watched them in silence, afraid that whatever he might say would only make things worse for Charity. He was still raging inside. Quickly he assessed the situation, wanting to sweep her up and carry her out of the house. Phineas and Hannah would have to be overcome, then there were at least two men in the hall. High odds against a successful escape, but not impossible.

Charity came towards him and he reached for her hands, pulling her close as he lifted them to his mouth.

'Come with me,' he whispered.

She gave a slight shake of her head, moving closer so that only he would hear her whisper.

'I am giving you time to find the evidence against Phineas. Pray God it will not take long—'

Phineas came towards them, saying angrily, 'Enough of that. What are you saying to him?'

He dragged her away. Ross's fists came up, but a word and a look from Charity kept him from attacking the magistrate.

'Your horse is at the back gate,' said Hannah, glancing out of the window. 'Go now, while you still can.'

'Yes, go, and quickly,' begged Charity. She gave him a last, wavering smile and her lips moved silently over her final words.

I love you.

Phineas opened the door. 'Rigg shall escort you to the yard.'

The constable and his assistant came in and grabbed Ross by his arms.

'I will be back for you, Charity,' he said as they marched him out of the door.

Phineas laughed. 'An empty promise. If you show your face in Beringham again, sir, I will have you arrested for highway robbery. Oh, and, Durden—my offer to buy Wheelston still stands. Perhaps you would like to sign it over to me now. That will give you a little money to take away with you.'

From the doorway Ross stared at him, his lip lifting in contempt.

'I would rather it was forfeit to the Crown.'

'And so it will be, now that you are an outlaw. No matter, I think I have sufficient standing with my fellows to make sure I can get it eventually. Take him away!'

Phineas closed the door and as silence fell over the room, Charity moved to the window. It was a moment before Ross appeared, but then all too soon he had crossed the yard, mounted his horse and was gone.

There was a rustle of papers behind her.

'Time for you to carry out your part of the bargain,' declared Hannah. 'Come here and sign this.' She added with evident satisfaction, 'It is the indenture for seven years' employment.'

Charity came slowly towards the desk. She signed her name on the paper, and when the constable and his assistant came back Phineas called upon them to witness it before sending them on their way.

'There, it is done,' declared Phineas. 'You are mine now, daughter. This is the Lord's will. I had given up on your soul, but clearly He thinks you may still be saved.'

Charity ignored his gloating voice and glanced out of the window. The sun was still high and Ross would have plenty of time to get away. She knew Phineas would keep his word over this at least. His plans for her required her co-operation. She was to humble herself— nothing less than her total humiliation would appease her father.

Oh, Ross, please God your naval friends find damning evidence against Phineas and you can rescue me very soon!

'And don't look for Durden to come back for you,' sneered Phineas, watching her. 'His fine words count for nothing. He is a blaggard. He will most likely go off to sea and never be heard of again. But mark me, daughter, if he does come back then I shall make sure he hangs.'

'Our bargain was that you would let him go free,' said Charity. 'If you do anything to harm him, I shall make sure that everyone knows what has gone on here today—do not forget how popular I am, Phineas.'

'But not for long. You are the audience's favourite at the moment, but how long do you think that will last, a year, two? Pah! They will have forgotten you by the winter. Then no one will give tuppence for your accusations.' He continued softly, 'And I think it is time you started calling me Father, don't you?'

'Never!'

He laughed. 'No, perhaps it is a little late for that. Then it must be "sir". What think you, madam wife?'

'She should call you "master",' declared Hannah. 'After all, she is nothing more than a servant now and should be treated as such. I shall have an attic room prepared for her. With a lock on the door, in case she thinks to give us the slip in the night.'

'I have given you my word,' said Charity coldly.

'And you have signed yourself over to me,' added Phineas, holding up the paper. 'I think now perhaps you should write a little note to Sir Mark, explaining that you have seen the error of your ways and decided to come home to your loving father and stepmama.'

She shuddered at the thought, but she sat down at the desk and pulled a sheet of paper towards her.

'I should write to Hywel Jenkin, too,' she

said. 'He will need to cancel my benefit night at the end of the week.'

'Benefit night?' said Hannah. 'What is that?'

'It was a special performance he was going to put on, where all the proceeds would come to me.'

'Well, you are giving up the stage,' Phineas told her. 'Your days as a symbol of lust and wantonness are over. From now on it will be a plain gown, and as for your hair—' He reached into a drawer and pulled out a large pair of scissors.

Charity's blood ran cold as he advanced towards her. Hannah laid a hand on his arm.

'Wait, my dear, let us not be too hasty. This… benefit night, how much does it make?'

'What?' Charity could not take her eyes from the shears clasped in her father's hand. 'Oh, it varies. A full house could bring in several hundred pounds.'

'Husband, I think we should let little Charity perform her benefit, do not you?'

Phineas shook her off.

'The theatre is an abomination,' he raged. 'It is a den of vice and iniquity. My daughter shall never again—'

'Yes, that is all very well,' replied Hannah tartly, 'But the proceeds would go some way to pay for the cost of keeping her here.' She paused. 'She might also announce to the audience her retirement and repentance for her wicked life. Think of that, Phineas, a public admission of her sin. All of Allingford would know of it, and a goodly proportion of Beringham people would be there, too, I have no doubt.'

Charity felt sick at the very idea, but she was watching Phineas put the scissors back in the drawer.

'Yes,' he said slowly. 'A very public renunciation of the theatre, from its principal player. I shall write your farewell speech—'

'You shall not!' retorted Charity angrily.

'Very well, I shall oversee it,' he conceded, 'but you will include a few lines of my choosing. And before you refuse, madam, reflect that it will give Durden more time before I levy hue and cry against him.'

Charity bit back a furious retort. A few extra days could make all the difference. At best it would give Ross's friends time to act upon the letter she had written out. At worst, Ross could be safely out of the country by then.

'Well, my dear, this is it. Your final performance.'

The curtain had just gone up and Hywel was standing in the wings with Charity. The past

few days had been agonising. Phineas had allowed her to return to Allingford to rehearse
and put her affairs in order. There had been no
news of Ross and, although she did not believe
he would desert her, Phineas's declaration that
he would save himself and leave her to her fate
remained at the back of her mind. After all,
even if Phineas was charged with treason, Ross
would still have to stand trial for highway robbery, if he came back.

When she had told Hywel she was giving up
the stage and putting him in charge of all her
properties and her money, he had been so as-
tounded that she had ended by telling him everything.

'At most it will only be for seven years,' she
said, trying to make light of it. 'I should be
thankful that neither my father nor his greedy
wife considered that I might have funds of my
own, or they would have made me sign those
over to them, as well as making me their servant.'

'If you think Phineas Weston is a spy, you
should take your information to Sir Mark Beverley,' he had told her furiously. 'There is no
need to put yourself through this.'

'He could not act on the contents of one letter, which is not even in my possession,' she
explained. 'And although the evidence against

Ross is equally insubstantial—more so, in fact—Phineas would make sure he was hanged. I could not allow that.'

Now, as she heard the familiar opening lines and prepared to make her appearance on the stage, Hywel squeezed her fingers and gave her a pitying smile.

'You are giving up all this for a highwayman?' he murmured. 'We should be repeating Mr Dryden's tragedy tonight.'

'All For Love or the World Well Lost?' Even through her sadness Charity managed a smile. 'Not at all,' she said, holding her head high. 'I shall leave my audience with the memory of laughter, not tears.'

The cheers, shouts and stamping would not stop. Charity made her curtsy again and again, and she brought back the rest of the cast to share the applause, but in the end she was left alone, centre stage, to say goodbye. She looked past the limelight and saw the flash and glitter of a bejewelled costume in the box nearest the stage. She knew it was Hannah, overdressed for the occasion as usual. She and Phineas had insisted upon coming to Allingford to watch her humiliation. Well, this was her world. Phineas might control her words, but not their delivery. She straightened her shoulders. Nothing she did now would help Ross. She could only pray that he was safe.

She began by thanking Mr Jenkin and her friends in the theatre. Then she expressed her gratitude to the people of Allingford for their kindness and generosity.

'And those of Beringham, too!' shouted someone from the benches.

'Of course.' She smiled. 'You have made my time here such a pleasure and I shall remember you always. Because this is to be my last performance.'

There were gasps and cries from the audience, a muttering that swelled to a roar of disapproval. Charity put up her hands for silence.

'Please, my friends, I am most gratified by your reaction, but it must be.' She began to speak the words her father had insisted upon and that she had sworn upon her honour to repeat. That she had sinned to show herself so brazenly on the stage, to allow men to lust after her body. That the plays encouraged fornication and lewdness and should be denounced by any true Christian.

The audience went quiet as the oration continued, listening to her with growing uneasiness. Angry mutterings began to run around the auditorium and someone from the pit called out, 'This ain't you, my dear. You don't mean what you're saying.'

She recognised the voice as that of her leading man, Will Stamp, and glancing down she saw that there were people standing in the aisles between the benches—people who looked suspiciously like her fellow players, although they were dressed in the rough clothes of working people. A woman ran forward, a shawl thrown over her head. It was the actress who earlier that evening had played Mrs Malaprop.

'Aye,' she shouted now, 'she's been bullied into this!'

Her heart swelled at their support, and it gave her courage to finish her speech.

'I am returning to my father's house,' she concluded, raising her hand towards the box where Phineas and Hannah were sitting in regal splendour. She drew herself up, curling her lip and declaring with all the derision she could convey, 'My father, Phineas Weston, Justice of Beringham. An *honourable* man, committed to bringing God's will to this land!'

Her voice rang to the rafters and was followed by a stunned silence. Peering past the flare of the limelight, she could see Hannah and Phineas leaning forward and smiling, her irony quite lost upon them.

'Weston's tyranny more like!' cried a man from the benches, jumping to his feet.

'He won't succeed in Allingford!' shouted another.

'No! By God, he can't browbeat you into leaving us!'

The protests were growing. The wrathful audience turned their attention away from the stage and began ranting at the box.

Charity slipped into the wings. Hywel was waiting for her.

'Did you plan this?' she said, catching his hands. 'I fear you may have caused a riot.'

'I could not let the audience think you were doing this willingly.' He hurried her to her dressing room. 'Quickly now. I have a coach—'

He broke off when he saw the three men waiting outside her dressing room.

Sir James Fryton stepped forward and made a bow.

'Ah, Mrs Weston. Hutton, Keldy and I are here to escort you to your father. Good thing he arranged it, for the crowd is rather boisterous tonight, what?'

Lights were blazing from the magistrate's house in Beringham as Phineas Weston's elegant travelling coach pulled up at the door. Charity ignored her father's hand as she alighted from the carriage and walked into the house with her head held high. Her nerves were at full stretch. She had spent the journey from Allingford crushed into a corner of the carriage while Phineas and Hannah gloated over their success, but beneath their smug laughter Charity felt the animosity growing and she wondered just what horrors awaited her.

Hannah led the way into the study and ordered Charity to take off her cloak.

'Hmm, very nice.' Hannah snatched if from her and threw it around her own shoulders. 'It will do very nicely for me, since you will not be needing a satin-lined wrap in future.'

'And just what have you in mind for me?' asked Charity, shocked by the hatred in the other woman's glare. 'A sackcloth gown, perhaps, or a hair shirt? And am I to sleep amongst the ashes?'

'It would be no more than you deserve,' growled Phineas, coming into the room and closing the door. 'But my wife is inclined to be merciful.'

'Yes,' added Hannah, although there was nothing merciful in the poisonous look she gave Charity. 'You shall be my personal servant. I thought of putting you in the kitchens, to help the scullery maid, but then who would know how low you had fallen? No, it is better to keep you with me, so that when we have visitors or when I am out of doors, others might see your disgrace.'

'As you wish,' said Charity. 'But it is past midnight, can we not continue this tomorrow?'

'We will discuss this whenever I choose!' snapped Hannah. 'And you will address me as "madam" in future, and with a curtsy. Do you understand?'

'Yes.'

Charity's head snapped back as Hannah slapped her cheek.

'Insolent girl!'

'It seems my daughter is still very proud, and "led away by divers lusts".' Phineas pushed her roughly down onto a chair. 'She needs humbling.'

Charity cried out as he grabbed her hair, pulling her head back so that she was forced to stare up into his savage, cruel face.

'Fetch me the scissors, wife. Let's see how proud she feels once her head is shaved like any doxy!'

She protested and he put his hand around her throat, squeezing tightly.

'"Let a woman learn in silence",' he snarled. '"I suffer not a woman to usurp authority over the man, but to be in silence".'

He released her. Charity struggled to breathe

and fought off the encroaching blackness. She would not faint.

'Here.' Hannah handed him the scissors. 'Cut off her hair, Phineas, but cut it at the root, the wig maker will give us good money for such fair locks.'

He was tearing the pins from her hair, all the time muttering texts from the Bible. Charity felt the familiar, shuddering terror freezing her blood, just as it had when she was fourteen, and she had sobbed, cried and begged for mercy. He had given none then and there would be no mercy now, especially not with Hannah at his side, urging him on. Summoning every ounce of courage, she threw herself out of the chair and ran behind the desk. Phineas lunged for her, his fingers missing her by inches.

As he came after her she grabbed the lectern and sent it crashing down across his path. He tried to jump over it, but the heavy Bible caught between his legs and brought him to his knees. It gave her the precious seconds she needed to reach the window and throw up the sash. She tried to recall what she had seen from this window when she had come to the house in daylight. A high wall, but not too high to be scaled, although her skirts might be a hindrance, but before that there was the drop into the yard. Twelve feet, fifteen perhaps, and she was likely to break a leg in the fall.

'Stop her!' screeched Hannah, helping Phineas to his feet. If she was going to jump, it must be now.

Phineas came roaring forward and made a grab for her just as she swung herself over the sill and dropped into the darkness below. Her heart had time to lurch up into her mouth, but no more. Instead of the bone-cracking jolt of hitting the ground, she found herself caught in a pair of strong arms. There was a grunt as some-one took the full weight of her fall and she heard a dear, familiar voice mutter, 'Faith, sweetheart, must you be always escaping from windows?'

Chapter Twelve

'Ross!' With a sob, she threw her arms about his neck. 'What are you doing here?'

Steadying his breath and uttering up a prayer that she was not hurt, he set her on her feet.

'I've just arrived from York with a party of officers to arrest your father. We came to the back of the house to make sure there was no means of escape and saw you at the window. When I realised what you were going to do I thought I should try to catch you.' His arms tightened. 'Foolish girl, you might have broken your neck.'

'I had to get away.' She shuddered against him. 'They w-were going to c-cut off my hair.'

He buried his head in the heavy locks falling over his hands, breathing in that subtle fragrance that was all her own. He loved her hair, but the idea of her risking her life to save it brought the rage boiling up.

'Your hair will grow again, but your neck would not mend, little idiot!' Immediately he regretted his harsh tone and held her close. 'Ah, love, forgive me, it is not you that deserves my anger. Come along, let us go into the house. The true villains should be under arrest by now.'

Charity was thankful for Ross's strong arm supporting her as the men with him forced the door into the house and they made their way up the service stairs. Anxious servants were pushed aside and two men detailed to round them up and explain what was happening. When they reached the main floor, raised voices could be heard in the drawing room. Ross held her back as the others surged towards the door.

'If you would rather not—'

'No.' She gave him a tremulous smile. 'I want to see this through, Ross. I am no longer afraid of Phineas, not anymore.'

They went in to find the magistrate standing in the middle of the room, his wrists shackled, and Hannah slumped on the sofa, sobbing quietly.

'Ah, so this is the young lady you told me of, Ross.' One of the officers limped towards her, smiling. 'Captain Armstrong at your service, madam. Thanks to your efforts we have stemmed this flow of secrets out of the country.'

'So Phineas *was* spying.'

'Yes,' affirmed Captain Armstrong. 'The Admiralty had set up an embargo around Yarmouth and was watching the coast for signs of anyone trying to send information *out* of the country, but they only made cursory checks on the cross-country mail, and no one questioned the mail sent to a magistrate in Beringham, innocuous family letters that attracted no attention at all until you spotted the discrepancies, ma'am.'

'I don't understand,' put in Phineas. 'What has she to do with this?'

'Mrs Weston memorised that last letter you received from your supposed brother,' said Ross. 'She knew it was lies, that you have no family.'

'But how did she see it, when—?'

'When she came to see me,' said Hannah, slowly. 'The witch inveigled her way in here and I left her alone in the study. But only for a moment. Phineas, I swear it was no more than five minutes.'

Secure with Ross at her side, Charity spoke up.

'That was all I needed. I wrote it all out as soon as I could.'

'And Durden brought it to me.' Captain Armstrong grinned. 'The navy can move fast enough on land when it has to. That letter was sufficient for us to arrest the French spy in Yarmouth, and enquiries at Filey soon revealed the fishermen who were carrying the information to France.'

'So even in this you defy me.' Phineas glared at Charity, his face suffused with rage.

She met his look boldly. 'Especially in this. But why should you help the French? Why would you betray your own people?'

'My people? Hah!' Phineas spat out the words. He began to pace the room, speaking almost to himself. 'This is a godless country. I have known for years that England is beyond redemption. Soon it will be consumed by the fires of hell and Bonaparte will be the means of it.' He stopped and glanced at the incredulous faces around him. 'You do not believe me? It was Bonaparte who reestablished freedom of worship after the Bourbon king had suppressed it. Bonaparte will ensure that the papists will no longer rule France, nor any of the countries under his dominion.'

'Nonsense,' said Ross. 'Bonaparte is using religion for his own ends.'

'No, I have proof—letters, assurances— that it is so,' declared Phineas. 'People are free to worship as they please, whereas here, the government is going out of its way to appease Rome!'

'But is that reason enough for you to turn spy?' asked Charity.

Phineas looked at her in surprise. 'I am no spy. It is only a matter of time before the Emperor is victorious. I am just doing what is necessary to speed up the matter. The sooner we are united under Bonaparte and this godforsaken government is brought down the better.'

'And just when did you start helping the French?' demanded Armstrong.

'Let me guess,' put in Ross. 'Five years ago, was it not? That is how you came by the money to buy this house and turn yourself from a poor preacher into a wealthy magistrate. You turned traitor, took French silver like a Judas. How do you reconcile that with your conscience?'

Phineas shrugged. 'It is the Lord's work and He moves in mysterious ways. I merely passed on the information when it came, and the money I received I made use of. I am helping the emperor restore righteousness to the world. I will be acknowledged as the new St Cuthbert, bringing light—'

Ross uttered a snort of derision.

'You deluded fool, you would betray your fellow countrymen for that?'

'What would you know of it?' snarled

Phineas. 'True Christians will revere me—it was because of my efforts, my exhortations, that the emperor did away with the Republican calendar last year—'

Charity shrank closer to Ross, staring in horror at her father's crazed face.

'He is insane.' She whispered the words, but Phineas heard her and drew himself up.

'I am the Lord's instrument. I have turned Beringham into a God-fearing place—'

'You have turned it into a drear, despondent town where people are afraid even to smile,' retorted Ross. 'The poor resort to illegal drinking dens and mills, while those who can afford it go to Allingford for their entertainment.' He put his hand on Charity's shoulder. 'And even there you would deprive them of their brightest star. But no more.' He stepped back. 'Take them away, John. The game is up, Weston. You and your wife will stand trial—'

'Not me!' screeched Hannah, jumping to her feet. 'I knew nothing about his spying.'

'But you colluded with him in every other way,' retorted Ross. 'You schemed with him to ruin me—'

'He forced me to it! Phineas wanted Wheelston. He came to me when I was nursing your mother, told me to run it into the ground so he could buy it cheaply.'

Captain Armstrong grinned at Ross.

'There's your proof, Durden. A confession in front of impeccable witnesses.'

Hannah flew across the room and threw herself against Ross. 'He forced me to give you up, Ross. He forced me to bring the blasphemy charge against you, he told me what to say, which phrases would do most harm, and he paid Sir James, and Keldy and Hutton to bear witness—'

Ross put her away from him, saying with contempt, 'And did he force you to marry him, too?'

'Yes! How could you think I would prefer him to you?'

'Easily, since he was so rich.'

Hannah clutched at his hand and gazed up at him.

'I was frightened of him, Ross. Terrified. But now he is found out and I shall be free, free to come back to you—I have always loved you.'

He shook her off and turned away. 'Pray do not shame yourself even further, Hannah. Anything I felt for you died a long time ago. You killed it.'

'So you will go back to that slut! She is a servant, the contract is signed, you will have to wait seven years for the harlot—'

'Enough, madam!' Captain Armstrong's

voice cracked like a whip across the room, bringing immediate silence. 'You have said enough to convict yourself of perjury. You will be taken to York, together with your husband, to answer all the charges.' He waved to the other officers to take them away, waiting until the door closed behind them all to turn to Ross.

'A good day's work, my friend, and it will be profitable, too, for you. With the woman's confession I think you have every chance that your prize money will be returned, and there is a reward for breaking up this little spy ring. Besides that, I visited, er, *friends* while I was in London. The blasphemy charge has been stricken from your record and you are reinstated as a captain in his Majesty's navy.'

'But the Dark Rider—' put in Charity.

Captain Armstrong regarded her with a serious gaze.

'Madam, I know of no evidence to link Captain Durden with highway robbery, do you?'

'Why, no, none at all.'

'Then the allegations are merely further evidence of Magistrate Weston's malicious intent to smear the name of this honest officer. And as for you, madam—' his eyes softened '— you need not worry about that contract. It was signed under duress and is therefore worthless. You are free to return to the stage, Mrs Weston.

I saw you play at Scarborough and, if you will forgive my saying so, it is where you belong.'

'Oh, no, it isn't.' Ross took her hand. 'She belongs with me, as my wife.'

Charity had been listening to it all and feeling slightly bemused, but now she tried to collect her wits. Her heart clenched as she saw the warm glow in Ross's eyes.

'Are you sure?' she asked him anxiously. 'Are you sure you want to marry someone whose father is a traitor?'

He pulled her closer.

'My darling girl, I have never been more certain of anything in my life.' He drew her into his arms and kissed her. She responded eagerly, leaning into him, feeling the hard arousal of his body against her own.

When he released her mouth she remained within the comfort of his arms, her head thrown back against his shoulder. He raised one hand and ran his fingers through the tumbling golden locks.

'"If a woman have long hair, it is a glory to her",' he murmured lovingly, then said with a sigh, 'I should take you home.'

She gazed up at him and said shyly, 'I am home, Ross. I am with you.'

She saw the flame leap in his dark eyes. He

swooped on her again, kissing her with a ruth-
less efficiency that left her weak.

'Ahem.'

They broke apart, Charity flushing vividly
and Ross giving a self-conscious laugh when
they remembered Captain Armstrong's presence.

'I take it you will not be escorting the prisoner to York, Durden?'

'Ah, no. I have a more pressing engagement,
unless you have need of me?'

'I shall leave a couple men here to search
the house, but I think a half dozen sailors will
be able to get those two safely to their destination.' He looked at them, a quizzical smile in
his eyes. 'May I be the first to wish you joy?'

'Oh, no,' cried Charity, flustered. 'That is—'

'*Yes,*' Ross interrupted her, grinning. 'Thank
you, John!'

'Good. Then I will be off—'

'Wait, John, I—' Ross turned to Charity. 'Do
you have a cloak, dearest?'

'Y-yes, it must still be in the study.'

'Then fetch it, my love, while I accompany
Captain Armstrong to the door.'

Charity missed the warmth and strength of
Ross's arm about her as she made her way to
the study to collect her cloak. The room was in

chaos, papers and pens scattered over the desk where Phineas had tried to reach across and grab her, one chair overturned and the lectern still on the floor. The family Bible was half-hidden under the desk, one of the covers hanging off. She had challenged her father, fought against the terror he had always instilled in her, and she had survived. He could not hurt her anymore; she could forget him and get on with her own life. Turning away, she picked up her cloak and went back to the hall.

Ross was in the doorway, talking earnestly with Captain Armstrong, but they broke off when they saw her coming towards them. The captain gave her a smile and a brief salute before striding away. Ross opened his arms and she walked into his embrace as if it was the most natural thing in the world. For a moment he held her close, his cheek resting on her head, then he took her arm and said briskly, 'Home, then, my love!'

It took some time to find a carriage to carry them to Wheelston, and dawn was already breaking by the time they arrived.

They spent the journey wrapped in each other's arms, and in the short periods of time between kisses Charity explained to Ross just what had happened to her in the days they had been apart.

'So Phineas never harmed you?'

She heard the anxiety in his voice. 'No. He had to let me go back to Allingford to prepare for my final performance.' She shuddered. 'If Hannah had not been so desperate to have the money from that as well as everything else, he would have shaved my head as soon as I had signed the forms.'

'Poor love.' His arms tightened into a crushing embrace. 'Phineas will never harm you again, I promise you that.'

'And you,' she said when she could speak. 'What have you been doing?'

A laugh rumbled in his chest.

'Riding! I went to London and met up with Armstrong, who had already arranged the whole, so then it was back here to arrest Phineas—praying all the time that he had not hurt you.'

'He did not,' she told him as the carriage bounced over the Wheelston drive and came to a halt. 'Not a mark.'

'No?' He jumped down and held out his arms to her. 'I am going to inspect you, inch by inch, to make sure that is true.'

She shivered deliciously, and with a laugh he stole another kiss before leading her into the house. A shadowy, expectant silence wrapped around Charity as Ross led her up the stairs. He stopped outside the door to the room where he had held her prisoner.

'I meant it, Charity, when I said I want you to be my wife. I love you, you know.'

She felt the light, breathless flutter of her heart when she heard those words, but anxiety shadowed her happiness. She could not believe he had considered the consequences of marriage to Phineas Weston's daughter. She reached up to cup his face with her hands, lovingly scanning every detail of his face.

'I love you, Ross. That is all that matters for now. Let us leave everything else until the morning.'

'Gladly, but…' He touched her lips with his own, a soft, gentle caress. 'I will not presume… That is, if you would rather sleep in here?'

'Alone?'

'Yes.'

She slipped her arms about his neck. 'I never want to sleep alone again.'

With something between a groan and a growl he swept her up and carried her the short distance to his bedroom. She clung to him, burying her face in his shoulder while the thought of what was to come filled her body with a thrilling anticipation. When he laid her gently on the bed she clung to him, pulling him down to cover his face with hot, fervent kisses, which he returned with a passion.

His hands stroked over her body, but when they became entangled in her heavy cloak she was as eager as he to shed the encumbrance. He bade her lie still while he untied her cloak and then wrestled with the ribbons around the neck of her gown.

'But this is foolish,' she told him, her voice trembling between laughter and delight as his fingers danced across her breast. 'I shall still have to get up to remove my clothes.'

'Quiet,' he growled.

She lay very still as he gently peeled away her bodice to reveal the twin mounds of her breasts rising above her corset. Under his hot gaze the nipples seemed to strain against the chemise, and when his fingers pushed aside the thin covering they became achingly hard. She gave a low moan as his mouth closed over one hot tip and her body arched when his tongue circled the nub and drew a response from deep within her body. She was burning with need; the layers of clothing irritated her tingling skin. She tore open Ross's shirt and slid her hands inside, running them over the solid contours of his chest, exulting when she felt his nipples harden beneath her fingers. She played with them as he had done with her, circling, gently pinching until he broke off from the delicious torment he was inflicting upon her breast.

'What are you doing to me?'

His groan elicited nothing more than a gurgle of laughter from Charity.

'Giving you your own medicine,' she murmured, pushing herself up. 'Let us get out of these clothes, Ross. I want to hold you properly.'

'I hope you will hold me most improperly,' he murmured, sending the heat rushing through her once again, but most especially it pooled between her thighs, reminding her of the sweet, sensual caresses he had bestowed upon her once before.

They slipped off the bed and scrabbled out of their clothes, Charity only pausing when Ross stripped away his breeches and stood before her, lean and muscled, his arousal all too obvious in the pale light of the early dawn. She stepped back and felt the edge of the bed behind her. She slid up onto the covers and began to move back until Ross stopped her, his hands on her ankles. Obedient to the gentle pressure, her legs parted. Ross dropped to his knees and pulled her towards him, settling a knee over each shoulder and leaning forward to kiss the tangle of curls at her groin.

'Ross! Don't…'

Her words trailed away as his tongue flickered over her, licking and kissing until she was writhing, wanting him to go farther, deeper. His fingers joined the incessant pleasuring until she could bear it no longer. Waves of pleasure were building inside her, rippling through her until she shuddered, arched and cried out, her arms thrown wide, hands gripping the covers.

Ross eased her onto the bed and stretched out beside her, wrapping her in his arms and holding her until the pulsing, throbbing convulsions had eased.

'Oh, I did not know,' she sobbed into his shoulder. 'I thought the first time was ecstasy, but this—'

'I am glad,' he murmured.

When he tried to pull her closer, she resisted.

'But you, Ross, you haven't—'

'Hush.' His arms tightened around her. 'There is time yet.'

She gave a shaky little laugh.

'I don't think I could...'

'Patience.' He silenced her with a kiss and settled her more comfortably in his arms, but one hand was stroking her thigh. It was a slow, gentle movement, but instead of lulling her into sleep she felt her body waking, the need growing in her again. She stirred restlessly and as the slow, sensual stroking continued, her body pressed against Ross. He began to kiss her face, leaving a trail of burning kisses over her cheeks and throat before turning his attention to her ear, where his tongue ran around the shell-like contours, teasing her into full arousal.

Charity wrapped herself around him and he gently rolled her onto her back, kissing her with a slow thoroughness that seemed to draw out the very heart of her. Her body was softening and she opened to him, inviting him in. He eased himself between her thighs and slid into her, moving with long, slow caresses that drew a rippling response she could not control. He took her mouth again, the rasp of his tongue mirroring those other slow, unhurried movements and driving her beyond reason. She was on fire, her body no longer her own as it matched his rhythm. He was thrusting deeper into her, deeper, harder, and she felt as if she was flying, arching and bucking beneath him as her body responded to his urgent demands.

It was too much; she bit her lip to stop herself screaming with the sheer joy of it as Ross gave an exultant shout and with a final, earth-shattering thrust took them over the edge and they clung together, suspended in time and space until at last the spasm passed and they collapsed together onto the bed, gasping, laughing and crying all at once.

They lay together, side by side, hand in hand. Charity gave a long sigh.

'That was…wonderful!'

He chuckled. 'And it will be better still, with practice.'

'Will it?' she asked him, wonder in her voice. 'Will it really?'

'Yes, really!' He laughed and rolled over to pull her into his arms. 'Oh, my love, there is so much I want to share with you, and not just the delights of the bedroom. I would like to take you to sea with me as my wife, to show you the wonder of a full moon sailing high over the water, to let you hear the wind keening through the rigging, taste the salt spray on your face— but of course if you do not care for the sea then we can make our home here, or anywhere you wish—'

She struggled and immediately he released her and fell back on the covers. She raised herself up on one elbow and stared down at him.

'You are smiling.'

The curve of his lips stretched into a full-blown grin.

'I have so much to smile about.'

She bent and kissed him. 'Being happy suits you,' she said softly. 'I like to hear you laugh.'

'Then you shall hear it a great deal. But not

just now.' He pulled her down beside him and settled her in his arms. 'Sleep now.'

Ross woke with the sun streaming through the window, hot on his naked body as he lay sprawled on the covers. He was immediately aware that he was alone and he sat up, stretching. Charity was kneeling on the window seat, wrapped in his banyan. She had her back to him and her thick hair cascaded down her back like a golden waterfall. He wanted to go over to her and let those heavy silk tresses run through his fingers, but something wasn't right. Something in her stillness, the slight droop of her shoulders, alarmed him. Tentatively he called her name.

When she did not move he slipped off the bed and went over to sit beside her.

'What is it, love?'

She turned to him and he saw the traces of tears on her face.

'Oh, Ross, I c-can't marry you.'

An ice-cold hand clutched his heart and squeezed it, hard.

'May I enquire why not?' He kept his voice calm, while fear made the blood pound in his ears. 'Do you find you don't love me after all?'

She averted her face.

'I do love you,' she muttered in a strangled voice. 'I love you too much to marry you.' She turned to him again, fresh tears turning her eyes the colour of polished sapphires. 'Do you not see how wrong it would be for me to marry you? My father—'

He bit back an oath. He should have known Phineas would be behind this!

'Yesterday you said you no longer feared him.'

'And it's true, but he is still my father.' The tears sparkled on her lashes. 'I am a traitor's daughter, Ross—if you marry me then you will be tainted, too. People would talk behind their hands about you. They might even question your loyalty.'

'Not when it is known that you helped to bring Weston to justice.'

'And th-that is another reason I c-cannot marry you.' Her voice trembled pitifully. 'What would everyone think of a daughter who would send her own father to the gallows?' She used the edge of the sleeve to wipe her cheeks. 'I thought I did not care what became of him, but it's not true, Ross. I was happy to think I need never see him again, that he would disappear from my life and not do any more harm to anyone, but when you were sleeping it came to me that the only way that is going to happen

is for him to d-die, and whatever he has done
to me I do not want that, Ross. I don't want to
see him hang.'

But I do! thought Ross furiously. *Not for the
injustice he has done to me, nor his treachery
to England, but for the misery he has inflicted
upon you, my love.*

He clenched his jaw, determined not to utter
the words, knowing they would cause her more
distress. He reached for her, but she gave a little
shake of her head and waved him away. A cloud
covered the sun and the sudden chill reminded
him that he was naked.

He rose, saying carefully, 'We will talk about
this more after we have dressed and broken our
fast.'

When she did not respond he put his hand on
her shoulder, giving it a gentle squeeze before
collecting up his clothes and dressing silently.

Charity sank deeper into her despair. He had
not argued with her, had made no attempt to
dissuade her, so he must agree, now that he had
had time to reflect upon it, that she would not
make him a suitable wife. Peeping through her
lashes, she saw that Ross had retreated to the
far side of the bed. She must be sensible and get
away from here with as little hurt as possible,
to either of them.

* * *

When Ross asked her if she needed help with her clothes, she said no and he went off to the kitchen to wait for her. She was relieved when she joined him a short while later to find that he was alone.

He was studying a sheet of paper, but when she came in he put it down.

'Mrs Cummings has shopping to do, so I sent her off with Jed. We will serve ourselves with breakfast.'

He waved an arm towards the table, which was covered with dishes, a raised pie, plates of ham and beef, fresh bread rolls and a dish of butter. Charity sat down and poured herself a cup of coffee from the pot near her elbow. Sensible, controlled. She could do this.

'I have been thinking what I might do for my father. I wonder if I should use some of my fortune to help him.'

'Do you want to do that?'

'No, of course not, but— Oh, Ross, when all is said and done, he is my father.'

'And a most unnatural one, to cause you so much misery.' He frowned across the table at her. 'He would have ruined your life without a second thought.'

'But I am not like him. I am not vengeful.'

'So you would be happy to see Hannah and Phineas walk free after all they have done.'

'Yes—no.' She shrugged unhappily. 'I do not want them executed.' She dropped her head in her hands. 'I feel like a murderess.'

'Well, you need not.'

Something in his tone made her look up. There was a smile glinting in his dark eyes. He picked up the paper.

'This has just arrived from Captain Armstrong. Phineas and Hannah, er, escaped last night.'

Charity jerked upright, one hand knocking her knife and sending it clattering to the floor. *'What?'*

The smile grew, but he kept his eyes on the paper.

'Yes, it seems they managed to get to the coast and escaped to France.'

His tone was perfectly serious, but she was not fooled and said sharply, 'Ross—just what is this? Captain Armstrong was taking them to York.'

He looked at her then and she could see the smile tugging at the corners of his mouth.

'I know, but I had a word with him before we left Beringham last night and we, er, changed the plans.'

'But—but how could you? Ross, that is

dreadful. Won't you— Won't he be in the most terrible trouble?'

'Well, that's just it. You see, he had already told me that the man they arrested in Yarmouth has friends in very high places who would be, shall we say, *embarrassed* if his part in this spy ring came out. The Admiralty were keen to hush up his part in it, so they can hardly complain if Phineas escapes justice, too.'

He saw that she was staring at him and laughed.

'John took Hannah and Phineas to the coast, where they were put aboard a small sloop along with an armed guard, who would make sure they were put ashore on the French coast. Phineas is so keen on Bonaparte's rule that he might as well live under it—although as an Englishman he might not find them as tolerant and friendly as he imagines.' Ross sat back in his chair, grinning at her. 'No, I think he and Hannah will have a very uncomfortable time of it, but Armstrong has made it very clear to them that if they show their faces in this country again they will regret it.'

'But what about your prize money? If Hannah is not here to stand trial…'

He shrugged. 'I will have to live without it.'

She looked at him, her heart swelling with

so much love and gratitude that she thought it would burst.

'You would let it go, let her go free, for my sake?'

'It is not such a big thing. Better to let her go with her husband and make his life a misery.' The smile that she had seen on his face almost constantly since yesterday appeared again. 'After all, I can't have my father-in-law dragged through a hideous court case.'

'Oh, Ross....' Her lip quivered. 'I don't know what to say.'

'Say you will marry me. Armstrong tells me there is a substantial reward on its way, which should help in restoring Wheelston to its former glory, but in truth, my love, the only reward I want is you for my wife.'

He came round the table and dropped to one knee before her.

'Well, Charity, will you marry me now? There may be rumours, but no one will know for sure what happened to Phineas. Not that I would care if you had a dozen traitors in your family. I would still want you for my wife, now and always.'

Happiness choked her and, mistaking her silence, he added, 'If you want to continue with your acting, then I will not stand in your way.'

She knew she must speak, and quickly, before he thought she was rejecting him.

'No, no, well, perhaps occasionally I might perform—but not if it conflicts with your own duties. Captain Armstrong said you would be reinstated in the navy, and I think you would like to go back to sea?'

He took her hands. 'I would, very much. There is work to be done there while this war continues, but not if you would dislike it.'

She looked down at him, hoping he could see the love she felt at this moment shining from her eyes and in the huge smile that was bursting forth.

'I should like very much to be the wife of a sea captain—'

Hardly were the words from her mouth than he was on his feet and dragging her out of her chair. She was in his arms, her face upturned for his kiss, which she returned with all the love she could convey.

* * * * *

Special Offers

Every month we put together collections and longer reads written by your favourite authors.

Here are some of next month's highlights— and don't miss our fabulous discount online!

On sale 21st March   On sale 4th April   On sale 4th April

The Regency Ballroom Collection

Scandal *in the* Regency BALLROOM

Louise Allen

Cinderella *in the* Regency BALLROOM

Deb Marlowe

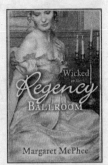

Wicked *in the* Regency BALLROOM

Margaret McPhee

Courtship *in the* Regency BALLROOM

Annie Burrows

Rake *in the* Regency BALLROOM

Bronwyn Scott

Rumours *in the* Regency BALLROOM

Diane Gaston

A twelve-book collection led by Louise Allen
and written by the top authors and rising
stars of historical romance!

Classic tales of scandal and seduction in
the Regency ballroom

**Take your place on the ballroom floor now, at:
www.millsandboon.co.uk**

Join the Mills & Boon Book Club

Subscribe to **Historical** today for 3, 6 or 12 months and you could **save over £50!**

We'll also treat you to these fabulous extras:

- 🌹 **FREE L'Occitane gift set worth £10**
- 🌹 **FREE home delivery**
- 🌹 **Rewards scheme, exclusive offers…and much more!**

Subscribe now and save over £50
www.millsandboon.co.uk/subscribeme

Discover more romance at

www.millsandboon.co.uk

- ❤ WIN great prizes in our exclusive competitions
- ❤ BUY new titles before they hit the shops
- ❤ BROWSE new books and REVIEW your favourites
- ❤ SAVE on new books with the Mills & Boon® Bookclub™
- ❤ DISCOVER new authors

PLUS, to chat about your favourite reads, get the latest news and find special offers:

- 📘 Find us on facebook.com/millsandboon
- 🐦 Follow us on twitter.com/millsandboonuk
- ❤ Sign up to our newsletter at millsandboon.co.uk